I0638572

PRAISE FOR ERADICATE

"With a brass-knuckled, blood-dusted prose style that picks up where brutal icon Mickey Spillane left off, author Jarrett Mazza pushes men's adventure fiction into darker territory. *Eradicate* pits mercenary Kyle Quinn against a sinister cult lodged in the bowels of the Louisiana bayou, and with no limits on his methods, bodies start hitting the floor at a rapid clip. Don a crash helmet and mouthguard, because Quinn's termination list is long and full of wrenching twists and turns. Highly recommended for fans of concrete-boiled, fast-paced novels. Mazza doesn't skimp on violence and thrills, and doesn't shy away from challenging the protagonist's—and the reader's—sense of right and wrong in a dangerous, grey world overrun by monsters."

—Jarret Keene, author of the *Kid Crimson* series

"Jarrett Mazza's novel, *Eradicate*, thunders ahead, gaining speed like a locomotive as protagonist and black ops assassin Kyle Quinn strikes a secret sect that harms children. Quinn also seeks to understand the demons driving him to kill. This intense tale entices readers to dive into scene after scene late into the night and even until dawn."

—John G. Bluck, author of the *Luke Ryder* series

"This book is a masterful, truly original work of suspense that has strong characterizations and clever twists. Eradicate is a quick, smart, engrossing read featuring a character in Kyle Quinn who readers will wish had their backs in any situation."

—Eliot Parker, award-winning author of *Double-Crossed*

ERADICATE

ERADICATE

THE CUSTODIAN
BOOK 1

JARRETT MAZZA

*ROUGH
EDGES
PRESS*

For Mom.
Always there, always prepared.

ERADICATE

CHAPTER 1
NIGHTMARES

IT FELT GOOD TO BLEED.

The bone-crunching wallop transformed Kyle Quinn from strong to weak in a matter of seconds. Awake at the crack of dawn, the former Delta operator was lucid after downing two shots of hard, black coffee.

"That all you got?"

The match was one Quinn had been fighting since before he could remember. It was against the man who made him, built him, owned him.

It was not his opponent; it was his shadow.

Not his attacker, but his abuser.

And it was not his foe, but his family.

"I am going to kill you...*Dad*."

The hard snaps from Quinn's father's lightning-quick legs were sufficiently distributed. The kicks connected with Quinn's chest while the others were countered with a low Kyokushin Karate block. They ricocheted off Quinn's arms as he dodged his dad's bawdy attacks.

"Not today."

Always opting for a rib-rupturing hit, Quinn indulged

in some good old-fashioned wind-knocking. He could put a person down from a distance. Quinn kicked, and his father staggered and grinned.

"Now we're talking," his father uttered with relish.

Quinn's ankle was wrapped up in a sleeve. This made his kicks more formidable because he felt less pain. After another strike, Quinn moved in for a second blow.

His father spun and unleashed a cascade of swiping blocks. He swatted Quinn's fists while Quinn's feet slid along the mats. Making whooshing sounds like papers zipping along a carpet, Quinn deflected all attacks and slipped into aikido.

Using the *kotegaeshi*, this was the art form's classic wristlock. In this case, Quinn had his dad by the leg. He dragged his father, twirled, and moved again. Straightening his arms, Quinn opened his hands and pushed. Now tipped over, Quinn delivered an uncomfortable sidestep in throw.

"Guh!"

It was the first sign of pain so far. Quinn's dad rolled along his shoulder like a bowling ball. Quinn's strategy was always to provoke, so he contorted his body and completed a judo hip toss.

"Ah!" His dad thumped the ground. Quinn climbed on top and to the back.

Executing a rear naked choke, Quinn seized his father's neck. Quinn's bicep bulged like it was being pumped with curdled milk. He heard his dad's wheezing as he continued to press. Quinn waited for his dad to tap out, but only spit dribbled down Quinn's arm, and not blood. His father refused to let go. The stakes were always high. If you didn't fight until the end, you'd never know who you really were. Quinn believed in this idea. More than this, he was this idea.

Quinn's teeth ground hard in his mouth. This was how most of Quinn's fights ended.

Never surrender. Never stop.

These were the words spoken only by Quinns.

Quinn clenched. He could still hear his dad speaking, except he wasn't there.

He never was.

He was a ghostly haze from a time long past. The fight was a ritual done only to satisfy Quinn's need to finish the mission that mattered most to him. After owning his opponent, the flashback ended, and Quinn realized he was not alone. Standing in a suit was his contractor, a man named Priest. Priest was at Quinn's farm in Wyoming uninvited, but he was smiling. Concealed by a wall of fading fog, Priest watched his best operator fight as though he was in a real match with a real opponent.

Heart pounding, aches surged through Quinn's deltoids. His chest felt inflated and tense.

It was not a loss. A loss only occurs when a person puts forth their best effort and fails. Quinn didn't. He would have if his dad were actually here. He could no longer hear his dad in his own mind. Now, the man had faded from Quinn's memory, almost completely gone.

Quinn dropped his hand and let the pain go. *Honor.*

He stood, closed his eyes, and made his dad disappear. *Risen.*

Quinn looked at his hand as it trembled. *Giving.*

Doing this, Quinn achieved what he—a former soldier and elite killer—hadn't in a long time. He knew what it was like to lose and knew what it felt like to know.

"So..." Priest said, giving his hand to Quinn. Looking at his boss's oily palm, Quinn accepted. Wiping the sweat off his face, Quinn waited to hear about this new mission, if that's what Priest was here to talk about.

"Got a new job for you, and it's a fight perfect for you."

Quinn breathed in. He wanted all the details.

"I found him, Quinn," Priest said. "I found...your father."

CHAPTER 2
THE JOB

THE FIRST CONSONANT IN THE TWO SYLLABLE WORD brought Quinn to a startling halt.

Fa-ther.

"What did you just say?" Still grinning, a tremor shivered through Quinn's wrist.

"Come inside. Let's have ourselves a drink first, yeah?" Priest asked. He followed Quinn into his lavish farmhouse.

———

Inside, the two mercenaries stood in Quinn's clean kitchen.

Broder Quinn was once a Green Beret training officer. A capable man, he bred his son to become the ideal killing machine. Kyle Quinn was sculpted from years of malice and brutality, which encased the mercenary in an impenetrable wall he spent years trying to break out of.

Born in Saskatchewan, Quinn was raised with a heavy hand and high expectations.

The way Tiger Woods's father trained his son to play golf, Quinn's dad taught Kyle how to kill. At the age of four, he was introduced to four martial arts and was trained in the basement of his home. Meeting every day for three hours, it was in the cold and in the darkness that Quinn was birthed.

It's where a Custodian...was born.

Quinn's father was a soldier, but other than duty, his neighboring passion was combat. Having learned from some of the world's greatest martial artists, Broder Quinn traveled the world, visiting places like Okinawa and Brazil. He learned everything from striking to grappling. Quinn's education began with the introductions of judo, jiu-jitsu, aikido, and Jeet Kune Do. Broder Quinn was adamant about making these the pillars of his son's style. Starting here, Quinn graduated to other fighting forms, such as Shotokan karate, wrestling, Krav Maga, and weapons training. Being a quick learner, Quinn embraced his ability to withstand pain and to continue to come back even in the most dire situations. Quinn would rise regardless of any challenges.

He knew how to fight until the very end.

"So...where is he?" Quinn asked.

Priest took a shot of malt whiskey and licked his lips.

"Well, I do have some news about your old man," he said, "but none of it is any good. See, he's been hanging out with some pretty bad dudes down in Louisiana. I have a list for you to look at, but before we get to all that, *some context* first."

Priest pushed off the counter and slammed down his glass.

"Context?" Either Quinn was going to be told where his father was or he was done with this conversation.

"Hmm," Priest replied, holding booze under his slick

tongue. "I know what you want to know, but before you can, we talk business."

"I thought we already were."

"Nah, we were talkin' curiosity," Priest corrected, turning toward this leather bag he brought with him. "And I do believe I've piqued yours. Now..." Priest removed a manila file folder and pressed it against his chest. "Time to grease it with something a little juicier, shall we?"

Reaching out, Quinn scowled. This was the common transaction done when conducting business. Talk first, brief second, and accept later.

However, there was a photo inside the folder, and next to it was a name.

Sirius Tenet.

Reading on, Quinn consumed more intel regarding this man.

Sirius Tenet was the current governor of Louisiana, and Alistair Tenet was his son. He was also the face of the sprawling family responsible for several outreach programs, including reconstructions and police fundraisers happening throughout the state.

Nothing surprising so far.

"So...a no-name politician? That's what I've been reduced to? What is this, Priest?"

"Keep reading."

Quinn sighed and returned to the folder. He turned the page and was greeted with not a photo of a man but instead with Polaroids of *very young* children.

"Well, the state, recently, has recorded the highest number of missing children in the entire country," Priest said. "Did you know about that?"

It was a rhetorical question. Quinn was not aware.

Yet, Quinn's father was not one for abduction. So, these new photos weren't about him. Harming children was a trigger for Quinn. He'd do anything to take out the people responsible. When Priest spoke again, it was only to clarify.

More than this, it was to *warn*.

"A new power is rising," Priest said, "and it's growing, Quinn. We have to stop it from spreading...before it's too late."

CHAPTER 3
ERADICATE

"CHILDREN ARE DISAPPEARING FREQUENTLY ACROSS the entire state of Louisiana, Quinn. Did you know that?" asked Priest. "And with so many classified as missing, not one case has been reported or gone statewide. Now does that sound strange to you?"

Priest leaned on the counter while Quinn kept browsing.

"And all these children have one thing in common," Priest said, "besides the fact that they all came from shit families and broken homes, and do you know what that is?"

"Let me guess," Quinn interceded. He stared at the photo under his thumb. It was taken at a school gymnasium. The students ranged from ages ten to twelve. The name Tenet was written in crisp, white lettering—officializing the building as owned by this family. "All went to one of *these* schools?"

"Very good, but that's only where this thing starts."

Quinn perused. If this was to be his next job, he wanted to know everything.

"The missing children all disappeared within a fourteen-mile radius of the schools that the Tenet family set up all across the state, as you can see."

"So," Quinn said nonchalantly as he came across some paper-clipped sheets. "Call the parish sheriff. I'm sure they'd be very interested to see what's been going on under their noses."

Quinn tossed the file aside and grabbed a glass from one of the cabinets. He filled it with water, took a quick sip, and exhaled. This was not the type of job that Quinn did.

Custodians—Quinn's classification in the black ops sector—clean. They did not investigate and they did not serve the courts or the people, not directly. But, if what Quinn was seeing was correct, then what Priest wanted was for him to go to the bayous and kill a bunch of clowns.

Did Priest not say he found his father? If so, where did he fit into all this?

"Now hold on there," Priest said, taking one step closer. "While the kids who have gone missing are *linked* to this family, I have reason to suspect that everyone is involved. Local PD, the sheriff's department, the whole goddamn state might know what's been going on, and still, they've chosen to do nothing about it."

"I see," Quinn said, glancing at the folder.

"It's a bloody growth, Quinn. A tree with roots that run deep. And to kill any tree, you have to go in and kill it from the roots up."

Quinn examined the innocent faces of all the children in the pictures. Not once was he required to deal with people who abducted kids and killed them without reason. He killed men who killed other men, and that was Quinn's world. That's what he did.

"This family seems to have their hooks into a whole lot

of other things too," Priest said. "I know that they've been linked to each case, and like I said, this is only just the start."

"So...they're kidnapping kids," Quinn said, his first actual engagement in regard to the mission parameters and its details. "For what purpose?"

"Well, I can tell you they ain't sellin' 'em," Priest said. "Not exactly."

This response forced a grimace from Quinn he quickly subverted. He wanted to conceal his emotions as best he could. Of all the terrible things Quinn imagined, grown men using children was as bad as it gets.

"I think this might be part of something bigger, something very dangerous."

Quinn considered the grander picture and wondered how much bigger.

"How do you know all this?" Quinn asked Priest.

"Same way I know all things," Priest replied. "I'm connected to all the bad shit happening in this glorious country of ours, which means I know how to ask the right questions to the right people at the right time. It's how I got this intel you've been peepin' through. Wasn't easy, but I got it."

Priest jerked his chin. He gestured to the folder. Quinn didn't bother to look.

"Sounds like a cover-up," Quinn said. "Powerful family like this could ensure that level of secrecy."

"Indeed, they could," Priest said.

"So what the hell do you need me for? Quit stallin'. Spit it out, while you still can."

Quinn asked the only question that mattered. He was rude because he was tired of the insinuations and the games. Being a man of few words, right now, Quinn wanted to say more. His interest was piqued, no doubt about that. Yet, he was only willing to hear so much prelude before wanting the full experience.

"Just get on with it before I lose my patience."

Priest cackled like a court jester.

"Well, I want you, Quinn. I want *you* to settle this. I want you to find every single maggot linked to this depraved family who call themselves the Brotherhood of Cyn, whatever the fuck that means." Priest gritted his teeth. Until now, Quinn had never observed such fury in his boss and overlord. Priest was usually stoic—straight to the point. "I want you to track 'em all down," Priest said. "I want you to hunt 'em all and make it seem as though they never existed, do you understand me?"

Cult.

This word was one Quinn rarely heard. Dealing with cults and removing them, as Priest articulated, was not in his realm of aptitude and understanding. But then that's why Priest was here now. He wanted Quinn to do this. It was all on the table.

"I see."

Finding his father was Quinn's only incentive. However, it was not Priest's. Therefore, Quinn was all the more curious.

What did this cult mean to his contractor? Why did he want *them* killed?

Did the cult *work* for Priest?

Quinn couldn't imagine this being true and, for now, he didn't want to.

From what Quinn understood, the Custodians were the only organization under Priest's command. It was his baby, his idea, *his guild*. He had formed this group of black ops assassins to protect the country at all costs. On the surface, the endeavor seemed noble and honorable, but they were essentially a group of killers and destroyers.

They weren't good or altruistic.

The Custodians were efficient but never kind.

They were real and usable but not good for much else.

However, Priest only looking after one operation was Quinn's assumption. It was something he only *thought* to be true.

He didn't know for certain it was.

Therefore, it might also be true that Priest was familiar with other organizations.

And, when Quinn thought familiar, he didn't think aware.

He knew Priest was *aware* of all the other crime syndicates and corrupt enterprises currently in operation. This cabal known as the Brotherhood of Cyn wasn't on Quinn's radar. They didn't seem to be powerful or interesting. By any other standard of criminality, they were boring.

Easy.

So, if Priest wanted them dead, it was because they were a threat to the country.

But they weren't, not in Quinn's opinion. And yet, Quinn didn't care why Priest wanted them removed or why. Quinn knew the world was better off without these pedophile pieces of shit running around. Quinn was willing and able to do the deed.

But Quinn knew Priest wasn't a good man.

Still, this cult was not what Quinn expected, and so he couldn't help but ask...why?

Why him? Why now? Why?

"And this is full-on, Quinn," Priest said.

Quinn's head tilted. He was intrigued. Full-on meant only one thing.

"This is an *Eradicate*."

Quinn gulped and was suddenly more relaxed.

"Eradicate?"

Priest's scowl and Quinn's stern demeanor both disappeared. They had each returned to a state of diligence and respect. Now they were talking business.

"Yep."

Quinn nodded and reflected on the order.

"No rules," Priest said. "No apologies. Just kill them. Kill them all."

CHAPTER 4
DECISIONS

A Custodian's duties are relegated to four main areas of expertise.

First, involves security. This was something Priest liked to call *checking*, as normal custodians performed a routine check each and every day. Then, there was reconnaissance. This was called *cleaning* because custodians did precisely that: they cleaned. There was also extraction or *guarding*. The reason for this was custodians generally guarded, preserved, and removed certain items from their place. And last, there was execution or *disposing*. Now this only had one meaning...

Therefore, the Custodian title made a great deal of sense, given its expectations.

Always unattached, Quinn would never fall for anyone or care enough to risk his name or his status. A *Custodian* was never permitted to tell any civilian what they did or how they did it.

When asked, the question: what do you do for a living?

Their answer was simple.

"Custodian."

Custodians preserved the country's ideas and values. They were more than just assassins. They were the gatekeepers and the watchers. They were the guardians of truths that could never be taken away or destroyed.

Without them, as Priest said, all we knew and loved would come to an end.

However, rarely did any Custodian receive an Eradicate order.

The classification, while self-explanatory, was the deadliest of all.

What was an Eradicate?

In essence, it was freedom. Little to no rules, oversight, or guidance. Mostly, it was the ability not to care and not to play by prime directives or objectives.

Other Custodial missions were regimented. They had protocol, like the rules of engagement, keeping civilian casualties to a minimum, and staying on target. Engagement, sweeping, and clearing all needed to be followed to a tee before said mission was considered complete. The bodies needed to be disposed of, and the kills needed to be reported, logged, and, in some cases, *reviewed*. No one could know of the job or the mission and especially, the assassin.

However, in the instance of an Eradicate, everything softened.

The scene was still left spotless and the job was done but all of those activities were at the discretion of the Custodian himself. It was a job done but done at ease and with little clean up. And the rules of the engagement were pushed aside in favor of obliteration and what was known as Old Testament.

The rules were there, but none are set.

Few organizations knew of the Custodians' existence, and even fewer knew what they do.

In the case of the Eradicate, none of that mattered. Someone needed to die, and it didn't matter how or why—it just needed to get done and it was entirely left to the Custodian.

On this day, it was left entirely to Quinn.

"What?" Quinn asked. He heard Priest clearly the first time but felt the need to ask again.

"You heard me right," Priest said. "I want all of these fuckers dead and gone, and I don't care what you have to do to get it done."

"Yeah," Quinn said disingenuously. In some ways, he was only pretending to understand. "But based on the intel you have here, this Tenet family looks like they have their hooks into a few things—government, education, law enforcement. Therefore, an Eradicate might be too much of a liability."

Quinn was lucid. His reaction was plausible. Nevertheless, Priest guffawed as he stood next to Quinn's refrigerator.

"Well, if this was a normal mission, you'd just take out the leaders, but an Eradicate will allow you to take out anyone linked to it as well as anyone else who stands in your way," Priest said. "You can also leave the bodies should you want to, and last time I checked, I was the one who gave the orders here and it was you who followed them there, Quinn. Sounds to me like you might be forgetting that."

Peripherally, Quinn looked at the folder. He could question Priest. He thought the mission somewhat suspicious. Even with his father added in, Quinn still was unwilling to accept. However, though he rarely questioned, it was not part of his job.

To eradicate a problem means to end it completely.

Quinn would need to leave everything more than *spotless*. This didn't mean literally spotless, only that none could survive. Everyone who was a threat was killed. Quinn was to complete a full sweep and bleach all the stains, so to speak. While Quinn did have more questions, he heard Priest again and peered at the folder for another look.

At the corner, Quinn spotted what appeared to be another photograph. It was a different color and right away garnered Quinn's attention.

"And you know why I'm offering this to *you*, right?"

Quinn removed this new picture he spotted. Drawn to it for no apparent reason, Quinn pinched it by the edge and slipped the photo out slowly.

"Because this family of bums," Priest said, "is linked to *another man*."

Priest's voice echoed in Quinn's mind like a baby's rattle.

It was as if every syllable provoked more pain and more trauma. At last, the words Quinn wanted to hear were uttered. And, although Quinn's interest rose as soon as Priest said these very words, "*I found your father*," it was not enough for the Custodian to commit.

"Someone who you know has had a long history with shaping the lives of people who desired power…"

Quinn held his gaze. He remembered the one who said it first—*desired power*.

He recalled the days of fighting to the death. Always, preparing for the war that might someday come, here was an image of the man who sculpted Quinn into a warrior of undeniable perfection. The photo showed a grizzled, tough guy with peppered hair. Donning two tags that dangled around his wrinkled neck, they peeked out of the man's unbuttoned Henley.

He was old, but exactly as Quinn remembered.

"This is him?" Quinn said.

"Yeah," Priest said, a few feet away. "*That's him.*"

A pair of aviator sunglasses with fat, black lenses concealed his dad's grizzled mug.

The last time Quinn saw him was years ago. It happened when Quinn left Delta and around the time when he had only just started to work for Priest. Lifting the photograph, Quinn replied to Priest in a raspy voice. Speaking in this tone, Quinn emphasized his opinion on this proposal.

"Where?"

"Last I checked," Priest answered, cheery and cool, "he was in Baton Rouge."

"Working?" Quinn lowered the photograph and looked at Priest. His lips curled and clenched.

"Maybe," Priest answered. "But he is there, as you can see."

Quinn glanced at the photo and said nothing. Yes, he could see.

"Look, I know the one thing you desire is to find this old fuck, your daddy, and make him pay for what he did to you, but to get to him, obviously," Priest explained, "you are going to have to get to *them*, and the only way you get to them..." A deep breath ejected from Priest's face. "Is... you have to accept this Eradicate and walk out the damn door, ready to do what you do best."

Quinn, looking pensive, rested his hand on his waist while the other was on the counter next to the folder. Quinn wanted nothing more than to find his old man and finish what he started.

"How long?"

Priest eyed Quinn while beaming with gross pleasure.

"Timeline is tight," Priest said. "But by the time you scratch one out, the rest will all scatter, so you'll have to move quickly. You'll have to find 'em all and take 'em all down one by one."

"I know that."

"But you can fly out tomorrow. I'll have a contact waiting for you. She'll set you up with the usual safe house, transportation, and all the other goodies you might need while you're knee-deep in the shit, you know? All you have to do is say yes."

Taking a moment to process everything, what Quinn envisioned was the only person he wanted to see. He could feel his dad as if he was actually there right now.

"Never let your enemies walk away. You end them right where they stand."

Hearing his dad's voice in his head, it was exactly like when Quinn experienced his severe moments of déjà vu. And, since he vowed to find his father, Quinn swore that when he did, he'd finish him once and for all. His dad was dangerous. He knew things and he built things. This was Quinn's purpose, and that's what made him so lethal.

"This is the only way you will end things, Quinn," Priest said by the counter. "The *only* way you will get what you want."

Quinn closed his eyes. He thought of all the years he wished he could make his father pay. At last, Quinn finally had the opportunity to do this. "I'm in."

Grinning the same maniacal smirk as before, Priest leered. And, with relish, Priest knocked his knuckles against Quinn's countertop. His smile widened and his eyes gleamed a sinister glare.

"Outstanding."

CHAPTER 5
HUNGER

Before Quinn began any mission, being former special forces, the necessary steps to prepare is more than an expectation for him, it's a duty. After agreeing to the Eradicate, Priest left Quinn's farm. Quinn watched Priest drive away and gave a soldierly nod, his usual way of saying goodbye.

Regardless of his designation or his abilities, what Quinn was addicted to more than anything was the thrill of the hunt. He relished in the tension and the split-second moments in between, all gifting him with absolute power and strength.

The deadlier the mission, the deadlier the thirst.

And the more dangerous, the more Quinn wanted.

And the more he wanted, the more he owned. The more he owned, the stronger Quinn became.

In the renovated basement, a steel table sat pressed against a paneled wall. Above it was a tool rack fashioned with a thick strip of pine. Resting on each shelf was Quinn's private arsenal. Each weapon was retrofitted to Quinn's liking. All were built to satisfy his particular tastes. When Quinn stood in front of the table, he wore a white shirt and a new pair of ankle-clinging sweatpants. He was shoeless. He wore a bandanna that secured his ruffled hair. Also in the room were four identical monitors connected to a mechanical keyboard and organized in a grid formation. Quinn also had binders with tactical notes, inkblot pens, and additional photographs taken from his time in JTF 2 and Delta Force.

None were from his childhood.

On the screen to Quinn's left was a map of Vermilion parish where the Tenets resided. And, while every job required much planning and diligence, every job Quinn accepted began this way. First, Quinn liked to know exactly where he was going. Then, he obtained all the details surrounding the location.

In this case, Vermilion was a parish located near the coast of Louisiana, included Erath, and with Abbeville serving as its main city. Browsing through photographs taken of all of these places, Quinn made note of the *red flags*. This was a term given to other criminal enterprises operating throughout a particular area. In this region, Quinn saw mostly small-timers—drug dealers and a few low-level biker syndicates. Nothing too hot for Quinn to handle. The police department was about as sizable as any. And, as far as policing was concerned, they were not nearly as equipped or as dangerous as Quinn. There were two main highways, LA 699 and LA 92. There weren't many others. Checking on the sheriff, Quinn investigated what he could. If he was going to take out a powerful family, police intervention was inevitable.

It was whenever Quinn performed a cleaning. But this was an Eradicate.

He could do as he pleased. Boss's orders.

With Custodial work, timeline is everything. The

clock starts as soon as a trigger is pulled. The parish's sheriff's department, from what Quinn could infer, seemed competent.

He highlighted a few articles about certain investigations. A journalist wrote about some notable crackdowns. Based on the reporting, nothing jumped out at Quinn. It was too small a district. The Tenet cult, according to Priest, did have a name.

The Brotherhood of Cyn.

Some name, Quinn thought. It sounded dumber than a cat with wings.

He hoped his safe house would be outside the parish limits. In other missions, safe houses were usually not in the general vicinity where the cleaning occurred.

This wasn't like other missions.

Things changed.

With the parish all mapped out and outlined, Quinn made note of the main roads and access points. It was then he moved on to his targets.

On his kill list were six names: *six* primary targets.

They were the key members of the shadow organization. They operated within this seemingly innocuous community. The pawns, like in chess, were at the bottom. These were the fall guys—the foot soldiers. From there, Quinn gradually rose to the rooks and the knights. These were the elite forces as well as the leaders.

In many of the photos, there was one man who seemed out of place.

This man didn't match in terms of style or presentation. He was tall and wore three-piece suits. Each suit was a different shade of red. Judging from the man's crossed hands and upright posture, he looked like the protector of the Tenet family.

The notes in the folder pertained to this person. Quinn pulled it up on the third screen.

The man's name was Frank Kardinal. He was Alistair's assistant but was clearly a protection specialist tasked with safeguarding the family. He was also someone who served and supervised. It was plausible that this was who the Tenets sent to cover up their many dirty deeds.

So, Kardinal was the *fixer*. He was *their* fixer.

The practice of fixing, although not explicitly stated, was a staple for every wealthy and privileged family. The job refers to someone who did the things no one talks about. It was a chore that extended well beyond the basic tasks and expectations of an employee.

It was a small detail, but it did help Quinn as he continued to peruse.

Obviously, he wasn't going to just walk up to Sirius or Alistair, Glock out, and shoot them both in the head. Such was never Quinn's style. No, should Quinn wish to proceed, he would have to nab this Kardinal fellow the same as all the others.

Hence the order. Eradicate meant everyone—everyone must die.

Therefore, Kardinal was as much a target in the game as the rest of the Tenet clan.

Holding his gaze, Quinn scanned this picture. Kardinal did not intimidate him, not even a little.

In order to be a Custodian, one must stand toe-to-toe with those who were highly lethal and dangerous. Engaging with the unstoppable was just another part of Quinn's job. Priest even encouraged his Custodians to take out those who were falsely under the impression they were untouchable. Priest also had a tendency to stroke the egos of his operatives. Often, he referred to them as the *best of the best*.

"You're my ultimate badasses. Ain't no one out there better than you."

As far as Quinn was aware, he had met many impressive killers. Yet, regardless of how tough or formidable one *thinks* one is, there is always someone out there who is tougher, meaner, deadlier.

Always.

Quinn had never met one who fell into this category. However, he knew one day that person would emerge. He already knew a few who might fit this criterion.

How Quinn's father connected with the Tenet family was something yet to be revealed. Now, Quinn suspected it might be these two commodities that fueled his father's interest. Particularly, it became popular in his later years, like profit and power. While he was ex-military and a mercenary, a pedophiliac family didn't fit his father's MO. Quinn could never see his dad participating in such things. It was too messy, too exposed, and too strange.

Despite being rich and powerful, the Tenet's inner sanctum was nothing compared to the Bratva or the Camorra. Hell, they didn't even compare to a level two criminal organization like the New Jersey outfit led by Tony Solantro, who was a member of the East Coast Mafia and ran a smaller, less organized group outside the Five Families.

None of Quinn's targets seemed compelling.

Based on the intel, the Tenets were all pitifully amateur. None of their credentials jumped out at Quinn. So far as he could tell, they were just a bunch of sick fools involved with a rich family. America had those for a dime a dozen. They weren't trained or motivated. They weren't interesting or exceptional. They were basically nothing.

Quinn had spent much of his career as a Custodian hunting sharks. Throughout America, he fought almost every major crime syndicate and succeeded in all his missions. He infiltrated the mob, fought the Yakuza, and was once charged with terminating the entire Russian Bratva single handedly. He murdered congressmen and state senators. He went head-to-head with other mercenary units and men employed by blacklisted governments. He did all of this without once compromising his identity, and so, Quinn began to wonder just how difficult this job in Louisiana could be?

If not for this father's name, would Quinn have accepted?

Therefore, he again returned to the same question.

Why did Priest insist he get involved?

Putting all this aside, Quinn thought about his father. The man was his sole motivation. Once Quinn accepted how the men on his list weren't very dangerous, then this job was technically a walk in the park.

Fine by Quinn.

In his basement, Quinn had all the Tenets memorized, as well as all the associates who had the most control over the cult. Among the materials Quinn had organized, there were *two* photographs of *two* different men. And, unlike their presumed cohorts, they were mug shots of two whiter-than-white assholes. Their hair was disheveled and there were tattoos on their necks. They looked smug even in their mugshots.

"Meres." Quinn read the name out loud.

Apparently, these boys were linked to the family by means of the father, Sirius Tenet. Quinn skimmed the info. According to the profile—and Priest did give an up-to-date family tree—it showed how Sirius had two children outside of marriage. They were linked by blood only.

Nonetheless, the Eradicate included them too.

Billy Lee Meres was the oldest. Sallow in appearance,

despite being big and brooding, he was a local heroin dealer and notorious throughout the parish. Among other things, there were a few rape charges laid on him and some other instances of aggravated assault. All of this was expected.

After Billy Lee, there was his brother, Brent.

Smaller and wiry, Brent was a Neo-Nazi, right-wing maniac linked to a few underground fascist organizations. He was also a meth head said to possess a penchant for gunplay and pyrotechnics.

The two were a pair of regular deviants. Obviously, they were the black sheep of the Tenet family. Byproducts of a refusal to take responsibility by their father, the boys were detached and shunned. Quinn examined their faces. He knew they'd been neglected and beaten. How they were raised might not coincide with the prideful Sirius Tenet philosophy, but did align with Quinn's father's ideology.

Brent and Billy Lee's statements were mostly belligerent and unintelligible. They did say they worked for *a lord*. Quinn sniffled and glanced at the last page in the folder. He knew the lord mentioned was Sirius. Quinn could also see the Meres boys had opted not to use the family's last name—not that anyone would see them as Sirius's kids even if they tried.

No, they were merely blood relatives.

CHAPTER 6
SUIT UP

Pure sunlight sheathed the field surrounding Quinn's farm. The Custodian's home was colonial. It appeared as three interlocked prisms stacked on top of each other. The outside was layered with a fresh coat of maroon paint while the barn itself was converted into an airplane hangar. The roof was shingled and the sides were winter-beaten. There were five solar panels connected to the shingles and the screen door was the oldest part of Quinn's residence. It was the only part was unchanged since his many renovations. A warm place comprised of only the bare essentials, with little luxury, here Quinn had everything he needed.

With the locations mapped and all his targets marked, Quinn saved all the intel he gathered onto a USB stick he slipped into his pocket. Quinn stood from his bench and walked over to another section of the basement. His black sweatpants dragged along the floor.

In his muscle shirt, Quinn stepped to a chrome table and turned on a lamp.

He liked this part.

Being a proud Glock owner, it was Quinn's favorite. His gun sat in the center of the table.

"Ladies."

Quinn's eyes twinkled in the presence of this valued arsenal. His penchant for firearms was one that, despite being a bona fide occupational requirement, was also a significant part of Quinn's life. They were as valued as the clothing on his back and the food in his fridge.

The best designer for customizing standard firearms was the company called TTI or Taran Tactical Innovations. Owned and operated by Taran Butler, his company had built its reputation from years of expert training and competition. Yet, the company's foray into gun innovation came as a direct result of Mr. Butler himself. He ensured his guns were made to be more than just effective. No, Mr. Butler wanted them to be the best money could buy.

There were six parts to Quinn's weaponry.

The first was his carbine. This was a fully outfitted AR-15 with a magnifying Trijicon scope. Next to it was the Benelli shotgun. Quinn was good with a Mossberg but never a Remington. His first choice was a Benelli and no other. Quinn also owned a Desert Tech Stealth Recon sniper rifle and two customized Glocks. His top choices were a 34 and a 26. He wasn't opposed to using an HK as long as it had the right mods.

There were Quinn's guns, and then there were his blades. His knife was an OTF used solely for close encounters, quickdraws, and fast attacks.

Quinn's selections were specific. They had not changed since he left JTF 2.

Whatever job Priest provided to Quinn, these were the weapons brought along for the ride. So far, not a single one let Quinn down. He planned to never let that change. He remembered the old saying: *if it ain't broke, don't fix it*.

Taking a second to marvel at the weapons' many brilliances, Quinn liked his Glocks the way he liked a cold beer. Refreshing and quenching, it was so satisfying to know there was something that always managed to get the job done. Although quite capable, with a wide range of firearms, Quinn's final weapon was one he took the most pride in.

He did because it was the most different.

On a separate table, Quinn lifted his tonfa.

These were sleek. The batons were constructed from a titanium alloy. Once called a *nightstick*, they were used by the police. However, their origins were based in Okinawan karate, specifically those who had knowledge of Shotokan.

The tonfa could be brandished in a number of ways. The first was to grip the short handle on the side. This was called the *nigri*. The tonfa could be used as a blocking weapon when secured against the forearms. The other way was to straighten the guard, which was the *monouchi*, and could be used to swat one's opponent. The last way was the least popular. It was to grip the tonfa by its shorter end. From here, the practitioner could wield it as a club. With variations provided, this weapon was diverse, light, and fortified.

Quinn's tonfa, like everything else, was given by the same person who taught him everything. Few knew how to use this weapon. Even fewer could use the tonfa the way Quinn did. In the end, the tonfa gave Quinn innumerable methods for protection and attack.

He stood in a basic stance and dished out a few practice jabs. He spun the tonfa in synchronous intervals, then

Quinn inserted them into two cases at the back of his armor. These weapons were mystifying to any opponent. This was an advantage Quinn never overlooked.

"Let's begin."

CHAPTER 7
FIRST BLOOD

In Louisiana, in addition to the Tenet family, Quinn was informed of three other men who were a part of the organization: Dr. Ameer Sauder, Cal Vickers, and some fool who went by the name Tulsa Monarch.

Ameer Sauder was a surgeon in Baton Rouge. Cal Vickers was an insurance agent with dark eyes and the pudgy fellow Tulsa Monarch. According to Tulsa's file, he was born and raised outside of Erath. In Quinn's opinion, the name was ridiculous. He was a slick fool. If he was a salesman, he would be downright sleazy. If Tulsa was a teacher and he was accused of being creepy, Quinn imagined the teachers on staff would agree. The students would fear him, but they wouldn't report him. They wouldn't because behind his eyes was something Quinn rarely saw. There was so little there, and that's why Quinn hated this Monarch the most.

Quinn knew the type. He was a guilty man filled with excuses and denial. He would gaslight anyone dumb enough to try and outsmart him. Tulsa's file alluded to all this. Quinn thought of Tulsa as a bastard, but also, he thought of how brittle and small he appeared. Barely part of the cult, Quinn looked forward to seeing him down the road.

Tulsa Monarch's execution would be swift and easy. This guy was less than nothing.

He was a fucking nobody.

The others Quinn examined seemed like normal, everyday folk. They were wealthy, yes, but unremarkable nonetheless.

———

In Louisiana, Quinn opted to buy a burly Dodge RAM as his chief mode of transportation.

It was a surprisingly well-furnished vehicle, equipped with heavy tires and leather seats. In fact, it was not at all different from the RAM Quinn had back in Wyoming.

Armed with his Glock 34, Quinn eyed a set of doors from across a parking lot. Quinn remembered the schematics of the hospital. There was a security guard poised at the front. He was armed but ordinary.

Quinn's plan, however, was to go in through the rear entrance.

There was a map on his cell phone. Here, Quinn had the floors memorized and knew exactly where Ameer Sauder was going to be.

His office was on the ninth floor, apart from the patients and nurses.

It would take more than two shots to finish the job.

Quinn entered the hospital as a man dressed in black. He left his usual gear in the trailer, which was his safe house. Rather than wearing what he usually did, Quinn was casual. Dressed in a plain shirt and a pair of baggy pants, Quinn strolled into the lobby with his

Glock secured in its holster and his OTF in his back pocket.

Both were easily accessible as Quinn passed through the bustling Emergency Ward. He walked with his head down to avoid being seen. Wearing what he was, Quinn could easily pass as someone going about their day. He stepped into the elevator. None would notice him unless they were given a reason to do so. Unlike the others Quinn was set to terminate, this first target would be nothing more than a step-in-step-out, quick-draw situation.

Soon as Quinn saw the doctor and identified him, he would fire and exit.

It was as simple as that.

Quinn's hand was on his 34. He walked by a sign with the name Ameer Sauder, Vascular Surgeon, carved into the placard.

He was close. Quinn turned left and then right.

He marched into the vacant setting and the room itself smelled of salty air freshener. As Quinn approached the door, he clasped the steel handle. It felt loose when Quinn pushed it in with his shoulder. Immediately greeted upon entering, the first sound he heard was a male's voice. Ameer spoke without the Southern drawl Quinn expected. In fact, it sounded a little Midwest.

"No more visits right now, thank you." Quinn ignored the refusal and stepped in with tender ease. The door didn't make a sound.

"Hey," Sauder snapped. "What are you doing? I said—"

Quinn had only contempt for the perverted, downright twisted doctor sitting in front of him. As soon as Sauder saw Quinn, he stood from his desk. His once perturbed expression morphed into a droopy, childish pout. "May I help you?"

"Ameer Sauder?" Quinn addressed the doctor before pulling out his weapon.

"Y-y-yes." And without hesitation, Quinn drew.

Equipped with a sound suppressor, the Glock 34 spat two clean shots into the doctor's chest. Thrusting him backward, Ameer Sauder fell into his swiveling chair and bounced back and down. He was dead before he hit the ground. Though his target was executed with precision and calm, Quinn spared nothing under these circumstances.

He completed his signature by putting another round in Sauder's head.

Fast and clean, this first name was crossed off Quinn's list.

Sauder was a foot soldier, a new recruit among the cult. Therefore, he was low on Quinn's list. Quinn knew straight away that the rest would not be as easy as this one. They wouldn't be. Killing never was easy. It was the most difficult job in the world.

CHAPTER 8
IN HER EYES

"Kyle!" Before Quinn executed Ameer Sauder, he needed to meet with the contact Priest had arranged. Quinn didn't admit this to Priest, but he was happy to see his contact was a woman he already knew.

Her name was Ally. Ally Shepherd.

Unlike Priest, Ally was enthusiastic and passionate. She was hired to be Quinn's *liaison*. When Quinn touched down in Louisiana, she was right there to greet him in a cool pair of aviator sunglasses and a big smile on her gorgeous face. Now, Quinn was only slightly familiar with Ally. He knew she served in the Army years ago and worked with the CIA for four years after that specializing in reconnaissance and espionage. A solid reputation, Ally always treated everyone with utmost professionalism, duty, and care. Even among those who were in the business of murder and disruption, always she was calm and professional.

Ally's background was similar to Priest's. She worked briefly for the FBI and the CIA.

Why she decided to switch was because, according to her, Ally felt the second job would be less dirty. Quinn didn't know what that meant. As it turned out, Ally liked getting her hands dirty. She also preferred to work behind the scenes. She was less of a field agent and more of an intelligence operative. In fact, Ally's forte was more trading secrets. She worked for the agency for almost three years before she decided to leave and do something different.

Stepping aside, Ally spent her years away gathering recruits. She worked with other people in the field too, not just with Priest.

She advertised herself as an *extra set of hands*. Growing her list of allies, it was unclear exactly how Ally met Priest. Quinn assumed it was because they had common enemies and common interests, but then there was nothing common about their goals.

Priest wanted power, and Ally desired perspective and truth.

When she worked with Quinn before, Ally spoke a little about her personal *journey*. She was adamant about her willingness to explore and discover more about herself and the country she served. Maybe that's what brought her to where she was today. Maybe helping Quinn is something Ally wanted to do. Unsure if it was, one thing was for sure...Quinn trusted Ally.

More than this, Quinn believed in Ally.

When Quinn stepped out of his Cirrus jet, he gave Ally a slight wave. He lugged his cases loaded with gear and proceeded across the tarmac. The Louisiana heat was like an impenetrable wave fueled by pockets of dry sunshine.

It assaulted Quinn the second he was exposed to it.

"Hey, want me to give you a hand with all that stuff you got there?"

"Thanks," Quinn said. "It's appreciated."

Quinn handed Ally a box and she dragged it over to her Jeep and popped the trunk.

"So was the flight okay?" Ally asked Quinn. She loaded one case into her Jeep. "Mr. Pilot!"

"Not bad," Quinn said. "Skies were mostly all clear."

"That's good," said Ally. "Last one?" she asked, referring to the last box Quinn had on his person. Quinn pivoted and eased the box away.

"No, thanks," he said and he pulled the box back. "I got this one."

Hands up, Ally politely stepped aside.

"Sure thing. Whatever you want."

With what Quinn had inside this box, he preferred it stay with him. Ally hopped into the front seat. Quinn closed the trunk and followed Ally. The interior of her Jeep smelled of pine and was fashioned with some expensive leather upholstery.

Not ideal for such a warm state, it was clean. Quinn appreciated that it was.

"Ready?" Ally asked, hand on the shift.

Quinn's chin moved. He wasn't quite nodding, but was more gazing up at the sky. He realized now he was far from home. The mission was now underway. Quinn adjusted his Oakleys and looked down the road.

"Let's go." Ally shifted her car into gear and drove out of the airport.

She and Quinn exited through an opening in the perimeter fence. Ally grabbed a water bottle from one of the cup holders and twisted off the cap.

"I've arranged to have your plane tagged by the way,"

Ally said. "It'll be stored in a private hangar for however long you're here."

"Right," Quinn said. "Thank you."

"Hmm," Ally said. She had a sip and held some water in her mouth for a second before swallowing. "Drink?"

Quinn noticed there was another bottle in the holder. This one was for him. Quinn removed the bottle and gulped down the cool liquid. He felt an immediate jolt as the water filled his stomach.

"So...you got an Eradicate, did you?" commented Ally, keeping her eyes on the road.

Quinn stared through his sunglasses and spoke quietly. "I did."

"Nice," said Ally. "I also heard you're going after the Tenets. A good fish, if I do say so myself."

Quinn squinted and watched Ally closely.

"It would seem so," he said. Quinn was still fatigued from the flight.

He hadn't slept well since he accepted this job.

"I take it you're familiar?" Quinn asked Ally.

"Everyone around here is," said Ally.

"So I've been told."

"I imagine Priest filled you in best he could," Ally continued, "but now that you're here, I've marked the area, so I do have some *red flags* for you."

"Thanks."

"Part of the job," Ally replied, swerving down the unpaved road.

A new smell sharpened Quinn's senses for reasons he couldn't quite explain.

Like smoke mixed with sewage, it contained all the intoxicants produced by the bayous and fat smoke stacks he was now passing by. What Ally had referenced were

Quinn's *red flags*. This pertained to the mapping and highlighting of things a Custodian needed to know. In this case, these were the people who might pose a threat to Quinn other than the Tenet family.

"Yeah, well, tell me what I need to know," Quinn said. "Countdown begins now."

CHAPTER 9
ALSO A FLYER

IN ADDITION TO QUINN'S MILITARY BACKGROUND AND martial arts experience, the Custodian acquired another useful skill.

"No shit. You're a pilot too and you have your own goddamn plane?! That's damn sweet!"

At the time, Quinn was escorting Priest to the barn at the back of his house. Priest rejoiced knowing his Custodian could fly anywhere he wanted at any time.

The hangar for Quinn's jet was once a stable used for horses and other farm animals. However, Quinn converted it into a hangar in order to make room for his Cirrus Vision SF50 jet. This was a sleek aircraft, low to the ground and it fit perfectly inside the once old barn. It was a single, top-mounted V-wing design and was Quinn's most prized possession.

When Quinn wasn't training or killing, he was working on his plane.

The inside of this aircraft was cozy. Quinn removed two seats so he could fit more cargo. Now used purely for business and rarely for pleasure, it avoided radar. The jet enabled Quinn to go anywhere he needed with minimal hassle. It was easier for his contracts and also for his employer. While the drive to Louisiana was manageable, flying was Quinn's most effective exit strategy.

It was another facet of his expertise that tickled Priest's fancy. Whenever he assigned work to Quinn, he had something few did, because one of his custodians could fly!

Before killing Ameer Sauder, Quinn went with Ally to a trailer, which was to be his safe house. In his hand, Quinn held on tightly to a black binder.

"Aliases," said Ally. She walked Quinn into the mobile home shortly after his arrival. Not one for these kinds of homes, this model was short and made of steel.

"Right." To be frank, when discussing the mission, Quinn forgot his next step.

"Open it," Ally said. "You'll see it's all in there. Exactly what Priest asked me to get for you."

"Right." Quinn slid up the zipper.

Inside this binder were items needed should Quinn come under fire. He had a driver's license, a fake social security number, and a crummy health card. Priest slid in some hundred-dollar bills as per diem. Flipping through the stack, Quinn skimmed. Intermittently, he looked at Ally. She smiled as she perused.

"You are now officially Quinn Masterson, janitor from Wisconsin."

Nodding, Quinn liked the sound of that. Yet, this was not really required.

Whenever a Custodian was sent to a new location, naturally, they could not go as themselves. Traceable yet also liable. Quinn didn't care, he was open to compromise. Still, he wanted to stay off the radar. False identities helped him to do that.

"Nicely done," Quinn said to Ally.

"Thought so too."

"Any other red flags or additional intel?" Quinn asked.

"What do you mean?"

Quinn eyed Ally. He was not only here for the Tenets. He hoped Priest made this clear to her. He wanted to tell Ally what he was thinking. He just didn't know how.

"Where's my father?" Now, Quinn wondered if Ally knew about this.

She would have told him if she didn't. She was always talkative. However, Quinn took Ally's current silence as an indication that this was all she knew.

"Never mind," Quinn said. "Thank you for all this. You did good. Real good."

Although it was Priest who obtained all of Quinn's information, it was Ally who delivered it. There was something about her, something difficult to place but very endearing, and Quinn wanted to think Ally might feel the same way about him.

Honestly, Quinn liked her too, more than she knew he did.

CHAPTER 10
ANOTHER ONE

Awake at four a.m., Quinn was back in his safehouse before the crack of dawn. For this next kill, he chose to arm himself differently. Sauder was executed with a clean shot from Quinn's Glock but now, the Custodian chose to wield something bolder and with more precision. For this, Quinn selected his AR-15. A classic rifle, he held it locked and loaded. When Quinn left the ravine, he kept the weapon stashed in the seat next to him.

When driving, Quinn reviewed the parameters of his next cleaning. Beneath this underbelly of depravity and greed, among the gathering of all the rats and filth, always there's a businessman who deals and steals.

Jeffrey Epstein was a sex offender who allegedly killed himself in his own cell. He was also the main flesh trader to some of America's elite. He operated out of an island. Supposedly, it was a land flourishing with underage girls and served as a frequent hot spot for the world's rich and famous.

While Cal Vickers belonged to the underbelly of Louisiana pedophiles, he was at the very bottom of this long food chain. His wife, Mary Anne Vickers, worked alongside her husband.

Both ran a chain of auto dealerships spread across Baton Rouge.

Quinn didn't care about his place within this Brotherhood of Cyn. However, he suspected neither his wife nor Vickers's children were aware of Cal's private life. They were oblivious to his interactions with the Tenets.

And yet, after Quinn took out the doctor, Vickers would likely scatter. He was not wealthy to the same degree as Sirius or Ameer. Therefore, Vickers might be willing to fight back if he had the skills.

Quinn had Vickers pinned as a coward.

He believed he would skip town after hearing of his friend's demise. However, before Cal could go anywhere, Quinn had him locked. He parked his truck outside of Mr. Vickers's house and watched. Thanks to Quinn's Nikon Prostaff binoculars, he had a solid view. These binoculars were the same model Quinn used when he was in Delta Force. He peered into the Vickers' two-story home with a gabled rooftop and a picket fence. It was so classic it could have been featured in a commercial for a mortgage firm.

Quinn spotted Vickers strolling through his kitchen. He was speaking to his wife and daughter. Quinn was allowed to remove anyone affiliated with the family, loosely or otherwise. So, should Vickers try and escape with his wife and kid, well then Quinn knew what he had to do.

He never wanted it to come to that. His orders were simple.

His decision was made. Quinn never proclaimed himself to be heroic. He was just a man following through on his words. He was a man true to his word who always did what he thought was necessary and maybe, sometimes, what he thought was right.

After completing a half hour of recon, Quinn's AR was ready. He stared up at the blistering sun as Vickers walked out the door. Dressed in a black suit, Cal carried a briefcase. He was the cliché epitome of an ordinary man beginning his ordinary day. He hurried to a silver Acura parked in the middle of the driveway. Quinn eyed the woman as well as the girl.

Both followed closely behind Cal.

"Shit." The wife and a daughter no older than ten walked alongside Cal. The girl was wearing a pink dress. She held an iPad and played with it as she walked.

Shaking his head for a moment, Quinn battled his conscience, which was a small entity.

He didn't like killing women, and he definitely didn't kill kids. Quinn's code was absolute, and so far, he had not broken it and he didn't plan on breaking it now. The Custodian's hand shifted from the wheel and then down to the seat beside him. Quinn brought his AR up to his lap.

Vickers entered the Acura and started its engine. If Vickers left now, he would be as good as gone. While Quinn *could* follow him, he was not one for delaying a target's death. If he had the *opportunity* to take out his target, then he was going to act on it, even if it meant doing something he despised.

Quinn gawked at Vickers. The sleazy fool snapped at his wife to quiet down and he raced toward the front of the car. With the rifle still on Quinn's lap, the strap remained tight on his shoulder.

Quinn gently touched the trigger.

Don't wait. Do it now.

About to open the door, Quinn's goal was to get out as

soon as the Acura began backing out. Quinn's basic plan was to spray the front seat in concentrated bursts and smoke everyone inside, including the wife. But, as Quinn eyed Vickers, he vacated the truck. Then, he noticed that the man was not moving toward the front seat like Quinn had expected.

Instead, Vickers was heading back in. He was returning to his house. He pointed to show his wife one digit, and Quinn could read his lips.

"I'll be right back."

With Quinn's target now turning, the Custodian's plan also began to turn.

Vickers was not *close* to the car. In fact, Vickers was not even *in* the car. Now, he was out in the open and completely exposed. Quinn could cap him on his way back to his home. If he did this, then Quinn could spare the lives of his wife and child, but *only* if the Custodian could get to Vickers in time.

Quinn trekked across the lawn. He scurried like he was about to conduct a raid. Quinn glided along the fence and his shoulder slipped across the wooden planks as he cut across. The searing Louisiana sun toasted the back of Quinn's neck. He kept a tight grip on his gun's textured handle.

All Quinn needed was two shots and that was it.

Quinn was not charged with confirming each kill. The Eradicate gave him full autonomy when it came to documenting those executed.

He had confirmed this was Vickers.

All he had to do now was pop him without being seen. With only a few more steps to go, Quinn heard the car door slam and listened as Cal Vickers called to his family again.

"Okay. Ready."

Vickers couldn't see Quinn. When the Custodian stepped out for the kill shot, the family would see him. And, if Quinn stepped even half an inch, the wife would see a man carrying a weapon. Should this happen, then the bullet Quinn put in Vickers would not be the last.

Quinn looked through the Trijicon scope. He glimpsed at Vickers's left shoulder.

Inching himself out farther, Quinn did as he always had whenever his target was looking in the other direction. He never executed anyone without staring them in the eyes first. This was not a question of honor or code. Quinn didn't like the absence of a challenge.

Vickers walked from his house to his car and Quinn made a clicking sound with his mouth. The original plan was to have Vickers whip his head around and shoot him square in the face. Yet, when Vickers heard the daunting sound, he stopped dead. His body stiffened due to the escalating fear brimming from within. Quinn pushed the stock of the AR-15 into his shoulder.

Hands up, Vickers turned. He knew someone was there.

Quinn was not entirely sure if he'd been spotted earlier, but he didn't care.

He knew Vickers would turn and the fool would see *who* was standing behind him. Expecting Vickers to do this, Quinn didn't wish to kill him in front of his wife or daughter. But, when Vickers rotated, he gazed at a man standing in full tactical gear and armed with elite weaponry.

Pulling his face away from the scope, Quinn observed his prey.

Then he shot.

Bang.

Quinn shot Vickers in the head with a bullet that

blasted out the back of his skull. In an abundance of caution and an antiquated need to confirm his kills, Quinn added four more to Vickers's chest. He dropped, and Quinn shuffled back to his truck.

Hearing Vickers's wife screaming for her life, the car door opened and she raced to recover her dead husband. These painful sounds were familiar to Quinn. And yet, he didn't flinch. Not a single strand of hair fluttered. He did not kill the wife or daughter.

In the truck, Quinn let go of his rifle.

Reversing the RAM down the road, Quinn rolled away and he became nothing more than a random resident leaving a normal suburb. He didn't think about the next or the first. No, Quinn simply crossed off another name. As he was nearly done removing pawns, Quinn would soon scale the pyramid.

He was well aware of how it would only get more difficult. His judgment would not be tested, and Quinn would come to understand his limits as he continued.

What he did was only just beginning.

Until now, Quinn hadn't once thought about killing a mother and her child. While Quinn always left a scene spotless, some of the custodians did kill bystanders. Sometimes, Quinn did too. It was rare and often unnecessary, but Quinn killed enough people in his life. He didn't need to broaden his horizons to include women and people who were there but did nothing wrong.

The Eradicate was not about killing arbitrarily. It was all about control and judgment.

It was about loyalty to a cause and ensuring that bad things didn't spread.

Nevertheless, what lay ahead of the Custodian, Quinn considered making some changes to. Drawing one step closer to his dad, he would do anything to get to him.

This desire blinded Quinn. He didn't lose sight of his mission, but he did struggle to maintain a clear outlook as well as his moral compass.

It was a tool he barely had. Mostly, all Quinn could see was vengeance. He wanted to see his dad dead. Killing these men was the only way for Quinn to see that. Quinn could see the face of his father again and squeezed the steering wheel until his fingers throbbed. He continued to drive the RAM and thought of nothing and no one.

As far as Quinn knew, the men killed so far were all dead and gone.

It was like they never existed at all.

CHAPTER 11
SAFE DISTANCE

Quinn's safehouse was a long mobile trailer set down in the middle of nowhere among bushes and a bayou. It was isolated, the same as his Wyoming residence, and Quinn enjoyed how he was often far from most things. This house, from what he could gather, seemed newer compared to the others Quinn had stayed in. Upon entry, Quinn was struck with air freshener and the smell of nasty cleaning chemicals. All of this gave Quinn the feeling of being in a department store. The safehouse's living room was just a sofa and a chair. Both were leather, and both were positioned by a window near a flatscreen. There were portraits stapled to the wall near a small round table and sitting area. The kitchen included black appliances, like a stove and fridge, and there were cabinets and drawers, but they were mostly empty.

"I found him, Quinn. I found your father."

Quinn was still trying to figure out how Priest made this discovery.

Broder Quinn was a cruel man. His terrible qualities

Quinn had come to know firsthand. His dad was capable of doing so much bad. As Quinn sifted through the intel, nothing discovered indicated Quinn's dad would go anywhere near the Tenets.

There was still no reason to do this.

The stories surrounding Quinn's old man began when he was a child.

When Quinn was younger, his father already had a reputation. None thought of him as an abuser or a killer, but as a decorated war hero and a man of very few words. He was rough around the edges, sure, but he didn't hide his scars. Should anyone pry too close or try to unveil the Quinn family's dark secrets, then Quinn's father revealed his plan for such interference.

He relied on his respect as well as his status in the special forces to protect him. Quinn's dad had achieved much during his time as a soldier. As a result, there were people in Quinn's community who thought his dad acquired equal status as a human being. This is a common misconception among people who are honored in one category and not another.

People automatically assume they are the same in every other capacity.

And often, there is nothing more respected than a soldier.

To the public, they are the ultimate representation of courage and heroism. Quinn's father understood this. He was humble. He never talked about his time overseas or what happened to him.

But should someone ask, then he wouldn't shut up.

He'd share his experiences like he was standing on a stage.

Sometimes, Quinn would go to school bruised and cut, and people would see him and question.

He fights in martial arts tournaments. That's the only reason he looks this way.

When asked if it was true by students and staff, Quinn would say it was.

The principal and teachers were comfortable to lean into their own ignorance. After all, there was not enough evidence to suggest Broder Quinn was abusing his child. If they only knew the truth, it would have forced them to see how Quinn's dad wasn't anything like he appeared.

Breaking Quinn down, abuse is a cycle that does not end. Quinn hated his dad but then sometimes he acted like he did. Quinn would sometimes follow the same pattern without realizing, and this only increased the Custodian's hatred for himself and his old man.

It drove Quinn's vengeance even further, to a place not even revenge should go.

Whenever Quinn refused to listen as a kid, most parents would take away their child's privileges or send them to their room. When Quinn disobeyed, his father was his most creative.

Occasionally, he would raise his hand to his boy and pound Quinn into the pavement.

He would strike hard and fast. Once, he threw Quinn across the room, and that was only the beginning. His dad's methods for ensuring obedience and maximum performance were medieval. If Quinn mentioned this to anyone, then his father became even more creative.

Making the claim his son needed to be strong, there was no denying the results.

Compared to the other children Quinn's age, he was stronger and he was faster. He was tougher and he could combat the things that would frighten an adult, let alone a kid. Disgusting as it all was, Quinn didn't process any of the pain until later in life. When he was older, he started to see the destruction his dad had caused. At the same time, Quinn was unable to process everything.

In high school, Quinn attended only to pass his classes. He graduated and enlisted shortly after. Heading into the military was not a new story for someone like Quinn. However, he hoped one day to close this chapter. He realized afterward there was no end to the military reign of his pain.

He was broken and there was only one way to fix it and forget it.

Yet, it was for these reasons Quinn couldn't understand why his dad would work with the Tenets. Everything he did was so secretive and well crafted. More than this, Quinn's father was independent. He was cut off from the general public. This cult might be hidden, but its methods were too redundant for his father to support. No, they didn't build anything. They wanted to gain only for themselves.

While Quinn's father was evil, he wasn't dumb or careless.

Under the leadership of Sirius Tenet, his cult was not out of control, but it wasn't all too impressive either. It showed no potential for expansion or posterity. It was just a group of perverts who wanted kids but then who made it about something else, something more sellable. They chose power and knowledge as their primary asset. Quinn's father was no pedophile and he wouldn't be caught dead working with anyone who was. It wasn't because Quinn's father was aroused when he abused his son. He was all about building better humans, not sex, pleasure, or ritual. Therefore, the connection Quinn was looking for did not exist. He was beginning to get distracted by there being no visible link.

But all Quinn asked was *why?*

Later, Quinn lifted the boxes and headed into the bedroom. He dropped everything onto the mattress and sighed. This room, like all the others, was nice. It was decorated with drawers and shiny cabinets. There was even another flatscreen mounted above the bed.

In Quinn's opinion, it was definitely a solid safehouse.

Swiveling his tonfa around like it was a balisong knife, playing with his weapons was often a relaxing task for Quinn. At this moment in time, he felt completely at ease.

He closed his eyes and breathed.

After Quinn executed a number of men, he would take time to think and to train. For someone as experienced as himself, the need to improve was always a chief pursuit and a pillar of his goals as a gifted killer.

No matter how good someone is, always they can be better.

This wasn't advice given to Quinn. It was something he learned on his own. So, when Quinn returned to his "home," he searched for any ways to improve.

In this case, he had a few ideas.

Although Quinn's tonfa handling was a marvelous tool, he practiced often to wield them more efficiently. He twirled the batons with his eyes opened wide.

He was thinking about how to better defend himself against multiple attackers.

While practicing, another memory surfaced in Quinn. It was the same but also different than the others.

"Let me show you."

Quinn's father now appeared in the mirror by the cabinet.

The tonfa was a weapon Quinn had chosen himself. Despite this, his father approved. He said he saw others use the tonfa when he visited Japan years ago. There, his dad learned from the best martial artists in the country.

To the right, Quinn's head shot around and he spotted his first attacker.

Although imaginary, like Quinn's father, it couldn't seem more real.

Quinn ducked and delivered a straight jab. He plunged the tonfa deep into the attacker's gut. With the opposite hand, Quinn finished with a hard uppercut. The blow was filled with so much strife it would have knocked the head clean off a neck.

Done.

Next came attacker two. This one was wielding a knife and looked the most like Quinn's dad. They all were in their own ways. Quinn used the tonfa to execute a straight block. Then, he flicked the baton out and back around. He popped the nameless attacker in the chin and Quinn listened to an imaginary exclaim.

His attacker dizzily bobbed side to side.

Quinn spun his tonfa. He continued to thrash all the demons spawned from his own dark imagination.

In a flash of quick-handed and unforgiving moves, Quinn clobbered until his enemies fell one by one. Breathing a little easier now, Quinn blinked. He was now back in the trailer. He was in the bedroom, alone.

That's how you use these weapons, and that's how you become better, my son.

Quinn heard his dad's voice. Releasing the tonfa, Quinn grunted. He remembered where he was and what he was here to do. He looked around the room and gazed at the bed in the center. Exhaling several heavy breaths, Quinn's muscles felt so sore it turned his limbs heavy.

It had been a long day.

His father was out there still and soon, Quinn would find him.

Quinn repeated this to himself again and again. He kept saying it until the sun set. He repeated it until his head sank into the pillow and until he fell fast asleep and could hear nothing but whispers and chants.

CHAPTER 12
THE TENETS

Louisiana was a state sculpted by a long, deep, and *complicated* history.

Along with its profound sense of patriotism, the state had to endure a thick wall of impenetrable heat that blanketed damn near the entire region every single day. The air itself, thickened by a beaming sun, offered a strange and omnipresent smell wherever Quinn traveled. He described the odor as a combination of cigarettes, rotting tree bark, and freshly mowed grass. This atmosphere was daunting to most newcomers. However, every person Quinn encountered informed him about the state's history.

Historically, Baton Rouge was discovered by a French explorer named Pierre Le Moyne d'Iberville. It was birthed when the traveler saw a pole covered in animal blood, hence the name *baton red*.

Vermilion parish occupied its own territory.

Apart from the parish, however, was another community just off the shoreline. Near the coast lay Vikaya or Victory Plains. This was not precisely discovered by the French. It was a place of refuge for a pirate brigade under the leadership of one man, Jacques Synthianas.

Said to be a pagan worshipper, Jacques was also known for kidnapping, murder, and other dirty deeds committed by himself and his merry men. According to Synthianas, all of this was done for the sole purpose of attaining a higher understanding. He sought to unravel the origins and mysteries of death. To the followers of his deity, named *Cyncero*, to sacrifice in his name was the highest honor.

If you give yourself to the Sun Lord, then in the next life, you will be given everything you've ever wanted. You will become a ruler and not a servant.

Now when you have nothing, as many people did during this time, Synthianas understood they needed other things to fill this void.

In this case, that filler was purpose and position.

And the greatest purpose granted to people who are feeling low is to give them the promise of one day having something better. Among Jacques's brotherhood, so many nobodies wanted to be somebodies, and the definition of a somebody, in their tiny minds, was a king.

And here, everyone desired to be kings.

Now, Synthianas was also a polymath. He believed in an ascension by means of producing specific energies. He preached this belief to his followers. He said a person never becomes more powerful than when they've killed another human being. In the pursuit of this dark and twisted knowledge, Synthianas began writing books that provided depth and understanding of such a disgraceful ideology.

It was a weird and vocal time and was enriched by stories of fire and death.

People died often and colonization was a story best told with blood and pain.

The reason for killing other humans varies depending on the weight of another person's hand. It is also determined by how much their heart can hold. Before either gets too heavy, the idea of murdering for a cause became quite appetizing to most people.

Everyone could kill if they were coerced or provoked. Most denied this being a possibility. For those who had nothing, death and murder was the only way to mark one's territory.

Everyone wanted to be successful and everyone wants a piece for themselves.

Death was not the end of anyone's journey, or so they proclaimed. No, it's actually the part of their journey that takes them back to where it all began.

In death, one didn't just learn who they really are. They also came to accept the truth that held the very fabric of reality together. There was no end, and there was no beginning. There was just here and now, and how much one could do with the time given.

Nothing else.

Soon, Jacques and *his guild* welcomed other unscrupulous characters into their organization. Some claimed to be doctors and nurturers, but Synthianas, like most settlers, eventually faded into the history books. Yet, what he left behind was a mess of bodies and many tall tales. Stemming from all those Synthianas had murdered in his rituals of appeasement, many followers continued to thrive and last.

Like the roots of a tree, they spread and ran deeply throughout the state.

With families choosing to follow the same traditions,

the tree continued to bloom and the belief system attached to it did not fade. While Synthianas's name did, new names emerged, and so did his message. It was simple.

Sacrifice requires pain.

Bowing to a sun deity called Cyncero, the brotherhood's name formed soon after.

The Brotherhood of Cyn.

Like all creatures of myth, the existence of a spiritual entity was dismissed as fantasy. The days of Synthianas, whereby one could sell such an idea, came to an end. Even so, it was shared among the people who were born in Vermilion. Some liked talking about the kooky, deranged pervert who settled in these parts long ago. There were others who claimed he continued to exist. There were places that still forced people into death and despair.

The Tenets shared this with all those who were willing to listen.

They had a new way of attaining power and authority.

They hadn't achieved much from this hard work. They learned to impress and how to shake hands. No, their journey toward ascension required more than just will and determination.

The Tenets were descendants of Synthianas.

They lived and died by the beliefs of put forth by his ancient cult. They pursued the same greatness and the Tenets found their tributes in the broken women and children lost and abandoned. Using these people, the Tenets sold them the same product once passed on to many others.

This was the easiest part of their endeavor.

I can make you great if you're willing to follow me. This was a Tenet family promise.

It polluted the entire parish and was gobbled up by

those who, like Jacques, desired more. Amassing more people each decade, Sirius Tenet became the brotherhood's chief architect. He now referred to it as *an organization*. But, as the cult began to assimilate, it dispersed into the higher echelon of citizens living in both Vermilion and Baton Rouge. Soon, the Tenets amassed a great fortune. Sirius had more power and wealth than he ever had before. And he sought to keep it any way he could.

"You want more?" Sirius said to his son, Alistair.

Alistair had been baptized in the cult the day he was born. He was involved in it as much as his father was. Often, he inquired about how these activities would continue and who would lead the brotherhood once he was gone?

The cult was not known for its size but for its reach.

The people who were part of it had to possess a unique set of skills that others did not.

For Sirius, his skills were his leadership and his knowledge. He was a success before he was elected governor. At one time, he was a volunteer sheriff's deputy. None of this was much, but after making certain sacrifices, Sirius's reward was being in a new level of prestige and power.

Sirius was granted the governorship—the highest anyone could go.

At least, it was as high as Sirius wanted to go.

Now Alistair was smart and he was cunning, the same as his father. Yet, it was Alistair's experience within the Vermilion school system that secured his place among the brethren.

What Alistair was good at was establishing trust and sincerity.

Always smiling, his role was that of a do-gooder and philanthropist. Sirius was an older man who had given much to his community, but what Alistair represented was the future—the future of the Tenet name. Always dressing classy, Alistair attended many events whereby he rubbed shoulders with other classy people. In doing this, Alistair did as his father instructed. He was mannerly, kind, and professional. He had the appearance of a Southern gentleman and knew how to use the right words at the right time. This led to many prosperous relationships. It also established a bond among Louisiana's high society. It wasn't long before Alistair used this to open two schools in his family's name and to secure their place as caregivers and selfless contributors.

Bring us your poor and your troubled. This was the invitation Alistair extended to the people of Baton Rouge and Vermilion.

It started with one school, which opened in the early 2000s. At the beginning, enrollment was small. Over time, it grew until every room was filled, every kind of education was offered, but most who were welcomed into the Tenet family's schools either came from abusive homes or were so impoverished they could barely afford food let alone pencils and papers.

The community itself wasn't prosperous.

The schools eventually were known as the *troubled* schools. The children who struggled in the regular classroom were sent to those owned by Alistair Tenet. As its unofficial director, Alistair was the one who decided who could attend and who could not.

He preferred to let in those who were broken and in despair.

The parents thought their sons and daughters would be granted a rich opportunity to improve. Alistair, however, knew they were welcomed for a different reason.

The brotherhood needed tributes. They needed children.

Every six months, a ritual was held. Their god required a blood sacrifice. The younger they are, the more prestigious the gift. This was an idea created by Synthianas. Where the Tenets found such hopeless and broken children was not just from their schools, it was from other places too. It was easy to target these children in these parts because their parents were already disconnected and neglectful. It was even easier to cover up their deaths because it could easily be blamed on their home life. Kids disappear all the time, and this was a fact Alistair and Sirius knew would help them as they searched for other tributes.

Whenever Alistair was looking for someone, he'd ask the teachers if there were any students that they were *worried about*. Often, Alistair promised counseling and assistance. Once the student was alone, Alistair would arrange for them to be picked up and then, they were taken to the Tenet estate so they could be *prepared*.

A dark practice, this went on for years and years and no one said a single word.

Children were left dead at Cyn's altar. Once they were killed, their bodies were buried or burned. No one cared or even noticed.

"Forget your place, boy. Forget who you are?" Sirius barked at Alistair.

He was silenced once after he questioned his father about the cult's activities in the last years. In many ways, he was and always would be a slave to his father's will.

"It's too risky now."

The risks were always clear, yet this didn't stop Sirius from doing what needed to be done. There weren't many schools, but there were enough.

Alistair would have to visit each one.

Whenever he did, he'd show up in his best suit and meet with the principal. One principal, Tammy Mark, was given the position because she once worked for Sirius as his assistant.

She didn't have any experience in education, not really.

She was employed at a daycare and also held other *positions*.

Mostly, she was just a woman who watched. While there, Alistair met the teachers too.

The way he selected tributes was based on two attributes: the child's cooperative ability as well as their home life. Some kids were naturally trustworthy. They didn't know how to react to adults because there were none at home. After all, Alistair was a larger-than-life man. He towered over all the teachers and staff. He wore expensive clothes and shiny shoes. When he spoke to the kids, Alistair did so on one knee so he could look them in the eyes.

The children knew Alistair because they respected him.

They recognized Alistair as the man in charge. For the ones he liked, Alistair brought them candy. For the ones he didn't, he also brought them candy. He was known as the candy guy, and his father, Sirius, advised against this. He didn't like how his son was making contact.

"It's good for us. Makes us seem affable."

Predators prey, but perverts stalk.

Alistair didn't think he was stalking. Mostly, he was just talking.

He looked for the kids who were too trusting and who had nowhere else to go.

Sometimes, Alistair would touch the children who had never been touched. He would hold the ones who were never held. They were willing to follow Alistair because none knew what was really happening. Alistair would work with the counselors and arrange for the children to be transported off the school premises. Using their home life as an excuse, it's easy to cover up the truth when the people who decide what's true are the same ones covering it up.

Sirius and Alistair were such people.

Children disappeared, and the cult continued to grow.

Alistair was the one who made it happen. Both continued their family's tradition and would continue so long as the tradition gave something in return. And it did. Always, it did.

"All of this is a small price to pay but look around. Tell me if you do not have what so many desire?"

Dead women and dead children were the tributes given to the great deity from the so-called higher realm.

But the sacrifice was real.

Sacrifice and pain to build yourself up was an idea preached by the cult.

Still, it was true among other organizations too. It was the philosophy of the military and in business and in government. Killing the weak in order to make yourself stronger is not only the principle among winners, it's shared among anyone who wishes for greatness. This was the reality which the Tenet cult was built upon and it did not change.

The more you kill, the more powerful you become.

And so, willing to attain greatness, none could bring an end to the family's cause or their practices. Alistair was told this on numerous occasions. If this was the way to achieve power, then power was gained, why stop?

Could he?

Must he?

Must anyone?

Cursed to go on, the impact of the brotherhood grew exponentially under Sirius's rule. He continued to recruit well connected individuals and the cult's activities and purpose soon became an unspoken thing.

While it might have been unspoken, it was not unknown.

The Brotherhood of Cyn was an extension of a fairy tale shared among the local community. Those who lived in Erath and Vermilion had their suspicions about the cult's existence. They knew its history and there were always rumors about those still loyal to the old ways. Few knew exactly what this meant.

There was a time when everything seen in Baton Rouge was green.

Before the buildings and the roads, before the boundaries and the laws, there were men and there were women. There were different people, different places, and ideas. The brotherhood only accepted those who respected their own histories.

They accepted those who loved their home.

None talked about it. And, because of its small size when compared to the Free Masons or certain branches of Satanism, the Brotherhood of Cyn was easy to hide. By being so compact, it only made the cult more exclusive and more difficult to access.

If there was ever a reason to expose its truth, it was easy to deny and easy to ignore.

Who's into ritual sacrifice these days?

It was a silly question for most. Pedophiles and perverts, in Quinn's view, were generally low-lives and bottom feeder fuckers. They weren't the rich people that were respected and admired, there were so few of those left in the world.

Even still, whenever any of the members decided to make a public appearance, always there was one man watching. He was a wiry fellow with olive skin who contrasted the generally pallid appearance of the other Tenets.

This man was not part of the family, he was only someone who served the family.

Every dynasty demanded its security.

Frank Kardinal fulfilled this role, and he did so perfectly, almost.

———

Once in the military himself, Kardinal served four years in the Army Rangers before he was honorably discharged. After this, Kardinal made it to Louisiana, which was not his home. No way. No, Kardinal was raised in Nebraska. Both his parents were college professors. He had two siblings, a brother and a sister. He was a world karate champion who competed in many tournaments. He had solid fighting experience and he thought when he left, he would have something to come back to.

As it turned out, Kardinal's father died of cancer, and his mother married shortly after.

Being the youngest, Kardinal didn't have much of a purpose other than fighting and hunting. He wanted to work for law enforcement and was a cop for a while, until Kardinal went too far and curb-stomped an innocent kid. He told his captain the perp looked like he was holding a weapon. No other officers testified to seeing the same sight.

In their eyes, Kardinal was too much of a hothead. He had his moments where he was not only unpredictable and dangerous, he was downright crazy. Kardinal had impulses he couldn't explain. It wasn't that he liked hurting people, but when he *did* hurt people, he felt tickled, almost aroused.

Now, this was a difficult sensation to grasp or explain.

But when it happened, something awakened inside Kardinal he could not deny.

It was like tasting a new food for the first time ever.

Now gifting Kardinal with a profound sense of wonder, he enjoyed the trade of killing. He relished in the power it granted to him. Coming back with almost nothing, Kardinal decided to return to his former trade. He found himself a new dojo and began training under a new sensei. Kardinal excelled in karate and taekwondo. He wanted to learn more so he continued to learn and found himself living in a new city, in a new state.

It wasn't until he was in his thirties that Kardinal met Sirius Tenet.

He was hired to be his personal assistant and valet. At the time, Kardinal was willing to take any job. His past had made him somewhat difficult to hire. With every interview asking about previous employment, Kardinal was forced to tell them all the truth.

However, Sirius Tenet didn't ask about Kardinal's past.

His questions pertained only to hours and skill set.

"How many hours would you be willing to work?"

"How well do you know local law enforcement?"

"How do you feel about children?"

The last question was the weirdest one for Kardinal. However, it wasn't until he answered all the other questions Sirius Tenet explained why he asked the last one.

"This family has traditions, its ways of weaving through the world. I am interviewing you because I know

you have a past, as do we. And, for now, that's all you need to know."

Kardinal didn't know what traditions his future employer was referring to. Yet, Kardinal was hired and he worked for the Tenets for six months before learning the truth about them. He first learned about the Brotherhood of Cyn when he found a little girl in one of the bedrooms. She was not a relative. If she was, Kardinal would have been notified.

Her hands were tied and she was crying.

Kardinal asked about the sobbing girl. He was told not to worry.

"She's our guest," Alistair said. *"Our queen. Our trophy."*

At the time, Kardinal had no idea. He learned that, working for this family, it was best not to ask many questions. The Tenets had their way of doing things. Kardinal enjoyed their methods of secrecy and subterfuge. He didn't understand their "traditions", but it wasn't his job to understand them.

In addition to being a protection specialist, Kardinal was also an expert in explosives. He was Sirius's aid. Thus far, he had not faced a single threat he could not handle or repair. But today, hearing of the two dead men, Kardinal had a feeling this was not always true.

It certainly didn't feel like it was now.

While he was a man who knew how to protect and to serve, he never questioned and always did as he was told to do. He served the family and his reputation grew because of this association. Kardinal hid children. He covered up their footprints and tricked up evidence. He had even worked with local law enforcement. When necessary, Kardinal removed certain people who were deemed a liability. With the hiring of Kardinal, Sirius was deep into sabotage and subterfuge. Kardinal was a killer, and so long as he prowled for new threats, the Tenet family and their secrets would remain safe. They would stay under Kardinal's protection. Mostly.

He was not the only protector of the family.

There was another. *One other.*

CHAPTER 13
WOKE UP THIS MORNING

Quinn woke at a quarter past six, so rested his body tingled. Back home, whenever Quinn woke early, he ingested a fat cup of coffee and stretched. Afterward, he'd jump into a CrossFit workout using equipment stored in his basement or outside.

Quinn fell forward and his hands slapped the ground. Completing a handstand, Quinn fought to stay balanced. Wobbling for a few seconds, it took time before Quinn achieved complete stillness. He kept his breathing under control by using small gasps and long exhales. He flexed his back and his shoulders and let all the blood flush to his face. This created a surplus of pressure. It hurt Quinn's skin and made his eyes feel like they were about to pop out of his skull.

Still concentrating, Quinn did his best to fight the pressure. Soon, he had balance.

Then he began to ease his nose closer to the ground. Going down, Quinn needed the strength to push his body back up *and* the strength to make sure he didn't fall. It hurt, but it was one of the most extreme physical feats a person could achieve. It worked. There was nothing holding him back. He performed some handstand push-ups until he collapsed. This was usually how most of his workouts ended. He pushed until he couldn't push anymore.

He didn't have any equipment. Quinn walked to a Keurig near the fridge.

He opened the drawers and found some canned goods. He uncovered a bag of oats and some breakfast cereal boxes. In the top cabinet was an old jar of peanut butter and some condiments, such as salt, pepper, and ketchup. Coming across a stash of coffee pods, they were likely left behind by the person who stayed there before Quinn did.

Whoever they were, Quinn imagined they weren't like he was.

He took a pod out of a cardboard box and inserted it into the coffee machine. He brewed himself a fresh cup and chose a bold brand of dark roast and Quinn didn't bother to let it cool as he drank. He wasn't dressed, but the wardrobe he had packed consisted of three pairs of sweat-pants and two pairs of jeans. Quinn also brought one belt, six socks, and several black t-shirts fitted to his torso. He placed his black Luminox SEAL diver watch around his wrist and walked toward the desk. Quinn pulled a folder from a binder and opened it to take a look.

Gasping, the coffee hit Quinn hard and gave him a glorious sensation.

The next name on Quinn's list was Billy Meres, one of the illegitimate sons of Sirius Tenet. Billy was an alleged rapist once charged with sleeping with three underage girls. Billy liked girls. More specifically, he liked young girls. From what Quinn could gather, the other cultists also liked children. However, Lee's tastes were more specific. His file showed a pattern. He liked girls between the ages of ten and fifteen.

No one older than that. Some Billy Lee had taken from their families.

Others he had simply stolen. When Billy Lee had obtained these girls, some of their families called the police. They demanded their daughters be brought back. However, since most had a history of coming from abusive homes, the onus shifted.

As Quinn was starting to realize, blame-shifting was the Tenet family's main strategy when protecting themselves. And it worked. Every charge laid on Billy Lee was dropped and every case buried and forgotten.

They were just girls, after all.

Quinn downed the last of his coffee and perused for more information. Due to Billy Lee's links to other criminal organizations, he served three years for aggravated assault and other drug-related charges. In addition, Billy Lee was also with a number of small-timers operating throughout Baton Rouge.

There were a few organizations overseen by Lee himself.

So far as Lee's father was concerned, he didn't exist in the family. Nevertheless, Billy Lee had his ways of making himself more known. When secrecy was vital, so was lending a helping hand along the way. Although Billy Lee went to several rituals, he didn't recruit tributes or look for ceremonial garbs, all he did...was make money. He set up a low-level meth lab outside Vermilion. Billy Lee had that ambitious Tenet family spirit. This Billy Lee attributed to his father. He knew how to cook and how to sell. He understood his family links would provide him with some security. His half brother Alistair knew the sheriff, and if anything happened to him, he would disclose valuable information about the family.

He was a blabbermouth and a royal pain in the ass.

Dealing crystal meth was a lucrative and effective profession, in Quinn's opinion. Billy Lee even managed to hire some local biker thugs to safeguard his house. All of this was part of establishing his individuality but it also was the beginning of breaking away.

He leaned on the family whenever he needed to.

A small timer, Billy Lee and his brother Brent didn't mind being referred to as such.

No matter what they did, they always came back to the man who oversaw everything and everyone. They returned to the one who knew who they really were. Billy Lee was a loose cannon, and so was his brother, Brent. The two were never photographed with the Tenets because they barely were with him.

Their connections were extracted primarily from bank statements and correspondence. They were connected only on paper, through records.

Also, there was the man in the red suit, the one called Kardinal. Quinn was unsure if this was the man's name or his call sign, and he didn't care which was which. Based on Kardinal's consistent presence, it was evident he fulfilled the role of the family's security.

So, Quinn had no choice and he made it quickly.

He added another name to his list.

CHAPTER 14
SON DOWN

BILLY LEE MERES WAS KNOWN TO FREQUENT THIS bar in Vermilion called Kinsels. It was one of the worst names for a bar that Kyle Quinn had ever heard but he headed over there a few minutes after eight o'clock.

Driving his RAM, Quinn filled the tank and drove with the windows down.

One of the most satisfying qualities about being in this state was its weather.

Quinn lived in Wyoming. He was not used to such a warm climate. Normally, he wore fat boots and coats made of animal fur. Quinn bundled himself up in many layers whenever he stepped outside. Here, everything was the opposite. The air instantly heated Quinn's skin.

When he vacated his truck, Quinn strolled to the squared windows on either side of the bar's door.

He was armed with his Glock and his OTF switchblade. He was wearing body armor under his shirt and looked bulkier than usual but not too heavy.

In jeans and light sneakers, Quinn sauntered.

The bar's exterior was complemented by a cheesy

neon sign. In addition, there was a wooden porch and all the windows were opened. Quinn neared the space and heard commotion, The entire time, Quinn stayed perfectly alert. With all hands on deck, Quinn was now a total stranger. He was a nobody going about his business and intended to say nothing to no one. Quinn exhaled slowly and blinked to take snapshots of all multiple points of entry and egress.

So far, Quinn counted only three.

He felt his gun against his waist and felt the weight of his vest too.

Everything about him was subtle and calm.

Now, Quinn's stature concealed most of it, and so did his pace. Quinn made sure he was moving fast but not too fast. He came close to the door. He made sure to remember he was not here to drink or speak.

He was here to kill one man, maybe two, or maybe more.

Outside Kinsels were three girls sitting on a porch. They were drinking beers and not wearing much. The barefooted one glanced at Quinn. She wasn't looking directly at him but she wasn't looking away either.

Quinn knew why they were looking.

Considering where he came from, Quinn carried himself with his own unique brand of confidence. It was one generated because Quinn could kill everyone in this room and still walk away unscathed.

Quinn listened to the girls giggling. He stepped in between two doors and, as soon as Quinn was in the bar, he was hit with the unapologetic smell of whiskey and cigarettes. In Quinn's mind, this was a run-of-the-mill, country-style saloon. Nothing more than that, Quinn gawked at all the faces.

Where are you, Mr. Billy Lee?

In addition to the bar, there were round tables with standing patrons and a few booths located near the rear exit. Quinn saw a pool table and a dance floor. It was occupied with gyrating fools and idiots strutting in cowboy boots and flannel.

Quinn saw two more men by the door.

They were smaller and definitely lighter than Quinn, but they were the security.

They watched Quinn as he looked for a place to sit.

Quinn continued to scope the scene and then he heard two people whispering by themselves. They were bickering about who Quinn was and who he might be.

Quinn made out a few words.

"Who's this asshole?"

"What the fuck's he looking at?"

"What's he doing here?"

Quinn ignored the comments and just moved on. He remembered why he was here. He wasn't going anywhere until he saw the man he had come to kill.

Quinn marched. It didn't take long for him to find the right face.

At the back of the bar, a skinny man sat slouched in a booth. He was so thin he reminded Quinn of a fucking rake. Along with his mullet and goatee, this man wore a Tartan shirt with no sleeves. Quinn blinked and took in more of the details. He observed Billy Lee Meres as he chatted with two girls in tight shirts.

Quinn went straight to the bar to reflect on his plan. He had it all figured out.

He was going to put two in Billy Lee's flabby chest and then another one straight through his forehead. After this, Quinn would holster his sidearm and exit through the back door. He would knock out some of the cameras and pummel the bouncer, if they stood in his way. From here, Quinn could get to his truck in no more than thirty seconds. This was all effective for now. All Quinn really needed to do was get Billy to look in his direction. Even with all the witnesses, an Eradicate order enabled Quinn to remove anyone he wanted. Yet, Quinn wasn't here to terminate anyone else.

It didn't matter if a threat was close or far away. And, if Quinn was going to pull his 34, then he would not turn his gun on the bouncers or the civilians.

He could. He had done it before. Quinn just didn't want to do it here and now.

Now by the bar, the gross smell of beer and meat lurked in the sultry space. There was this, as well as a hint of bad perfume lingering in the crevasses. Quinn suspected there were sex workers roaming in search of clients. With his elbow resting on the counter, Quinn had no desire to sit down.

No, now he was waiting. He was waiting and listening as a calming, totally unexpected voice, spoke into his left ear.

"Can I get you somethin' there, sweetie?"

The music was not too loud. Quinn was surprised he was actually being addressed.

He turned and stared at a blonde-haired beauty with tanned skin and in a pink top stood next to him. She spoke to Quinn like she knew him. Quinn looked her up and down. Her shirt was unbuttoned and her breasts were ample and totally out for all to see.

"Shot of whiskey," Quinn decided. "Thanks."

He didn't plan on drinking but he didn't plan on saying no to a hot woman either.

"Great." The bartender walked away. Quinn focused on the depraved man he was here to kill.

Billy Lee Meres held one girl by the hips but Quinn held his position and laid low.

"One whiskey," said the bartender.

Scoping Meres and his *girlfriends*, Quinn looked again at the blonde barkeep.

Her name was Kindly. She handed Quinn his drink. Truthfully, Quinn really didn't want one, but part of him thought he might need it. While cleaning, Quinn couldn't ingest anything capable of disrupting his focus or might take him off course.

In fact, Quinn ordered something he felt would not draw more attention to himself.

Leaving the glass, Quinn inhaled. His mind and his body were ready.

The plan was set.

Quinn thought of Billy's cohorts, none were on his list, but all of them were likely to interfere. He recalled the order.

Eradicate.

Quinn knew to draw Lee out of the bar and take care of him outside. Depending on this kill position, Quinn would douse Lee's body with whiskey before lighting a match.

Once again, Quinn noted another Priest recommendation.

If you can burn 'em, burn 'em.

Quinn wasn't much for said method, and he didn't need to do it. The Eradicate was about killing, not about cleaning up afterward, but then that was a Custodian's duties: clean and leave a scene completely spotless.

Tonight, however, Quinn would continue that tradition.

"Ya gonna drink or not?" Stepping forward, the tip of Quinn's shoe pressed into the wooden floor, but he stopped when he heard Kindly's voice. Now, Quinn couldn't think of a reason why a bartender would inquire about whether or not a patron was going to finish their drink. Clearly, she did.

"What?" Puzzled, Quinn glanced at his glass.

"Your drink. Ya gonna have it or not?"

"Oh," Quinn said, sighing. "Right."

Picking up the small glass, Quinn downed the shot and kept the whiskey in his mouth. He wanted to spit it back up soon as Kindly walked away. To Quinn's surprise, she stayed and actually waited for the Custodian to finish.

"Good, huh? Top shelf stuff you got there."

Quinn gulped.

His lack of alcohol consumption was part of what kept Quinn in such good shape. Kindly leaned over the counter, and Quinn, no longer shocked by his choice, was repulsed by it.

This was *not* his mission.

And yet Kindly insisted on being quite verbose. This was weird for Quinn. She was just being too nice. Then again, her name was Kindly. It was well suited, all things considered.

"Thank you," Quinn said.

Billy Lee's table was now starting to clear. The people around it all stood up to exit. Quinn hadn't moved, but he would soon.

"You're not from around here, are ya'?" Kindly asked Quinn.

And there she was again, talking despite Quinn's inability to make eye contact. He was being absolutely clear. He was *not* interested.

Still, she insisted.

"Excuse me?" Quinn asked.

Now Quinn played it cool. His eyes felt heavy and he

was deadpan while expressing his dissatisfaction. However, despondency was part of the Custodian's demeanor. He was not trying to be rude. Quinn did have an idea about why this Kindly was being so insistent.

Quinn perused the bar.

What Quinn saw was a swarm of obese, sluggish men. These were the kind of dudes who came and hit on Kindly every week. And she, being who she was and how she looked, she likely played into their grovels but never indulged in any offer.

When Quinn came into a room, his brooding persona made him look more dangerous. He appeared more unique compared to some of the other patrons. Apparently, Quinn looked newer to the women too, and newer was good.

Quinn kept a safe distance. This was also effective and endearing.

"Never seen you here before," Kindly said to Quinn. "Visiting?"

Quinn smirked. The question was actually decent.

"Yes. You could say that."

"Nice. Family?" Kindly asked.

Quinn shook his head and kept his eyes on Billy Lee. Quinn spoke with Kindly for a few seconds. Although a nice guy, his focus was understandably elsewhere.

"No."

"Oh, so work then, maybe?"

"Actually," Quinn replied. Again, he was entertained because almost every question the bartender was asking was correct. "Yes."

"Cool," Kindly said, almost cheerily. "And what do you do?"

When asked this question, Quinn could not say he was a black ops assassin here to kill a powerful Louisiana family. No, he was required to keep everything a secret by relying on half-truths only. He gave the answer he always did, and this forced a pleasant smile to sneak out of Quinn

.

"Custodian."

To Quinn's surprise, Kindly's face lit up and she chuckled.

"That's cool."

Quinn was poised. He couldn't help but wonder if this was the first line in a longer conversation? Wasn't she busy working? Nonetheless, peripherally Quinn could still see Kindly. She was mixing drinks and ogling Quinn from far away. She was interested, but in what? Quinn had some ideas.

"Another three cold ones, babe!" an irritating voice rang into Quinn's ear and he immediately stepped back.

It was time for him to get back to work.

Quinn's head bobbed and he gave Kindly a humble nod. He acknowledged her, at least in part, and he was listening despite not looking in her direction.

"Nice talking to you," Quinn said. "Stay safe."

This phrase was one Quinn gave often. But when Quinn said anything, *generally*, he meant it exactly as he said it. And, as Quinn moved back, he continued to stare at Billy Lec. The lost Tenet son was making his way toward the back door. Being an experienced lip reader, Quinn interpreted a few of Lee's words.

They consisted of *fighting, finishing, fucker*, and *get away from me*.

Quinn eased from the sweet bartender known as Kindly. She was certainly more dignified than those Quinn met before. Seeing this, Quinn recalled another one of Priest's cardinal rules. *"Never stay long, always get the job done, and never get too attached to anyone. Keep it*

simple and don't draw too much attention even if the atten-
tion is warranted."

Quinn understood this. Therefore, he knew he had no choice.

He walked out the back door and headed to the parking lot.

Along the way, Quinn removed his OTF. Ejecting the blade, the handle was clamped between Quinn's thumb and index. Quinn held the knife down and crept along. The inebriated fool moaned and was completely unaware of what was about to go down.

Billy Lee fumbled for his keys and tried to open his car. Quinn stepped in and snatched Billy Lee by the collar. He pulled this fool in and, in a second, jabbed the blade right into Lee's back.

"Gah." Billy Lee gasped. The wound produced a pain Quinn knew firsthand.

He'd been stabbed before.

With the OTF's razor-sharp edge, Quinn plunged it deeper. He could feel air expelling from Billy's gaping mouth. It was a hard exhale done only to vent the brutal agony he was now enduring. Billy Lee was a pedophiliac monster who was dying in Quinn's arms. The Custodian's hand remained clamped over Lee's mouth. Quinn squeezed harder before pulling out the blade.

"Ah!"

The wound in Billy Lee's torso was deep, wide, and full of blood. It was not Quinn's quickest kill. The loss of blood forced a convulsion from Billy Lee as he died.

Quinn felt Lee's face starting to tremble. He cocked his hand and wiggled the knife around to adjust the position. Quinn then waited for two seconds before he jabbed Meres in the throat. Quinn jimmied the weapon and dark arterial blood oozed from Billy Lee's solid neck. It dripped along Quinn's hand as Lee slid down the wall.

With each inch gained, Quinn moved closer to the floor. He waited until all the lights went out in Billy Lee's face. It didn't take long for him to stop hearing his target's faint breaths of dead air.

Quinn soon felt a calming chill.

He didn't think at all about Meres now that the deed was done. He wiped the last of the blood off his chin and slipped the OTF back into his pocket.

After dousing Billy Lee with lighter fluid he kept stored on his belt, he lit a match and walked away. Roaming as the fire scorched Lee's corpse, the shadows ensconced Quinn as he stepped slowly into the night.

He faded away almost like he was never there.

In so many ways, he never was.

CHAPTER 15
MEETING

THE ENTIRE CONGREGATION OF MONSTERS AND maniacs were summoned for an emergency meeting to be held at the house of their great master. As soon as the brotherhood was informed of Billy Lee's murder, a meeting was to be held in order to determine whether the organization was *under attack*. Sirius hadn't conducted a meeting like this in over a year. Such a practice was deemed too high risk and too much of a liability to take place. Despite this, an assembly did occur at a secret location only a few were aware of. After the death of Vickers, Dr. Sauder, and now Billy Lee, Alistair Tenet encouraged his father to address all the other cult members.

Alistair's encouragement paid off. He and his dad welcomed the entire Brotherhood of Cyn in the basement of their decadent home. Gathered in an ornate room, the room was decorated with the heads of the animals Sirius had hunted over the years. In the middle of this wide space was a broad desk. Surrounding it were leather sofas and a projector positioned on a table.

The light from the projector flashed as Sirius stood in his long robe. At the head of the room, Mr. Tenet watched as the other members began to pour in. Among them was Brent Meres. He wore a torn jean jacket and dragged his leather boots across the carpet. Along the way, Brent received a glare from his estranged father.

Still, he was the man's child and he had lost a brother. Part of Sirius hoped his illegitimate spawns would stay alive longer than even he had expected. However, another part of Sirius was glad to see that one of them was now gone.

There was less for him to worry about and even less for him to take care of.

"Everyone, take a seat, please," Alistair said.

The others in attendance were known as rooks among the cult. Just like in the game of chess, they weren't the pawns but the soldiers. They were the people who wanted in but who had not yet earned their rank or right. They didn't quite believe in the cult's ideology entirely but they did believe in its ideas of power and achievement. Acting as security for the brotherhood, the rooks were the reinforcements. They were just starting to prove their loyalty to Sirius and his son and were expected to fight and defend.

By the door, Kardinal stood watch with his arms crossed.

He said nothing to anyone. His job was to be on guard and to make sure no one entered without permission. With everyone present and accounted for, Kardinal nodded at Alistair. The second-in-command moved into the center of the room and joined his father.

"All here? Good. Let's begin." Sirius grunted to clear his throat. Looking ahead at those in his company, the boss held the remote to the screen. "In the last two days, three of our own have been killed."

The room was silent as the TV cast three pictures of the recently fallen brothers. The pictures displayed all of them slain in cold blood, and were taken as evidence from the crime scenes. It looked like they were taken after the bodies were discovered.

Alistair grimaced and looked away. The sight was brutal, but he had seen worse.

"All were found dead," Sirius said. "One in his place of work, the other was at his home, and the third happened by his car. Now, while we do not know who is responsible for their murders as of yet, one link is undeniably clear. They were members of our age-old family ...*tradition*."

Brent Meres produced a cackle as he sat slouched over. At the head of the room, the father of all things glared to express his hate for this kind of disrespect. Kardinal marched vehemently toward Brent and stood before this boorish oaf and gawked. Brent needed to remember it was his brother who was killed.

"I'd listen closely if I were you."

Brent submitted to Kardinal's warning. Sirius's hands slid down to his hips. With everyone now watching attentively, he was about to deliver the most significant part of the exposition.

"Whether we want to admit it or not, we are being hunted," Sirius declared.

What he said couldn't be more true.

"Any suspects?" Brent queried. "So far?" Brent was smarter than his brother was, no doubt. His question made sense. It was the same one on everyone's minds. "Leads?"

"Not as of yet," Alistair answered for his father. "But we're currently looking at some of the security footage taken outside of Sauder's hospital. We are checking to see if it provides us with anything useful."

"But if we *are* being targeted then that means someone knows about us. They know who and what we are and they know what we do. And the only way for that to have happened is if someone here is not too good at keeping our secrets," Sirius expressed.

Brent bowed his head and tsked.

Sirius's eyes were on everyone now. He inspected his fellow brothers and attempted to read their expressions. At the same time, Sirius was assessing their loyalty. The main cultists were close to ten members, four of which were direct descendants, while the rest were rooks. They were far from major players and others were too low in the hierarchy to be deemed as *traitors*.

The only people who had all the facts were Sirius and Alistair. This was information capable of exposing and compromising all of them, and it was held by the higher-ups. In this case, the *higher-ups* were those who fell directly into the Tenets' immediate family.

"We need more time to figure things out," Alistair said, breaking the tension. He stepped closer to his father. "We don't know who is targeting our family, but rest assured, we are doing everything we can to find the one responsible."

Alistair stayed quiet after he made this staunch declaration. Now next to his father, Alistair acted all graceful and kind while Sirius remained cold and stern and continued to glare at the crowd.

Someone dangerous was looking for Sirius's family.

It was someone who threatened everything he had achieved. It jeopardized power, prestige, wealth, and status. Above all else, it risked the cult's prosperity. Some of the rooks in the room were too far down the totem pole to ask any specific questions.

The real onus, however, fell on those at the very top.

Now, the brotherhood's defense was exacted by those who wanted to fight the hunter. They wanted to seek, and they desired the death of the one attacking their family.

"In the meantime," Sirius said to Tenet, "what we need to do is stay sharp, keep our eyes open and our ears close to the ground, in a manner of speaking."

This was not intended as a joke, and no one laughed.

Sirius kept himself poised and almost lawyerly. The entire time, he declined to show any emotion at all. When Sirius made the announcement, Alistair wanted his appearance to showcase the seriousness of this situation. He abandoned his emotions and stood like a soldier next to a general.

"And if anyone does see anything or hear anything, you will let us know so we may take the necessary steps to..." Alistair's eyes began to drift. Now, he was considering the brutality of the situation. "Neutralize."

Alistair stared at Kardinal. The fixer was at the back, by the door.

What the Tenets meant when they said *neutralize* was actually to pay another person who could take care of problems. Therefore, Alistair was not referring to himself at all. Instead, he was speaking of a man whom he thoroughly relied on.

"For now," Alistair continued. "We put all *activities* on hold until we sort this thing out."

The activities Alistair mentioned were the cult's ritual sacrifices. No more from here on.

And taking control of the gathering, Alistair was a much better speaker than his dad.

"Now, does everyone here understand what I'm saying to you?"

With no one saying a word, Alistair assumed all understood the cult's orders. They were clear. Somebody knows who they are and this person is capable, cunning, and dangerous. They are willing and resourceful, and coming...*very soon.*

There was not much else to discuss other than that. For now, it was wise for everyone to lay low. Everyone was to keep themselves at a distance until a solution was found.

"Good," Alistair said. He looked again at his father. Sirius nodded before a hand was raised up by the door.

Few actually did raise their hands. To do so was both childish and strange. Still, it was the proper protocol. Everyone here was an adult. Even so, when Alistair saw this hand, he pointed directly at it.

"Yes?" Alistair asked.

One man cleared his throat as he stepped out of the shadows to reveal himself to those watching. He was a short man with a pointed goatee and nicotine-stained teeth. His eyes were gray. Seeing him, Alistair nodded and gave him permission to speak.

"Tulsa?"

Tulsa Monarch was a higher member who'd risen through the ranks of the cult due to his connections to the Louisiana shelters. Most were those overseen by Alistair, the same as the schools. Tulsa, however, was also someone who gained notoriety for finding a way to get parents to stop asking questions about their kids. Once, he threatened to expose a mother's criminal past if she pursued her missing son.

Ruthless and savage, Mr. Monarch adhered to the brotherhood's code.

Even now, with his hand up, Sirius and Alistair expected Tulsa to offer something worth hearing. They wanted a solid question because now, everyone was listening.

"I take it this means that there will be nothing for our approaching *solstice*?" asked Tulsa.

The room was still dark. There was enough shadow to conceal Tulsa as he stood at the back. When everyone saw who it was, Alistair and Sirius exchanged glances. They knew it had to be Tulsa who made this inquiry.

Together, there was one thought on both their minds.

"No, Tulsa," snapped Alistair. "Nothing now, do you understand?"

"Drat." Tulsa Monarch was an oaf, no doubt. He was also so lanky and thin he was practically a scarecrow walking on his rigid legs. "Guess we'll just have to wait until this is all over then, huh?" Chortling, Tulsa slouched in his chair.

He dropped his hand down to his lap and blushed to the point where he was flourishing. On his way back to his seat, Tulsa garnered looks from those around him, particularly Alistair and Sirius. Both were familiar with Tulsa's behavior. While everyone else could contain themselves, wait, and hold off for further instruction, Tulsa was someone who struggled to stay silent.

As a result, he was a huge liability. Often, Tulsa was kept out of sight because of this. Although three men were dead. In the back of Sirius's assertive mind, he was quite surprised to see Tulsa still alive.

Tulsa didn't belong in the field doing chores. He was a cockroach who belonged in the cracks and out of sight. He was just a guy who was good in close situations. He didn't need to be used for anything more than that. He walked on the inside and was good at locating lost and lonely children who could be used for something better.

In fact, he was the best.

While other members of the brotherhood would watch before they touched anyone, Tulsa was different. He always touched first. Tulsa used his hands to inspect and to hold the ones he liked most. He was quick. People saw him sometimes but then they could never identify him.

Always, he had a way of changing his face.

Tulsa was a chameleon. He could blend in and he could sneak out. Often, he would change his wardrobe. He would hide his face using a variety of items, such as fake sunglasses and teeth. He'd go to great lengths to hide himself, and it worked.

Eventually, Tulsa was brought into the brotherhood precisely for this skill set. Tulsa was a pedophile. He couldn't explain why he liked kids, he just did. He also hated the question, why do you like kids? In response to this, Tulsa would ask, why do you like men, women, or fucking dogs?

So far as Tulsa Monarch was concerned, no one told other people why they liked what they did. Therefore, he shouldn't have to either. Since his welcoming into the Brotherhood of Cyn, Tulsa remained close to the Tenets. Like their personal dog, whenever Tulsa was ordered to do something, he always did it.

Tulsa Monarch always would be part of the Brotherhood, still he was a slippery one.

He was so slick he couldn't even keep his own hands on himself. He couldn't go anywhere without touching something that wasn't his to touch.

"Guess so." Tulsa scoped out the room for the last time. The rest of the brotherhood stood back and all that was visible was their stern, cold faces. Sirius glared. The orders given were clear.

"Watch your back," Sirius said to everyone in the room.

"You are not as safe as you think you are," Brent hissed.

If he didn't know any better, and he didn't, he'd say he was the next one to die.

CHAPTER 16
PREVENTION MEASURES

IN SIRIUS'S OLD AGE, HE FELT MORE SECURE THAN HE did when he was a younger man.

No, he didn't fear those who tried to harm him or his family now. Unlike his son, who was protected since the day he was born, Sirius knew what it felt like to be vulnerable. He understood what it was like to have to attack and to defend.

In this case, what Sirius was forced to face was something he hadn't before. Someone was here, and Sirius Tenet had no idea who they were or why they were coming. As his hand started to twitch, Sirius raised it to wave at Kardinal.

This meeting had now come to an end.

Everyone vacated the Tenet manor and Kardinal marched toward the front of the room. He met with his boss and politely lent his ear.

"Sir?" Like a diligent soldier, Kardinal waited for his boss's command.

"I want you to keep an eye out, do you understand?" ordered Sirius.

Kardinal nodded in agreement. He knew exactly what this meant. Kardinal was also prepared to carry out whatever Sirius requested of him.

"I was told by Alistair to speak with state PD," Kardinal informed Sirius. "I'm going to take a look. I assure you I have, but—" Sirius lifted his hand and showed his palm.

It was not the lord's intention to silence his head of security. It was done to politely indicate that—while all of Kardinal's actions were admirable—it was *not* all Sirius wanted.

Kardinal leaned closer and waited for his boss to explain.

If not this, then what?

"I want you to keep an eye on *him* too."

Sirius pointed at the doorway to where Brent was now. This man was still Sirius's son. He was also a hoodlum and a bastard. Sirius knew, sooner or later, he would have to deal with Brent. Although he cared little for his foolish boys, they did serve a purpose.

If there was an assassin going after the Tenets, then they too were part of this same pursuit. And, should whoever was hunting them find Brent, then they would come to find Sirius too. They would find him and Alistair and anyone else affiliated with the Brotherhood of Cyn.

Everyone was at risk. And, as much as it pained Sirius to admit, he was not safe either.

"Whoever this man is who's hunting our own, he will continue to do so. And I have a feeling where he'll be striking next."

Sirius focused on Brent while Kardinal was turned.

"And when he does," Sirius said, "I want you to be there, waiting for them."

"Yes, sir," Kardinal said. He turned to face Sirius. "I understand."

"Good," Sirius replied, his hand was on Kardinal's shoulder.

Kardinal was reliable and capable. Knowing this well, Sirius gave his fixer a gentle squeeze before moving on. Ending their time together, Sirius left and Kardinal glared at Brent.

He envisioned Brent already dead and bleeding. Now, Kardinal could do much to protect his master, Brent would be a different story. Kardinal began to think perhaps even he would not succeed. The main question on Kardinal's mind now was not whether he could protect Sirius. No, the real question was whether he was better than this assassin?

Who was he, and what did he want?

The answer was irrelevant. Kardinal wanted to know who was killing the family and needed to do what Sirius said to be done.

That was his true purpose.

It was this code that kept him and his family alive and safe.

Yet, that was then and this was now. And now, Sirius didn't know.

Now, Sirius was more than uncertain. Now, Sirius Tenet was very much afraid.

CHAPTER 17
UPDATES

Whenever a Custodian is deep into any mission, a conference call between themselves and Priest is usually an expected task. But, since Quinn's mission was classified as an Eradicate, it was not mandatory, just recommended. After completing previous ops, Quinn was expected to report on all his kills. Usually this was done via a phone call. Yet, given the scale and the classification of this new mission, Quinn was free to do as he pleased.

He could keep doing this so long as he continued to amass the right bodies.

So far, he did, and he would continue to do so.

When Quinn returned to his trailer, he placed all his weapons into the closet and sat in front of a folded laptop. The computer was older. It was a flat, rectangular prism with the only purpose being to communicate with Priest. The machine was voice and password protected. Should someone wish to scramble its data, a kill code could be added. If entered, it would reduce the computer to nothing more than a brick of circuit boards and scrap metal.

Quinn opened it slowly. After he did this, a voice-recognition entry-key greeted the Custodian. Speaking clearly, Quinn uttered his classification number, slowly.

"Quinn, Kyle. 11315." This was a number all custodians possessed. As soon as it was given, the computer beeped. The black screen transformed to show a few icons as well as a mouse-arrow.

Now secured, Quinn clicked a swirling cartoon of an inverted broom. This was something Priest created back when the group was first conceived.

Quinn looked at the blinking ellipses and drank from his canteen. The screen altered and a straight line appeared in its center. This indicated that, although Priest was not visible, he was still present. He was listening.

"Entry passage?" The voice was muffled and troll-like. Quinn knew right away what to do.

"The walls are high," Quinn said, reciting the secret phrase. It was one unique to him and the other Custodians. It was also another requirement from Priest. "But the sky is higher. We climb until both are below us."

"Accepted. That you, Quinn?"

With everything approved, Quinn was allowed to speak.

"It is," he answered. Quinn was terse. He didn't wish to engage any more than need be.

"See you felt the need to check in. Any changes?"

Quinn's head moved side to side and he reflected on those he'd killed so far.

Quinn had removed three members of the family. This happened within the first forty-eight hours. He planned on taking out two more within the next two days, maybe even sooner.

It all depended on location and security.

"None that need noting," Quinn said.

"Good. And proof?"

As Quinn was well aware, he was not required to give proof, it was not expected at all. The same could also be said for Quinn's compensation. There was a standard salary for all Custodian jobs, regardless of risk or importance. One receives half upfront while the other half is held back until everything is completed.

"No."

"Could you acquire it or did you just choose not to?"

Quinn shrugged at Priest like he could see him through the screen. He couldn't. Quinn could have easily gathered the proof. However, given the order, he didn't quite feel the need to deliver on this. He was here to destroy, not to record or remember this mission as anything more than what it was. It was revenge. It was retribution.

"Didn't want to."

"Okay then."

Holding his breath, so far, there were no signs of Quinn's father.

This bothered the Custodian very much.

Although Quinn was supposedly linked to the Tenet family, according to Priest, none of it reeked of his father's stench. It still didn't carry Quinn's dad's signature. It was still early in the process, but Quinn believed he would have found something by now.

As it stands, there was nothing.

"I haven't found him yet."

Priest declined to respond. Quinn's elbows were pressing hard into his knees. He gazed at the black screen as well as the line appearing across it. Quinn pictured his father. He was still out there, somewhere, hiding and doing God knows what. Quinn considered the future. He thought about how he would *actually* end his dad's life when gifted with the opportunity.

Such was something Quinn felt he was owed. It was something he absolutely needed.

"Keep an eye out," answered Priest, after pausing. "Still early, but as I showed you, he's there. I know he is, and I know you'll find him soon enough."

"Soon enough," repeated Quinn, as if reiterating the phrase made it all the more likely. "I hope so."

There was another pause and Quinn reflected on how to end this conversation. His intention was for it to be nothing more than a simple exchange, and this was about as simple as it could be.

"Is that everything?"

"Yes," replied Quinn.

"Well, any further updates would be appreciated. Stay frosty there, Quinn. Over and out."

Quinn closed the laptop. The conversation between him and Priest was now said and done. Next to Quinn were the remaining names on the list. The main players and the future of cult leadership. There were three crossed off. The next ones were a major priority. Quinn was closer to the person at the top. But, as he knew when removing the first few, it was not going to get easier. Should his father be alive by the end of all this, then it was Quinn's guarantee that the mission would only get more intense.

Still, Quinn was ready. Thanks to his father, he always was.

———

The Tenet estate was an ornate mansion poised on a hilltop in a neighborhood reserved only for Vermilion's elite class. At this hour, a white Pontiac passed through an iron-wrought gate and rolled up to a winding driveway. It proceeded to the arched entrance that guarded the property. In the driver's seat sat Kardinal. He chose to drive very slowly and also chose to park next to Sirius's Lexus and Alistair's Cadillac. While this was a dated car, it was quite detailed.

Alistair customized it with shining rims.

It was waxed and displayed like a model for all to see.

Kardinal's residence was in a house owned by the Tenet family. It was located only a few blocks from theirs. The shortened distance made it easier for him to come by for a visit.

And tonight, they *needed* him to be here now.

Stepping out of his transport, Kardinal glanced at the estate. It had been in the family for generations. The Tenets assimilated most of their wealth through various real estate holdings. Sirius also had much luck in business. He exploited his contacts and used this to gain more territory. This allowed Sirius to make a number of shrewd investments that paid off.

It was after midnight. Most of the lights in the Tenet house were still turned on.

Kardinal steadied up the broad steps and entered the front door. He glided his dusty boots along the glossy marble. He entered the house's grandiose foyer. It included high ceilings and a crystal chandelier. Kardinal overheard chatter in the other room. He walked until the lights were brighter and there, he saw three men standing in the den.

Faint sounds of laughter could be heard among the wafts of smoke. Kardinal knew right away who was there. He stopped by a leather sofa and grunted to get the attention of Sirius.

Sirius was sitting by the fireplace.

At attention, Kardinal's cold expression was his chief method when communicating. And Sirius Tenet, who was an old and decrepit man, his wrinkled skin hung off his brittle bones. He stood in a silk robe. His hair was oily and his teeth nicotine-stained and wet. Kardinal felt chills seeing his boss in this light.

"We need to talk, sir." An ominous silence emerged in the fiery room. A burning log crackled as Sirius lowered his cigar.

"Yes." Sirius sounded groggy. He spoke like there was a marble jammed in his throat.

"Any leads?" asked Sirius.

"I know that PD is looking into Billy Lee's death," replied Kardinal. "Couldn't find much. His body was burned, but I'll do some of my own searching as well."

"A pattern is starting to emerge. As I said at our meeting, we are being hunted." Sirius Tenet was drinking near the fireplace. Kardinal didn't know this for sure, but he assumed Sirius was thinking of his dead son, Billy Lee Meres, and Brent too.

Both boys were the byproducts of Sirius's self-indulgence. These particular offspring were created whenever he engaged in the sins of the flesh. And, although Billy Lee was Sirius's bastard son, he was slain in cold blood.

Sirius stood and slipped his hands along his robe to flatten the fabric. He roamed across the fine carpeting and circled the fireplace.

"This family has done a good job of keeping its secrets over the years," Kardinal said, "but as our family grows, which you know it has, it will be possible for someone to let a few things slip that shouldn't have."

Even saying this was too much.

No one spoke of the Brotherhood, not unless Sirius did first.

Kardinal's job was to analyze possible threats. It was not to make comments or criticisms on the cult's activities. He did this now and he was doing it without permission.

"We don't slip," alleged Sirius. His hand rested on a stone mantle. "And we do not surrender either."

Sirius nodded. He was less describing his family's unwillingness to back down and more providing Kardinal with a new list of expectations.

Kardinal read his boss loud and clear. He sternly replied.

"I think we should hire more security. We need to contact them and tell them what has happened."

"Yes," Sirius said. "Very good idea."

"Okay," Kardinal acknowledged.

Sirius sighed and he removed his hand from the mantle. He fastened the robe against his chest and glimpsed over his shoulder.

"Make the call," Sirius said to Kardinal. "Then I want you here as often as possible, on near twenty-four-hour watch until we get this thing resolved."

"Understood," Kardinal added.

He received an off-the-collar glare from Sirius. Still, Kardinal stood by and said nothing. He agreed to every order. Going forward, he knew it could only get worse.

"And I want you to go see our friend Sheriff Stillwater," Sirius said, his eyes began to narrow. "Take what you must and then move on."

"Aye," Kardinal said. "Anything else?"

"No," Sirius said, eyes on Kardinal. "But do you have any ideas at all about who is trying to kill us?"

Now by the door, Kardinal was about to step through. He stopped when he was asked this next question.

"No," Kardinal responded to Sirius. He was gripping the door handle and turning it slowly. "But I'm going to find out, sir. I swear to you, I will find whoever's responsible."

"Hmm," Sirius said. He downed the last of his drink and sucked his cheeks into his face.

"I hope so," he said. "I really...hope so."

Moving away, Kardinal proceeded out of the Tenet house. He chose to leave his master alone to mourn his loss and thought about the days ahead. To Kardinal, all of this was far too complicated. Therefore, Kardinal could not predict its end.

Prepared as he was, anything could happen. Nothing was impossible now.

CHAPTER 18
QUESTIONS

KARDINAL MET WITH THE PARISH SHERIFF AT THE crack of dawn as he was ordered to do. There to fulfill Sirius's request, he did not come to interrogate or to pry.

No, he had come only to understand. Dressed in a black suit, and not his usual red, Kardinal entered the station where he was spotted by several deputies. They knew who Kardinal was and who he worked for. The other cops were without a single clue as to why he had chosen to come now, at this time. And those who knew Kardinal always referred to him the way Sirius did.

When they saw Kardinal, the cops stopped and gawked at the unfriendly man.

"Hey, you here to talk about that benefit bash that old Sirius has planned for us at the end of the month?" One deputy said this after Kardinal entered the room.

Kardinal ignored the question and scoped the office. The benefit mentioned was an annual event, but no, he was not here for that. The best way to be perceived as a good person was to do good things. For the Tenet's, the annual police benefit was their good thing.

They often praised the efforts of local law enforcement. They complimented their service and how their sacrifice made the city a safer, better place to live. Such praise was appreciated. Few ever gave it to the police. The fact that the Tenets were one of the few who gave it granted the police both friendship and glory.

Sirius was once a deputy himself.

At the event, Sirius often spoke about his experiences, how it was the police force that taught him the importance of discipline and determination. All the police ate this up. In doing so, the Tenets were welcomed and protected by everyone who wore a badge.

They were, after all, their allies.

"No," Kardinal said. Now, Kardinal was not law enforcement. He had no authority or jurisdiction that could grant him any privileges. He also didn't have the authority or the right to interfere in an ongoing investigation.

However, what he did have was status and money. As of now, that was all Kardinal needed. He was invited into the sheriff's office and was direct about the reasons why he was there. Kardinal mentioned how Sirius Tenet was concerned about what happened. Kardinal mentioned to the sheriff how any information would be appreciated. Sheriff Peter Stillwater was a newer sheriff in Vermilion. He was a plump fellow who carried an old revolver and met with Kardinal because he was afraid of what would happen if he didn't.

Even without jurisdiction, Kardinal insisted Stillwater submit what he had uncovered so far. However, there wasn't much to recover. Billy Lee's body was burned to a crisp. Aware of Sirius's position as a philanthropist and as a politician, Stillwater did as he was asked.

"What, he wanna open an investigation of his own,

does he?" Stillwater was half-kidding, but he was also not kidding.

It wasn't entirely uncommon for Sirius to interfere with local PD. This was not the first time he did.

"No." Kardinal was not interested in providing further details.

As soon as he had what he needed, Kardinal was gone as quickly as he came. Now with a file in his hand, he stepped into his Pontiac. He placed the papers down on the seat next to him. Only few knew of Billy Lee's link to the Tenet family, he was still part of its *inner circle*. And now, with Billy Lee dead and Brent Meres classified as another possible target, Kardinal's duty was to stave off the infection.

Kardinal removed his iPhone and dialed.

On the other end of the call, he heard Alistair's voice, not Sirius's.

The two did live in the same house. Few commented on this notion. A fifty-year-old man who shared a residence with a man in his late seventies was odd, but that's how it was. Nevertheless, Kardinal, who did find it odd, also knew that the Tenets were an odd family. In fact, they were a sick family.

"Kardinal?" Alistair crackled on the other end of the phone.

"I have it," Kardinal immediately said.

"Well, what does it say?"

"I only just got it," Kardinal said. He looked at the work submitted by the parish detectives. With only a few details listed, none of which were intuitive or interesting.

There were few eyewitnesses, but not many were questioned. There were also notes that pointed to a few possible suspects.

"There isn't much here," Kardinal said. "But I will

stake out Brent's place for now. If there's a pattern, he'll be next on the list."

"Yes," Alistair said. "Wise decision. Very wise decision."

Saying nothing after, Kardinal didn't care what Alistair's opinions were about his *decisions*. In the end, he worked for his father. He was the one who was giving the orders.

"Yes," Kardinal said. "Tell your father I will give him the files when I see him next. Make sure you tell him that."

"Okay. I wi—"Kardinal dropped the phone and then he left the station.

———

Brent Meres lived in a ransacked apartment he shared with five other junkies. Not quite a crack house, it was a house whereby everything inside of it was cracked. With no leads at the crime scene, this said more to Kardinal than the execution.

The same could also be said for the death of Sauder and Vickers. According to ballistics reports, they were both shot in the head and the chest. In fact, the notes were clear about this. It was always two in the chest and one in the head.

Each of the wounds were discovered very close together. They were incredibly precise.

This strategy, as Kardinal knew, being ex-military himself, was training. It was a tactic done by someone who had experience, who knew where to shoot in order to ensure absolute death. The executions were solid and clean. When completed, the person left the scene in a haze of fog, or so the notes detailed. On his way to Brent's apartment, he traveled toward the gray horizon. He clutched the sidearm in a holster around his belt. He wasn't on his way to protect Brent. He was going to find the man who wanted to kill his employers, and he was going to kill him first.

That was all. That was everything.

CHAPTER 19
NO MERCY

OUTSIDE THE RUINED COMPLEX WHERE BRENT MERES lived, Quinn looked at two trucks parked along the curb. With rusted wheels, and windows glazed with soot and grime, these cars faced each other like a pair of angled feet. The door to the building was ajar. Beyond it was Brent's primary residence. The setting was impossibly dark and each room looked like they were painted black.

Nothing was visible.

Quinn heard commotion on the other end of the sidewalk while next to him were the photos of Brent Meres.

Quinn tucked them into the glove compartment. He came out of the RAM dressed in full gear. In black track-pants and with a muscle shirt tucked into his body armor, Quinn also wore gloves and a mask. Secured in the back of his vest were two slots for Quinn's tonfa.

This was a detail that never changed for Quinn.

Although he had not yet used the tonfa since beginning the Eradicate, he believed that the time would come whereby they could be put to good use. Quinn meditated in the car and estimated there would be at least five men inside. All were set to be eliminated the same as Quinn's primary target.

It was a quiet night so far. The streets were vacant and there were only a few homes in this decrepit, piece of shit neighborhood. Resting against the chair was Quinn's Benelli M4 shotgun. The weapon was thick and surprisingly light for its size. It was loaded with eleven rounds and also included a match-saver should Quinn need any extra shells.

Fitted with a fixed stock, a lightened bolt carrier, and a customized grip, this Benelli was the ultimate blow-you-in-half kind of gun. It was loud but at the same time deadly accurate. Quinn had an ammo belt strapped on too. With this on his person, the Custodian had officially crossed into overkill territory.

' Quinn opened the door and vacated his RAM. He grabbed the Benelli and brought his Glock 26 along for the ride. He didn't imagine he would need this gun. It was small and easy to keep hidden. In addition to the pistol, Quinn's OTF knife was also brought. Quinn trekked up to the door and kept the Benelli behind his arm. As bouts of drunken laughter echoed from beyond Brent's door, there was one light turned on above the frame.

Quinn waited.

"What?" The person shouting sounded like they were trying to sing soprano.

Ignoring these boisterous sounds, soon as the door opened, this fucker had only a second before his face was lasagna. Quinn used the barrel to knock once, but not more than that.

"Who's at the fucking door!"

A new voice said, it was squeakier yet just as frail as the one that had come before. Inching away, Quinn listened to the door peel open.

"Open that shit, bro," a third voice followed.

Quinn heard the creak, and then he raised his Benelli.

Now face-to-face with a known associate, it was one of Brent's standby thugs. This fool looked at the Custodian and the barrel of his epic shotgun. Both were visible, but so was the idiot's face seconds before it was blasted to smithereens.

Bye bye boom.

CHAPTER 20
BOOM BOOM POW!

Barreling brutishly into the space, Quinn was strapped and ready to go. He cocked his Benelli and loaded in a fresh round. In Brent's crowded living room, on the crummy sofas sat five people.

More than Quinn had initially anticipated.

All in leather and all heavily bearded and gruff, they were possibly bikers but then Quinn recalled the *red flags*. Quinn knew all the *One Percenters*. He could list them all offhand, in fact. Quinn respected outlaws, but he wasn't afraid of them. He had encounters with a few gangs, yes, but all of those encounters ended in the same way. He shot them all dead. Generally, however, the bikers were tough and they were also strong. What they lacked, however, were the necessary training and skills.

Often, they were too brooding, too slow. Quinn was above them.

He was better, and he didn't know if these men *were* bikers, but they did fit the profile. Quinn was given some background intel from Ally about certain clubs operating in certain areas. These fools looked like they belonged to a few, but Quinn didn't know for sure.

And he didn't care either way. His mission hadn't changed. Eradicate.

When these men saw Quinn standing there, all of them scuttled like roaches. They reached for their weapons and scampered. Quinn held steady. He was prepared for this. Fortunately, he brought a weapon that reacted well to surprises. One man with a long beard reached into his jacket and Quinn pumped him through the chest. The dude soared through Brent's kitchen and collided with a table before landing hard on his back.

"Ah!"

Shooting another maniac in the face, Quinn immediately pivoted after the blast. Swinging his body in a circular motion, Quinn kept the shotgun tight in front of his chest. He was ready to fire again, so Quinn shot a third man with another clean shot to the face. The boom split the man's skull apart like a cantaloupe as grimy handfuls of brains splurged in a great vomit of gore.

So far, Quinn counted three.

He scanned the room and spotted one more.

This next fool was wielding a Smith & Wesson revolver. He peeped out from behind the couch. Due to the Benelli's textured grip, it remained taut in Quinn's hands. It didn't slip, not once. Quinn thrust the barrel aggressively into the boy's chest. He figured so long as he was close, Quinn might as well make a statement. The Benelli's match-saver was loaded. With this, Quinn pumped a clean shot straight into the fool's abdominal cavity.

It produced a muffled pop as Quinn decimated the man's heart.

Another down.

While Quinn eliminated everyone in this area, still he had not executed Brent.

Quinn circled and lifted his Benelli. He returned the gun to his shoulder and exhaled as he motioned through the kitchen. He was not tired. For now, Quinn's heart rate remained steady. He was unfazed but he still didn't have eyes on Brent, not yet. Quinn moved around the corner and stepped into another hallway. He was cautious. Quinn's gaze touched everything around him. At any moment, Brent could pop out. As he would likely be armed, Quinn's finger rested on the Benelli trigger. He was ready.

Quinn's shoes were messy with blood, so much so that they slid along the tiled floor.

The Custodian crept and Quinn heard a squeaking from the end of the hall. Initially it was faint, but it was still audible enough for Quinn to catch. Hinges screeched and the sound of a door tapping the wall sounded shortly after.

Brent Meres sprinted across the room. Wielding an Uzi, the fool screamed in a wild fit of madness as he charged.

"Guh!" In a display of sheer absurdity, the junkie weasel held down the trigger of his automatic weapon. Spraying bullets, Quinn ducked and rolled.

"Fuck you, motherfucker!"

As soon as Quinn glimpsed at the weapon, he collected himself before making his next move. He kneeled to avoid the gunfire. Quinn waited a millisecond before shooting back.

Boom!

Quinn popped Brent Meres in the leg. He severed the fool in half with two quick blasts to the kneecaps. After shredding Brent's calves off his puny thighs, the asshole's legs broke off the bone like an action figure being pulled apart. Blood sprayed in a messy expulsion reminiscent to a thumb clamped over a garden hose, and now so slick and so wet, Quinn looked into the eyes of the man whom he had come to destroy. Taking out Brent's legs, Quinn could have easily left him alone to bleed out and die. While an ambulance may have prolonged Brent's life, Quinn wasn't in the saving or the prolonging business.

He trampled over the gooey mush as patches of blood squished against Quinn's shoes.

Quinn marched straight over to Brent, ignoring his screams of pain. Bringing the Benelli to his face, Quinn cocked the weapon again. Another shell was loaded into the barrel, and Quinn raised it up to Brent's head at a snail's pace. Brent gasped and then he gagged. He shivered and stared into the mouth of the gun now so close to his mouth.

"You...don't..." Bubbles of grimy spit had gathered along Brent's gray lips. He attempted to provide Quinn with a warning that, while well-placed, was also expected.

Everything here was expected.

Know what you're about to do?

Quinn was never given the opportunity to say this, but he could speak it in his own mind. When Quinn fired, Brent's head exploded in another juicy display of glorious carnage. With the kill finished and done, Quinn crossed another name off his kill list and he did this as he walked away.

Brent Meres, brother to Billy Lee Meres, was now deliciously dead.

CHAPTER 21
THE FAMILIAR

Quinn exited Brent's obliterated apartment and a newfound calmness ensconced him as he became one with the night. Quinn reached for his keys, and the entire time, continued to hear the rage in Brent's voice. For some reason, Quinn was struggling to forget it.

You don't know what you're doing.

"Maybe," Quinn said to himself. "Maybe."

Quinn unlocked his RAM. He was about to step in when he reached forward to place his Benelli in the passenger seat, he realized the night was still very young. Then Quinn lifted his leg and glanced at the rear-view mirror.

He always used mirrors, even when his car wasn't moving. Reflections, in Quinn's mind, were sometimes the only way to get a good look at things. He was about to go to his safehouse when he noticed a man waiting by the curb, holding a firearm.

Ducking before the man could fire, a bullet pinged Quinn's mirror.

Too close.

Quinn leaped out of his truck and took cover behind one of the street poles. Holding the Benelli, Quinn listened to the pitter-pattering of footsteps. Quinn counted only one shot as he glimpsed past his shoulder. Before the shooter fired again, Quinn somersaulted and peered through the broken window. From there, he spotted the shooter. Now seeing him in full view, the shooter was a man in a suit armed with a SIG.

He fired again, and the glass shattered, and shards sprinkled Quinn's chest.

Quinn exhaled and then began to push himself up.

He whipped his body across the hood. In mid-air, Quinn stretched his leg and performed a sweeping side kick. He aimed for his attacker's arms. Quinn kicked with his shin and hammered the shooter's gun.

Quinn knocked the weapon out of his hands and accompanied the first hit with another.

Quinn elbowed the suit-wearing man in the face and knocked him straight down. Doing this, Quinn had effectively disarmed his attacker.

"Ah." Quinn stared at the backside of the man he hit.

From here, he considered a number of follow-up techniques. Quinn was now depending on Jeet Kune Do. In bai jong, a basic stance, Quinn gawked at Kardinal.

Staring down the Tenet's main bodyguard, Quinn was the one whom Kardinal had come for tonight. Nevertheless, the Custodian began to circle. Quinn squinted through his mask's visor. He started the fight by kissing Kardinal's mouth with a few rapid jabs. Kardinal's head bobbed, and Quinn hopped. He was enjoying this.

The hits were not knockouts because what Quinn wanted was to establish control. He needed to do this before he got crafty. Let's see what this guy was made of, Quinn thought, and then decide what to do next.

Kardinal spat after each punch. Later, the fixer struck his own stance.

Kardinal, however, was sloppy. Quinn could see right away he was off balance. Although Quinn was a decent striker, he was also a damn good grappler. Quinn assessed the potential of the one he was facing down.

Strong as he was, Kardinal swayed.

He kept his hands up but Quinn spotted a significant weakness. There was too much weight in Kardinal's shoulder. He was dipping too far forward. As a result, his strikes appeared visible *before* they were delivered.

Quinn switched to Shotokan.

What he sought now was distance and aggravation. Distance provided time and aggravation clouded the mind. One of the most difficult tasks in any fight was for the fighter to stay calm.

You needed to keep calm and always keep your head in the game.

As Quinn learned from experience, only a few fighters could handle or live up to this expectation. There were few operatives who could handle the pain and who could stay as focused and play with much intelligence and assertion. If you aggravate, then you can get your opponent to slip and you gain the upper hand.

Quinn knew this. In fact, he knew it all too well.

And now, he was seeing it.

Everything Quinn knew to be true was confirmed as he pummeled Kardinal's knee with a solid front kick. Afterward, Quinn established a new striking position. Watching Kardinal stagger, Quinn knew his jabs hurt but his kicks hurt more.

"Aw!" Kardinal shrieked.

Quinn shuffled and performed a tiny hop. Then he powered his opposite leg again into Kardinal's ribs. It was an infuriating blow as Quinn completed a new, stunning sidekick. Even as a tyke, Quinn could break boards like they were nothing.

Kardinal wobbled and fell down to his knee. He pushed himself up before he was straight again. Kardinal spat a second time, and Quinn lowered his arms.

From here, Quinn switched to aikido. Now in kamae, right foot out, left leg straight and flexed, his back tense, Quinn waited for Kardinal's next attack.

In response to the fight, Kardinal resorted to more bombastic techniques. There was little direction and little power. Kardinal was a feral jungle cat. His fighting style was there but incomplete. Kardinal charged at Quinn in a bullish stampede and rammed the Custodian.

In a second, Quinn pivoted. He spun one hundred and eighty degrees and performed a quick wheel throw. Such a throw is only feasible if the opponent is willing to attack with full force. Generally, the move is done against more careless fighters. It can also be morphed into a deadly wrist lock or an armbar. In this case, Quinn nabbed Kardinal's forearm. On the spin, he locked Kardinal's limb and obtained control. Once Quinn had him, he sent Kardinal head-first into the truck.

Kardinal smacked the car, and Quinn thought that would be the end of him, but Kardinal collided with the steel doors and raised his hands to protect himself.

Observing this toughness, however, it was grounded in something Quinn didn't expect. Kardinal was experienced. In fact, his abilities and his style were *strangely* familiar. And with Quinn out in front, he stared at the Tenet's fixer.

Kardinal marched after Quinn and his voice was a boar's roar.

"Ah!" Kardinal was a beast venting his frustration.

Yet, Quinn continued to keep his body open as he snatched Kardinal's tie and hammer-fisted the fixer hard in the chest. Quinn pummeled with quicker, unrelenting strikes and was now pounding nails into plywood. Quinn struck using the outside of his palm and kept on until Kardinal's face was littered with bruises. Quinn could see Kardinal's hand in his pocket.

Here, Quinn expected to see a pistol. This would make sense.

However, Quinn was shocked by what Kardinal had removed instead.

He pushed his jacket aside and Quinn spotted a leather sheath. Kardinal's hands were next to it as a shiny, fat Jim Bowie knife slipped from his back. Kardinal looked like a croc wrangler. And, given his location, Quinn thought this was appropriate.

A Bowie, unlike Quinn's OTF, was not very common in knife fighting.

Consequently, it was hardly a concealable one.

The Bowie was thick and heavy, basically a butcher's knife and the kind brought into the wild or a blade one carried in the Old West. While bigger and more solid, the weapon itself was not ideal for combat. It was made for chopping wood and cutting meat. Quinn could see how this spoke to Kardinal's inexperience in the knife fighting game.

This was *not* something you did because it could not be done.

In Quinn's opinion, Kardinal was no knife fighter. Right now, he was way out of his league. Kardinal held the Bowie upright and tried stabbing Quinn. But the angry bodyguard depended on the power of his fierce, upper-handed jabs whereas Quinn aimed only for the chest.

"Argh," yelped Kardinal.

With the knife drawn low, Quinn snagged Kardinal's wrist and squeezed. Losing one arm, all of Quinn's strength shifted to the hand now preventing the blade from moving.

As soon as it did, Quinn flipped Kardinal to his feet. In aikido, the kotegaeshi wristlock is difficult to perfect, but done in the right way, is one of the most effective blows in the entire pantheon of martial arts. And, as soon as Quinn managed to get Kardinal down, he retrieved his tonfa.

Clubbing time.

A passionate and elegant draw, Quinn yanked the weapon, and stood in Southpaw.

"So, you like swinging clubs, huh?" Kardinal toyed with Quinn.

He heard the heaving sounds of Kardinal's heavy breaths. He gawked as Kardinal held his Bowie. Stoic, Quinn was a phantom prowling in the night. He said not a word.

"Never bring a knife to a gunfight. You ever heard the saying?" Kardinal barked.

Silent again, of course Quinn heard it. Kardinal lunged.

Quinn noticed the attack and his arm shot down. Rotating his hand, Quinn used his forearm to deflect the incoming blow. He clashed Kardinal's wrist, yet Quinn's block was so clean the knife didn't get anywhere near his body. Quinn used the other arm to deliver a straight punch that struck Kardinal in the torso. Quinn pummeled Kardinal in the belly with the tonfa handle.

"Gah!" Kardinal shrieked for a third, possibly a fourth time.

Now at the mercy of the weapon, Kardinal shuffled and Quinn made sure to keep moving. The batons stayed flush against Quinn's meaty forearms. The technique driving Quinn's moves was clear to his advantage. He dipped down and then up again. After this, Quinn hit Kardinal again in the ribs and again in the chest.

"Motherfu—" Kardinal's voice faded out again.

Now Quinn had the fixer right where he wanted. He rammed the tonfa directly into Kardinal's chin in a devastating uppercut of epic proportions. Kardinal dropped like a wounded soldier. Although Kardinal made an excellent effort, what he was seeing now could only be stars.

Quinn spun the tonfa and circled Kardinal.

Delivering another vicious combination, the Custodian kicked Kardinal's side and turned him over. Quinn switched the tonfa back and slipped them into their slots. He stared at his attacker and patted Kardinal's pockets using his weapon and searched for useful things.

Quinn scoured Kardinal's body and soon found a wallet. Quinn reached for it. And, while he was about to pull out the leather case, Kardinal—once thought to be unconscious—suddenly woke up.

"Gah!" Kardinal screamed as Quinn jumped back and moved his tonfa back behind him.

He had nothing other than his hands and so, nothing else to use but his hand. With a straight kick, Quinn knocked Kardinal's pointed chin.

"Uh!" Kardinal emitted another beaten sound. He was sent straight to the pavement while Quinn sprinted toward his RAM. The license plate on the truck was a fake one. It couldn't be traced even if a person knew every single digit. Once Quinn hopped inside, he started the engine.

The truck skidded.

A vehicle like this one, in Baton Rouge, was standard.

Many locals owned trucks that looked precisely the same as Quinn's did now. This one provided excellent cover.

Quinn pushed his foot down and accelerated the truck to sixty miles per hour.

Sirens rang as three patrol vehicles passed one another in the opposite lane.

Though Quinn was not winded or injured, he was thinking about the recent tussle. He reflected on Brent as well as the other casualties. Primarily, Quinn thought of the one who had arrived at the scene.

Kardinal was the one who was willing to throw down without hesitation. There were few who could stand toe-to-toe with Quinn, and some he could name offhand, like Khabib, GSP, and Royce Gracie to name a few. Quinn once had the opportunity to fight Khabib in a "friendly contest" when he visited an MMA gym in Wyoming. It ended in a draw. And, while Kardinal was an imperfect fighter, he was tough enough to fight despite being outmatched in every way.

Quinn admired the audacity and grit in every one of his opponents.

This was a significant part of the Custodian's growth and learning. It was also the part that made Quinn more complete. As he drove, he heard the voice of his father.

"You want to be the best; you have to play with the best. The biggest shark stayed the biggest until the day it was hunted and killed," Quinn's dad had proclaimed.

Should one wish to make themselves into anything better, then one is required to find those who are supposedly bigger and better. In essence, Quinn needed to find the messes that were too much for anyone else to clean. Then, he needed to go in and mop it up like it was nothing but a stain on God's beautiful green earth. But those other missions had rules. Eradicate had only the rules that

Quinn himself created. It was what he decided to do. Therefore, what came of this new surprise—this unexpected and deadly fighter—was intriguing.

His style was too familiar for Quinn. He could identify all the techniques and all the tricks too. None were mainstream. They had all likely come from the same source.

Quinn's style was somewhat unique. And yet, all Quinn could hear now was his father coaching him as he delivered his many punches and kicks. Based on what Quinn observed in Kardinal, the Custodian felt like he was not the only one hearing the voice of his dad.

Whoever this Kardinal was, he was no Quinn. Goddamn it, did he ever fight like he was.

He did in almost every way except one. Kardinal was still alive and he shouldn't be.

No, as far as Quinn was concerned, Kardinal should be gone.

He should be fucking dead.

CHAPTER 22
PROBLEMS

KARDINAL WADDLED UP THE TENET'S DRIVEWAY AS IF in a drunken stupor in the middle of the night. Understandably exasperated and very sore, he motioned to the front door, so weak he could barely stand. At this time, both the father and the son were asleep. To disturb them now was unacceptable. Kardinal walked into the foyer battered from the encounter he experienced earlier. And what he just endured, he hadn't in a very long time.

Kardinal fought many people in his youth.

He participated in tournaments, but Kardinal wouldn't describe himself as a *professional* fighter. He did, however, have some experience in the trade.

Now, being older, Kardinal's fighting days were mostly behind him.

Still, Kardinal knew how to deliver some powerful strikes and how to block as well. He was never the best fighter despite his martial arts background. He moved hard and he moved quick. Yet, this new man hunting the Tenets was more than just skilled.

Kardinal would not describe him as talented. No, this man was so much more.

This man was gifted.

No matter what Kardinal attempted to do to bring this one man down, he adapted instantly. The assassin had either absorbed each punch or he stepped aside and locked up Kardinal's joints. And, if the assassin wasn't doing this, then he was striking Kardinal immediately after.

In the end, the fight was brutal. It was one Kardinal would remember for the rest of his life. Kardinal moved on and he thought back to when he was engaged with a similar opponent. There was one instance that continued to surface in his mind. Kardinal had encountered only one person who truly scared him in his life. At the time, Kardinal didn't know exactly who this man was. However, he was someone who Sirius Tenet had been meeting with these past four months.

Kardinal labeled him as *an outsider*.

He was present once at a meeting with Sirius. This was a peculiar occurrence because it was one Kardinal had not been informed of. This man there was taller and he was older. He might even pass for Sirius's age, but appeared more rugged, more brooding and tough. His shoulders were fat and his arms were too.

When Kardinal met this man, he was wearing a black trench coat and was always smoking a cigar. He did all of this in front of Sirius and broke one of the main rules of his house. No one smokes outside the den. And yet, Sirius said not a word to this man as he did.

So, who the hell was this guy?

Kardinal asked himself this question as the man left the Tenet house. The man never gave his name. He was, in effect, a complete stranger. When visiting the Tenets, the only word Kardinal could discern from their conversation was an easy one.

Children.

This man, like Kardinal suspected, was someone whom the Tenets were turning to for advice. Maybe for more tributes? It was possible. Yet, all of this was something Kardinal only assumed. However, to turn to someone who was not a member of the brotherhood was never done.

Ever.

Therefore, something else was going on that Kardinal wasn't being told about. He consulted Sirius about who this man might be but received nothing in return. As the family's head of security, Kardinal was entitled to know the identity of this visitor. However, when Kardinal inquired, he received only a pat on the back followed by a boyish grin.

"Don't worry," Sirius said to Kardinal. *"He's not looking for what we are. He just wants to know more about what we do and what we like."*

What we like.

Until now, Kardinal hadn't heard anyone in the cult phrase the family's tastes in such an odd way. What the Tenets liked were young, impressionable kids who could be molded and shaped. They liked children who came from broken homes and who could be tempted and sacrificed all in the name of some dumb demigod.

However, this was *not* what Kardinal said this *man in black* wanted.

There was no mention of sacrifice or death. According to Sirius, he only wanted to know more about what the Tenets liked. At the time, Kardinal had no idea how to interpret this. The man had no interest in entering into the family's cult. Kardinal knew this because he asked Sirius if they were taking new members.

When Sirius heard this, he responded by saying, "Nothing like that at all."

"So...what is it like then, sir?" *Kardinal felt obliged to ask.*

Sirius lit a cigar and continued to grin.

"It's just not like that."

It was then that the consultation between Kardinal and Sirius ended. Despite the fact that Kardinal worked for the family for years, it was not enough for him to get the truth out of his master.

Sirius wasn't going to tell Kardinal why that man was there.

And so, if Kardinal wasn't going to get these answers from his master, then he had to look into it himself. He would get closer to this man on his own terms. He would make his discovery by doing what he did best.

He would stay close and he would keep his eyes and ears open.

He knew, one day, Kardinal would see this mysterious man again. In fact, Kardinal continued to recall the day he first encountered this other man. He remembered leaving Sirius's office and stepping past Kardinal like he was as inanimate as a bookshelf.

Kardinal studied this man from top to bottom.

Walking by a man like Kardinal without acknowledging him was the epitome of disrespect. So, this man's prowess and alpha male persona were noted and loathed. It was Kardinal who occupied the space around here. He was the one who guarded this family and he was the one responsible for their safety. Therefore, whoever this new visitor might be, he was in no position to treat Kardinal with such derision.

And the fixer refused to stand for it.

"Hey!" Kardinal shouted and followed the man out of the Tenet house. Kardinal trailed closely, and when he reached for the man's shoulder, the man in the trench coat stepped aside.

For a second, Kardinal thought he disappeared.

His movements were so sharp they bordered on the precognition.

The man in black knew where Kardinal's hand was before it was placed there. With Kardinal's arm now extended, the man in black reacted with precision and speed. He snagged Kardinal's wrist and clamped it tightly. Kardinal was then sent flying over this man's shoulder before he clacked the pavement.

Kardinal wanted to get up because he wanted to fight back. Once he was down, this man in black stiff-armed Kardinal. Doing this, Kardinal was unable to move or escape. Although the man was older, he was undeniably strong. Kardinal soon found himself at the mercy of the man's fortified grip. He kept Kardinal pinned until he settled.

While on Tenet property, not a single person had come to Kardinal's aid. It was almost as though they had chosen to ignore the altercation. Apparently, they feared this man in black more.

"Nice effort," the man commended Kardinal's recent attempt.

His breath smelled of tobacco and cologne. Kardinal squirmed, but it didn't do any good.

"But you're too eager to attack, see?" said the man in black. "You're too bold, and that makes whatever you're trying to do too obvious, too readable, and so...too damn easy to fuck with."

The man's hands unfastened and his hold on Kardinal

loosened. Acting like a sensei, the man in black was critiquing the moves of his fellow student. When he was done with this, the man smiled and then he let Kardinal go.

"At least you got guts, though," the man said. "And guts is worth somethin'."

Kardinal didn't know what to do.

The man was proficient in self-defense and advanced combat. He was so capable he dropped Kardinal like a bag of dirt. Though older, the man knew how to fight better than anyone Kardinal had come across before.

This did more than frighten him. It intrigued him.

Kardinal was fascinated.

"Who are you?" Kardinal barked while catching his breath.

The man smirked and lent his hand so Kardinal could stand back up again. The man didn't say his name. He also didn't make an appearance on the Tenet grounds again.

Nevertheless, Kardinal remained curious. Who was this man?

He was so fast, so assertive, and calm. In fact, he was so calm Kardinal struggled to think of him as human. He was, but only barely.

So, where did he come from?

From what Kardinal could gather, the man seemed military. Yet, this man was less former military and more former *former* military—so old school he'd come from a breed of soldier that no longer existed in the realm of brutes, grunts, and mercenaries.

But why was he here?

This question was answered from the encounters the man had with Sirius. During this time, Kardinal overheard some other words that piqued his interest. They did because they were words the head of security hadn't heard in Sirius's office ever.

Kinetic. Youth. Program.

Kardinal knew the meaning of these words. He just didn't understand why they were being spoken of now. He knew the definition, but as far as the link they provided to the family...that was as mysterious as the man.

It was because of this that Kardinal had to ask himself a question he could not avoid:

What are you building?

Were the Tenets building something I'm unaware of?

Was this cult about something else, maybe something bigger?

All of these questions mattered to Kardinal. However, they didn't matter nearly as much as the one Kardinal refused to forgo any answer. The man he faced at Brent's place was similar to the man Kardinal fought all those years ago. The two could have been trained under the tutelage of the same master or perhaps they were the same person. Kardinal doubted this.

They did use a similar fighting style, no doubt.

It was similar, but different in only one way.

The one Kardinal faced today was faster, smoother. He was more tactical, more multi-faceted. In essence, he could perform multiple things at the same time. And, while they were so close in terms of technique, the two still passed for master and apprentice. Yet, all of this was true *if* they knew each other. Kardinal didn't know if they did, but every part of him suggested this was true.

Kardinal returned to the Tenet residence and went straight to the bathroom. He stood in front of the mirror and wiped off most of his blood. Later, Kardinal heard the voice of Alistair Tenet. He was calling to Kardinal from the second floor of the mansion.

"Cardy, where are you? What happened?" Kardinal glared.

He hated the nickname. He hated it almost as much as he hated seeing Alistair in his silk bathrobe, with his gut hanging out for all to see.

"We have a problem," Kardinal said.

Alistair stood poised near the banister. He gasped and leaned forward. Rarely was there ever a problem so severe it could not be handled by Kardinal. In addition, the problem was never so severe Kardinal had to come to the house. He did all of this while the issue remained unresolved. Normally, Kardinal would fix and go away. He was, after all, *a fixer*.

Nonetheless, here was where Kardinal stood now. He was standing in front of the man he served and he disclosed to him something he never wanted to hear.

"We have a very *serious* problem."

CHAPTER 23
HUNTERS

Sirius Tenet stood in a pair of platinum loafers and a silk bathrobe that was the same as his son's. He waited before the brick fireplace, silently sipping his drink, and gazing at the crackling flames.

"A problem?" Sirius asked. "Is that what we have now?"

Sirius's question was directed at Kardinal. It was given as soon as he disclosed precisely what he had observed to Sirius Tenet. He described what happened during his attempt to protect Sirius's other illegitimate son. Once informed, Kardinal told Sirius the details surrounding the attack. It was all bad.

"They're all dead, sir."

Alistair knew Brent almost as well as he knew Billy Lee. He was aware of the other family that, while linked, carried a different name. As a result, neither Billy Lee nor Brent were granted the same privileges or the respect.

Nonetheless, they were *still* Sirius's children. He did nothing to show he cared.

"I'm sorry."

Kardinal offered his condolences despite the fact that he loathed Brent. Sirius could be kind. He could also be quite terrible. However, Brent Meres was more than a troubled child and a criminal. He was reckless. If he wasn't killed tonight, then he would have been sometime in the future. And this was the problem.

"Someone was there."

It was the most vital piece of information Kardinal could provide. Tonight, he had encountered the man responsible for the deaths of both Meres boys. He was also the same assassin currently hunting the family—*his family*.

"And did you see his face?" Sirius's question was generic. If Kardinal had seen the man's face, then he would have said he had. He didn't.

"No." Kardinal's response was cold as ice. It was no fluff, just facts.

Whatever was asked could be answered using just a few short words. Still gazing at the fireplace, it was Sirius who ordered Kardinal to protect Brent. He also wanted Kardinal to see if there was a pattern. He was searching for a possible link between Brent's death and Billy Lee's. Hearing Kardinal, Sirius continued to review the murder of the boys he had known.

As Sirius did this, he came up with a new question.

"Who? Who...did it?" Sirius's lips quivered as he made the inquiry.

Kardinal was prepared for this. For now, he had only stated he did *not* see the assassin's face. He also didn't discuss how the man had tossed him around the parking lot using a fighting style superior to Kardinal's.

Again, Kardinal didn't know how else he could make his news any clearer.

"I didn't see his face," Kardinal said, "but I did see what he could do."

Silence emerged as Sirius and Alistair stood next to each other.

"I have reason to believe," Kardinal said, "it was a *professional*."

Mentioning the word professional was a trigger for Sirius. However, when hearing Kardinal say it, Sirius Tenet peeped over his shoulder. Flames lingered in his pupils and his expression began to fill with hate.

"*An assassin*," Sirius said. He wanted to clarify even though the word required no clarification at all.

"Yes."

Kardinal's reply was only a confirmation. It resolved the issue at hand and made the current news abundantly clear. The Tenet family was being targeted. More than this, their brotherhood was now compromised.

Sirius looked scornfully at Kardinal.

This was his way of telling Kardinal that his job was far from over.

Kardinal was also telling Sirius it was about to get so much worse.

"I will discover who this man is but given the situation..." Kardinal's eyes turned downward. Kardinal considered more about what had transpired and what needed to be done going forward. "I think calling in our asset might be the wise thing to do. If we want to stop whoever is making a concerted attack on your family, then we might need to bring in some additional assistance."

There was tension in Kardinal's response, specifically when he mentioned this *assistance*.

The fixer bowed his head. There was only one person whom the family was considering bringing in, and Kardinal knew him. He also hoped it was the same one Sirius was thinking about now. He was the man whom Kardinal had feared. He was the only one capable of making Kardinal look foolish besides this new assassin he met back at Brent's.

He was, as Kardinal called him, the man in black. *The Dark Man*.

"You believe it's come to that?" Sirius asked.

Kardinal avoided eye contact with his lord. When things *come to that*, it means desperate times call for desperate measures. Kardinal was straight and he was honest, like always. He prided himself on being this way all the time.

"Yes," Kardinal said. "I do."

The Brotherhood of Cyn, as real as the sacrifices made in the name of their so-called deity, was still an organization bound by its laws. There was respect and there was a strict adherence to those laws. This was an obedience of its leaders, for it was founded on the undeniable belief in its pursuit of higher learning and understanding.

These were the facets that must be upheld at all times.

Yet, of all the rules that the members were expected to follow, none went as deeply as the devotion to secrecy. One was to never speak or allude to the brotherhood or the lord or the legions outside of Vikaya. Even in private conversation, the topic was still forbidden. Therefore, to bring in this outsider was a risk rarely indulged in. However, Kardinal and Sirius both understood the threat was real. To conquer it, they would need to exhaust all their options. This, while not a traditional strategy, was the best one they had. A new threat had emerged. They needed all the help they could get to stop it.

"Bring *him* in then," Sirius said. "Tell him what we need him to do."

Kardinal nodded and replied.

"Understood."

With nothing left to say or do, Kardinal proceeded toward the door. The passage was within his reach. Kardinal stopped moving after he heard Sirius's voice again.

"Wait." Sirius was stern and halting. His voice beckoned as Kardinal stood by and waited.

Right now, Kardinal didn't know when another order was being given. He didn't know if there should be another detail, and Kardinal only chose to stay and to listen.

"If you hear anything else about this killer that has come into our state, I don't want you to immediately execute him, do you understand? If it's possible," demanded Sirius, "I want you to bring him back to us, to me, *alive*. I want him placed at my feet."

Kardinal closed his eyes. Doing this only further illustrated his adherence to his master's orders. At the same time, Kardinal was conflicted. He expected his boss to know more than just this.

"I told you, sir, this man is *not* to be underestimated."

"Of course," Sirius acknowledged. He spoke with the same urgency as Kardinal. "But then again, neither are you, and neither are we."

Kardinal nodded again to comply. If there was ever a time whereby he was earning every last dollar of his job, it was right now.

"Find him," Sirius ordered. "Find him and bring him to me."

These last words could only come from a megalomanic hell-bent on destruction. Even in spite of Kardinal's warning, his orders remained. And now, Kardinal was required to work with a man he once feared. He was also required to locate a destructive force swallowing all the people he was working for. When he did, Kardinal was not to kill him. No, he would capture him. He would place him at Sirius's feet. This could be done, but not until Kardinal himself was connected to the only one stronger than him. Kardinal walked out the door and to his car. With all he had to reach this Dark Man, Kardinal dialed. Waiting until he heard the click, Kardinal chose his next words carefully. He kept his greeting as short and as professional as possible. In fact, Kardinal spoke so softly he could barely feel his lips as they moved. "It's me. Right now...we need your help."

CHAPTER 24
FRIENDS

When Priest informed Quinn of his mission to eradicate the child-murdering cult, the reasoning behind the extermination was eerie, open-ended, and ripe for interpretation.

Quinn had questions.

The first began with: how the hell did Priest even know the Tenets, and why was he so adamant about having them killed?

At the time, Priest said he wanted the Louisiana family removed because they were a sinister and terrible organization. He said they were a plague infecting his great country and they needed to be exterminated. Although this was an explanation Priest had, it was also not one thought of as substantial.

To the Custodian, it housed the same logic as all the others.

For starters, there were many groups worse than the Brotherhood of Cyn.

Quinn counted several that were larger and thus, more powerful than this new deranged cult of pedophiles.

In the pantheon of criminal organizations, there were various levels of superiority and capabilities. Quinn refused to call himself a *hitman*. He hated the term because, while Quinn did kill people, that didn't mean he was one. In Quinn's professional opinion, hitmen worked for criminals. The custodians were *not* a criminal enterprise. They were a government-sanctioned operation that was perfectly legal, well-financed, and organized.

They were just unspoken of and kept a secret.

Therefore, hitmen worked for crime syndicates, some of which Quinn had tangled with before. And if he had to classify the most dangerous groups in the world, it would probably be the Yakuza. Existing for generations, the Japanese Mafia was vast and expansive. They were comprised of hundreds of followers, all of whom were dedicated to the cause and who fought to uphold the clan's values as well as their honor.

Quinn supposed the Brotherhood of Cyn possessed a similar attitude to the Yakuza's. Still, they didn't have any of its resources or numbers. As a result, the brotherhood wasn't even close to any of Quinn's former foes.

Then he remembered the truth. This was an Eradicate.

Priest himself expressed a deep animosity toward outsiders. The way he saw things, America belonged first to those who were born here. Priest tolerated the Italian mob.

In some ways, they built America. And there was nothing Priest loved more than America. However, he loathed any outside organization setting up shop where they didn't belong, the Yakuza included.

When Quinn was sent to exterminate them, the job wasn't easy. Still, it did get done.

The Yakuza were attempting to smuggle weapons

through the Port of Los Angeles and were jeopardizing the business of other local manufacturers. This threatened employment as well as the economy. More than this, it was going to put hardworking Americans out of work.

Priest refused to stand for this. So, he sent Quinn to fix the problem.

The Yakuza weren't known for child sacrifice or the slaughtering of women.

Certainly, they did some nasty stuff. As guilty of human trafficking as any other criminal organization, they didn't kill women and children because they needed to or wanted to.

Sometimes it was business, and so unavoidable.

In the end, the idea of taking kids and killing them was wrong, even to them, but not to this cult. Why?

The Yakuza, in terms of lethality, were the worst for Quinn. After them, was the Sinaloa Cartel, which operated mostly out of Mexico. They were the most terrifying group in North America in Quinn's opinion.

Now, Quinn was familiar with them from the stories told.

While he didn't cross paths with them yet, part of him hoped someday he might get a taste. There was the Camorra. This was an older Mafia that operated out of Naples and the Bratva. Quinn had tangled with the Bratva. There was actually another Custodian whose origins were linked to this pack of brutal Russian killers. And yet, as Quinn reflected on how many bad guys there were in the world, none were similar to this cult. None prided themselves on killing children. To go out of one's way to seek and find little ones to butcher and maim, not even the most godless of men would commit such a heinous act. To comprehend this level of evil, Quinn chose not to try. He refused to grasp the practice, for he had come face-to-face with the worst of the worst. He couldn't understand it and he couldn't explain it. However, it wasn't his job to understand it, as Priest assured him many times before.

His job was to clean.

"You don't need to know how or why. You just need to do what you gotta do and leave the rest to us."

Before this mission, Quinn was content to go along with the process.

Now, he was struggling.

He thought maybe it was because his father was involved. Honestly, Quinn didn't know why he was suddenly asking himself so many questions. All he knew was he looked forward to seeing every member of this sick, demented cult dead soon. He couldn't wait to look into his father's eyes as he said goodbye and pulled the trigger.

Both days would come soon enough.

As Quinn was starting to now see, he was so close he could already feel his dad. In his chair, Quinn looked around and scanned the inside of the trailer. He sipped more of his black coffee and reflected on the mission as it was now. The safehouse, which was surprisingly homey, its cabinets glistened and the area with the sofa bed and the flatscreen was absolutely immaculate.

Quinn yawned. He felt grateful he had a good machine.

He scoured the cabinets for pods. He found a few stashed in a box on the top shelf. He pulled one out and placed it into the machine. While brewing another cup, Quinn did his best to stay relaxed. The trailer felt like a timeshare. It was filled with things left by the other people whom Ally had helped before. Quinn suspected they might've been witnesses or other people of interest. They were likely families in hiding, maybe CIA or maybe NSA agents. Since the entire location was technically government property, it was clean and it was quiet.

Quinn missed home. His house in Wyoming was top-of-the-line. His farm was a sprawling twenty-five-acre sect of prime real estate. It was also the last gift given to Quinn by his mother. She died five years ago. It was Quinn's private lair, out in the middle of nowhere, among nature and the quiet. He never considered himself wealthy, but he did have more money than most. Quinn spent it wisely and saved and invested. On the farm, Quinn had his pickup truck and his defense automobile. His choice for defense was an AMX American Muscle car, his Cirrus Vision jet, his weapons, and most importantly, his purpose.

Financially, Quinn had it good. Then again, he also didn't have the things most people had. He didn't have freedom, safety, family, or love. He didn't have that most of all. Quinn did have moments whereby he retreated to some dark places and had very dark thoughts.

Sometimes he felt low and weak.

Then, Quinn remembered he had what some men never would. He had a mission and he had a purpose. Always, Quinn was trying to be better, to be stronger. Always, he wanted to be the best. And for now, that was enough. Whenever Quinn did feel the bad things coming on, his main strategy was to house these feelings for later. He would throw them back and swallow them down, and he never once ever felt sorry for himself.

In this life, you didn't have time to look back or to break.

You could pause, skip, and you could slide, but if you fell once, then you're gone.

You're dead.

CHAPTER 25
REST

QUINN FILLED HIS COFFEE MUG TO THE TOP AND stood tall in his joggers.

The fabric lagged around his ankles and brushed against Quinn's surprisingly well-kept feet. He wasn't wearing socks. Every window in the safehouse was now open. A gentle breeze flowed into the trailer and Quinn drank more as he looked out into the open field. He stared at the mowed grass and the gravelly walkway where the RAM was parked. The trailer was the only manmade structure throughout the dense bayou. Quinn was secluded among green and he could hear nothing except the chirping of birds and the scuttling of rodents.

Quinn walked down the wooden steps and felt sore as hell.

His body was knotted and decimated from exhaustion.

When Quinn motioned along the grass, he felt the stalks grazing his toes. The mossy soil squished beneath his feet. Quinn sat and spread his legs. Bending down, Quinn pushed his elbows into his inner thighs and performed a nice squat hold to open his groin. He exhaled and arched back his head.

Quinn was under the impression he was alone.

Two seconds later, his phone began to vibrate.

Quinn kept hold of his own cell. The only calls he made during missions were using a laptop, which connected him with Priest. Flakes of puss lingered in the corners of Quinn's dull eyes, so tired and worn.

There was a message. It was from Ally.

Hey.

Quinn replied shortly after. They exchanged numbers after the safehouse.

Hey.

Quinn blushed. He was amused by the greeting that Ally sent to him so early in the morning. Quinn hadn't kept her posted on his progress. Checking in wasn't mandatory.

Yet she did choose to check in, for some reason.

Morning.

Quinn, who was about to put the phone back into his pocket, didn't expect a response, at least not right away. At the door, Quinn hopped along and felt a new vibration. Straight to the point, Quinn didn't want to waste any time. He was always testifying that, should anyone ask, Ally was nothing more than a contact for Quinn. But, if he had to say anything more, he would say Ally was smart. He would say she was sweet and more capable than he thought.

On top of all this, Quinn liked her. In fact, he liked her a lot.

All good?

Quinn texted using his thumbs. Quinn had misspelled

most of the words he was writing. He let autocorrect do its thing, and when he was done, he sent one important message.

All good. Quinn waited. Much to his pleasure, Ally responded.

Good to hear.

Quinn's grin stretched across his attentive face. The Custodian found himself stirred by the interaction. Quinn wasn't familiar with the feeling of having butterflies in the stomach. If he had it, it wasn't because he was smitten. No, it was because there was something else going on that demanded Quinn's attention.

Something like this didn't exactly qualify.

What did was how enthusiastic and joyous Quinn could be while receiving these messages. He wanted more. He wanted as much as he could get.

Good.

Thinking that was the end of Ally's texts, it wasn't.

Quinn read the next.

See you soon.

Quinn blushed like a schoolboy. He was embarrassed. He never felt this way, but he liked it.

CHAPTER 26
ORIGINS

IN HIS YOUTH, SIRIUS TENET WAS MORE THAN JUST A citizen of the great state of Louisiana. He thought of himself as a guiding and noble force. He was a leader and he was a teacher. He was a voice that needed to be heard and it was a voice heard by many. It was because Sirius was a man who never stopped talking.

In public, Sirius was staunch and charismatic. It was known to most that Sirius Tenet began his ascent toward greater glory as a volunteer sheriff's deputy. It commenced when Sirius was nineteen and ended when he was elected governor. Now Sirius's family was nothing to speak of. All Sirius ever said about his mom and dad was they were poor—impoverished. At least, this was the story he told to others. And, when asked about his childhood, Sirius said he was born and raised in Vermilion. He said he lived in a two-bedroom house where he and his sister shared a room. However, when Sirius was nine, his sister drowned in a river behind the family's home. They were both swimming there and Sirius saw her struggling in the dark water. She kicked and screamed and begged to be saved. And, while Sirius said he tried to save her, her head went under too fast and it never came up again.

This was another story told.

Afterward, Sirius's father and mother stopped talking to Sirius. He didn't like to discuss his sister's death and he didn't like to talk about his parents either. They died too. Oddly, they died together in bed. Sirius said they committed suicide. This was another story, however. Continuing the fable, Sirius said he was so young he barely remembered what happened. He also said tragedies like that are impossible to forget.

Of course, Sirius fucking remembered everything.

Coasting through life as a teenager, Sirius asked the local sheriff how he could be of better service to his community. The sheriff touched Sirius on the back and told him he could come by every now and again to help. He said he would always find something for Sirius to do. Sirius was under the impression this included helping the other deputies with their jobs. He wanted to be with them on the front lines, protecting and serving just like the old motto said.

But this isn't at all what happened.

Most of the time, Sirius was tossed aside. He was sent to do boring tasks, like take out the trash or just run and get shit for the cops on patrol. He wasn't law enforcement any more than an FBI secretary was a fucking agent.

He was just a fall guy, and once again, Sirius Tenet was back to where he started.

He had nothing, and he was nothing.

He wasn't the smartest or the strongest. He wasn't the wisest or the cleverest. In fact, he wasn't anything, really. He wasn't tall or handsome, skilled or unskilled. He spent his entire life in this territory, at the bottom, where no one could see, or none could notice him. Always broken and always continuing to break, what Sirius Tenet desired was a place in this world. And the place he wanted to be was where the sheriff, the governor, and the state senator all sat.

He wanted to be higher. He wanted to be above the rest.

Sirius never knew what it felt like to be powerful or feared. He would watch other powerful and intimidating men, and all he would ask himself was why.

Why could he not be one of them? What did they have that he didn't?

Asking himself these questions, Sirius began to work and work and *work*.

He gave and he gave. But even then, nothing was ever given in return. He was still the smallest and weakest one in the room and he refused to take it.

The time for being ignored was now over.

It was time for Sirius Tenet to become more. Greatness was now upon him.

Sirius learned a lot from his days as a sheriff's volunteer. He learned how to pay attention, how to respond, and how a police department functioned. He did this while also looking for new ways to broaden his horizons and open his mind. Most people would do this by taking classes or getting an education so they could become real cops.

Not Sirius. This was not part of his plan at all.

He was too poor and too busy, and he was never good at school.

However, his desires and his drives remained the same.

He wanted more. He wanted to be better. And, as Sirius strived for something greater, he looked for better options. Such an ambition had caused him to re-evaluate his entire life.

Where did it go wrong and how could it improve?

What did he, Sirius Tenet, really want?

What Sirius wanted, he would never have. People like him weren't entitled to big things. From what Sirius learned, they weren't able to pursue the same opportunities either. And so, they couldn't have what they wanted, not in the traditional sense.

Sirius just knew he didn't want to be himself anymore.

He wanted a way out.

He was twenty-two when he first discovered the work of prophet Jacques Synthianas. When he did, Sirius couldn't stop reading about his tales about a world beyond this one. He spoke of a red world and a place teeming with life. He spoke of hidden powers, of legacies, of signs, and the way to obtain a power unlike any that walked this earth.

This was *the new way*. And, from then on, it became Sirius's. It was his for all time.

The rituals to reach this world were found in the pages of Jacques Synthianas's many books. Each book was hidden in secret sections of his local library. Sirius checked them all out but never returned them. His town was born on indifference. This was a legacy Sirius understood and one he could also embrace. He wanted to know more about this new god. Sirius desired to learn his ways. He wondered if even the most hopeless of people could be transformed into something better. This was the promise of their god, Cyncero. It was a path that spoke to Sirius in ways few things did.

After reading the books, Sirius couldn't get the thoughts out of his head.

Sirius refused to keep them buried there, and there

was only one way for him to get rid of them. He could either deny them or he could accept them. He could either run from them or he could face them.

And Sirius was done running.

Running was for the weak and he wasn't weak, not anymore.

He would be better. He would be stronger.

He would be a king.

After Sirius underwent his studies and training, soon he became the one giving orders. He did this while building a new and vast organization. Doing this carefully, Sirius was able to conceal himself and his interests. Sirius's pursuit of otherworldly powers grew as a result of what was a tormented and disturbing childhood. Sirius Tenet always felt weak and small most of his life, but now he was told he could have power and authority. Therefore, Sirius craved them both the way a rat craves when it nibbles for a piece of cheese. It wasn't until Sirius began to delve into the power of human sacrifice that he began to obtain what he wanted above all other things.

Nonetheless, like all men who desired power, Sirius also wanted control and freedom.

Being a natural leader, he knew how to rally others and so, Sirius's journey forced him to cross paths with other hopeless people. Like Sirius, they too wanted more. This, in turn, brought Sirius close into the lives of other dreamers, namely women and those who required more than just charity and guidance.

As soon as Sirius had this, more attention was granted in return. The recognition he always desired eventually became his for the taking. It was at this point that Sirius stopped asking for permission. It was here where Sirius finally ignored what other people had to say about rules and standards. Once Sirius became more than just an ordinary citizen, fewer people held him accountable. There were few who challenged Sirius's new status or his position. It was then that Sirius became free, free to do as he pleased and take whatever he wanted.

And so Sirius's power began to grow.

He evolved into a new and seemingly improved person. Rising higher, Sirius eventually met another man similar to himself. This man was not born in Louisiana, nor was he someone who had the same intentions. Still, Sirius remembered this new man quite well.

He could recall him because this man *was* different. He was very different, in fact.

To begin with, this man wasn't rich.

In fact, this man stated this proudly when money was first mentioned.

Despite not being among the higher echelon, this new man fearlessly stood among Louisiana's finest citizens. Sometimes, this man was confrontational, defensive, and even cruel if necessary. Among all these classifications, this man's vocabulary included words like *princess*, *daddy's boy*, and *trust fund fuckers*.

Sirius never heard talk about Louisiana's elite in this way, but this man did. Sirius felt it was very brave or very stupid to talk like this.

But this man didn't care.

He had a name, but at the time, Sirius found it odd. And as Sirius began to draw closer, he found the identification to be just as intriguing as the man himself.

His name was Priest.

Now, this man didn't give his full name, but that was not a problem for someone like Sirius. He didn't need to know people's full names in order to see who they were and what they wanted. However, everything about this Priest seemed suspicious. He was confronting Sirius for information. And, being the governor, he had everything Priest desired. Sirius knew about the missing children and their families. And should this Priest guy want kids, for whatever reason, Sirius could provide them to him.

And yet, Priest didn't request children for reasons that Sirius was familiar with.

"What exactly do you want from me?" Eventually, Sirius had to ask Priest this one question. When it was provided, Priest smiled.

"From you? Nothing. What I want is for me."

With this as Priest's answer, it didn't help Sirius to understand anything more. In the end, there were *very* few people in the state who knew what Sirius was truly up to. None knew what he did in his spare time and Sirius never revealed the truth to anyone. The only people who were aware of the cult's existence were its members. Consequently, none of them would speak about it because to do that would be to expose themselves as well.

Although Sirius did not utter a word about the cult to a man like Priest, Sirius suspected he knew the truth. How he did was not known. It seemed as if Priest's intentions were not to expose the brotherhood, it was only to take a part of it for himself. Sirius knew this practice better than anyone else. It was the reason why he started the cult in the first place.

Priest did frequently mention kids. It wasn't for sacrifice or for sex, but then Sirius had to ask...what else could it be for other than that?

Sirius didn't know, and he didn't care to know either. He didn't trust Priest. In fact, Sirius didn't even like him. Yet, here he was, and he was not going anywhere.

Both Sirius and Priest met at a governor's ball. Why Priest had chosen to come to his event was unclear at the time. Still, Priest was fearless. He moved around the room with his chest out and a constant grin on his mad-dog face. Sirius could only speculate about Priest's access to power.

To Sirius, it had to be a power drawn from a different source.

During these interactions, Priest alluded to Sirius that he worked in DC. Priest suggested he was some kind of manager or something along those lines. The reason he crossed paths with Sirius Tenet was centered on only one topic in general:

"I want to build something," Priest said, "and I'm looking for information surrounding the ones who have gone missing in your state. I need as much information as you can give. I want it all from you." As Priest inquired about the growing number of missing children in Louisiana, Sirius believed their interaction was not an interrogation either.

It was about curiosity, research, examination.

But why? Why kids?

Sirius made this inquiry only to himself. If Priest didn't like children the way Sirius Tenet and his friends did, then why was he asking about kids so often?

"We're working to get that number down as much as we can," Sirius said to Priest at the time.

Now his response was false, it was actually a damn outright and shameless lie. Of all the people who knew where the missing children were, Sirius Tenet was the most aware. Still, Priest didn't dive into this all too much. Instead, Priest segued into a new topic. He wanted to know where the missing kids had come from. He wanted to know their backgrounds as well as their stories. Generally, most were from poverty, as Sirius had explained. Before this, Sirius thought Priest's question to be endearing. He knew right away Priest wasn't asking because he actually cared for those who had disappeared.

"Any information you have would be most beneficial," Priest said.

It was the last conversation Sirius could recall having with this Priest character, whoever he was. After that, Sirius never saw or heard from him ever again. And, as far as the concern for the disappearance of children, it was something that greatly stood out in Sirius's memory. *The Suit*, which was how Sirius referred to Priest, worked in a different industry. He was not interested in the cult's activities as much as he was interested in what fueled their wants and desires. But it was Priest's confidence that grabbed Sirius's attention most of all. It was also how, regardless of any room he was in, nothing made Priest change his manner or his tone. It was in this way Sirius Tenet found Priest to be a most compelling individual.

Above all else, Sirius asked himself, how was he not in the least bit intimidated by anyone?

Was he a pedophile? And was he the one hunting his family now?

Yet, Sirius Tenet knew the behaviors and signs of certain people. Priest did not fit the profile of his cult brothers. Well, at least Priest didn't so far as Sirius could tell. With more questions raised, Sirius soon realized he might never discover who this Priest really was.

Sirius, however, imagined it was why he would never see Priest again.

Sirius also suspected Priest might be someone even more powerful than him, than his whole family.

To Sirius, this Priest actually might be...a fucking god.

CHAPTER 27
HEAD IN THE GAME

BACK IN HIS TRAILER, QUINN STARED AT A MAP HE had laid out on the table. So far, he had eradicated four members of the Tenet clan. Now a wanted murderer, the police were looking for the one responsible. Thankfully, Ally was keeping it all under control, or so she told Quinn. They texted twice during his time here, in Louisiana. However, this was *not* why Quinn had crafted this collection. No, there was something else he was searching for now. It was the whole reason for being where he was today.

"Where the hell are you, Dad?" As Quinn learned already, Sirius Tenet was well connected. From what he gathered, his dad *might* be too. Since Sirius was a former volunteer deputy, the lieutenants, and the commissioner were people whom Mr. Tenet knew. Although this was a long time ago. Still, it was possible for Quinn's dad to be involved somehow. Soon, all of the Tenet's closest allies would be together at the annual police charity auction.

This was an event the Tenets hosted each year.

Quinn's knife pierced a picture of his father. It was

the same one given to Quinn by Priest. How exactly Quinn's old man was involved with this Tenet clan, the Custodian had yet to figure out. However, Quinn's primary motive for accepting this job was to find the one who made him.

He would find him, and he would kill him. Mapping out each target, Quinn continued to search for his dad's link. Quinn was accessing other skills besides those that involved him using a gun or knowing how to fight. Quinn was good with clues. He was even better at keeping his eyes open. Quinn hoped to find something useful about his shrewd enemy. Yet, in regard to his final assassinations, Quinn's weapon of choice was his Desert Tech Stealth rifle.

His plan was to post up across the street. He had pictures of the location and he would be there. Then, as Alistair was about to leave, Quinn would pop him and then he would wait for Sirius to follow. Although Sirius was traveling in a separate car, Quinn would vacate the building and run down the adjacent alley. After removing the pawns and the knights guarding the entrance, he would switch to his AR-15 and wait for the car to drive down the bordering street.

In essence, Quinn was going to flush the Tenets out of the hotel and cap them all upon escape.

On paper, it all looked easy. In principle, however, it was not quite so.

On the road, Quinn would take out the driver. After this, the bodyguards were certain to move in and attack whoever was in their way. It was here Quinn would show Sirius a picture of his dad and demand Sirius surrender Broder Quinn's location. If he didn't, then Quinn would kill him. And, when all of this was done, Quinn would finish Sirius the same as his sons regardless of his choice to reveal it or not. This would conclude the eradication of the cult known as the Brotherhood of Cyn.

Like Quinn had established, this entire endeavor should be easy.

As for an exit strategy? Quinn's plan was to use the alternate alley separate from the hotel itself. There, he would pack all his guns into a briefcase, strip off his gear, and leave it all behind. Quinn would then return to his truck and head back to the safe house. Once he had his dad's location, Quinn could track him and then finish him, thereby ending their rivalry for good.

Of course, this was only a plan as it existed in Quinn's head.

While it was suitable, there was little time to comprise the remaining details. It was riddled with variables and Quinn needed to spend more time scavenging for clues. He also wanted to use more of Priest's intel.

Time was a luxury Quinn did not have. What he needed was to be ready.

Quinn checked his watch. It was almost eight o'clock. In just twenty-four hours, he would commence the most difficult part of the Eradicate mission. He was coming to the end of his journey, and Quinn thought of nothing except the hotel. He had memorized the locations. He was familiar with all points of entry and re-entry.

Quinn also knew where all the security would be situated.

Quinn wouldn't be a Custodian if he didn't consider all alternative measures. And he always did. Always, Quinn planned for the worst. He felt thirsty. He walked up to the sink to fill a glass of water. The safe house was suitable by most living standards. Quinn was now only beginning to adapt to it. Filling his glass, Quinn's mind circled around a single idea: I am about to kill an entire family and I don't care.

Keeping his glass down by his chest, Quinn heard the voice of the man who introduced him to the morality of murder.

And it was not Quinn's father.

Make peace with death and you will never be afraid.

Unlike other advice given during Quinn's formative years, most of it had come from his dad. This one he learned while in Joint Task Force 2.

Before being a part of Canada's elite special forces division, Quinn grew up in rural Saskatchewan and completed his training in Nova Scotia. There, his instructor was a man named Henry Moahan. He was a wise man who contrasted his father's unrelenting personality. No, Moahan was kind and he was direct. He was also quite potent.

Most think the best military instructors are fearsome and berate their trainees constantly. Although this did happen to Quinn on a few occasions, what he remembered most was Moahan's voice and his honesty. During weapons training, Moahan recited to Quinn an unforgettable ballad about life and death.

"*No one is above dying,*" he said, "*because death always wins. Therefore, all you have to be certain about is... you can live with that. You have to understand it and ensure that you've done all you could to survive. If you've done all that, then death will never be a bad thing.*"

"*And how do you do that?*" Quinn asked his commanding officer after he'd crawled through muck, ran twenty miles, and spent hours shooting a single target. Moahan closed their conversation with one last valuable takeaway. Quinn could hear him even now just as he did that day.

Live. Just live.

Although it was a simple answer, it was not one Quinn had expected. It was, however, precisely what he needed to hear. Since that day, Quinn reflected on death before concluding any mission. If this was to be his last day alive, then Quinn was going to clear his mind and remember how he was prepared to fight and to win.

He would not surrender. He was ready for anything.

Grown to always expect the unexpected, Quinn's head was forever in the game.

The more Quinn remembered how the game was played, the more he could foresee the outcome. And he was a winner, so he was going to win.

CHAPTER 28
EASY EYES

QUINN WOKE EARLY THE NEXT DAY, CLEANED HIS guns, and performed a quick ammunitions check on each one. Still healing from the fight before, he was not in as much pain as he once was.

The less he thought about it, the better.

With the 34 in hand, Quinn cleaned the Glock's barrel with a small brush and then heard a knock at the door. Clicking the chamber, Quinn sidestepped toward the sound. No one knew of the location except for one person.

It could be Ally, but then it could also be someone else.

Quinn peeped through the curtains. His weapons were set. As soon as he caught a glimpse of the outside, a familiar voice eased all Quinn's tension booming from inside.

"Relax. It's just me."

After seeing who it was, Quinn unhinged the locks. Although a trap was still quite possible, Quinn's gun stayed in his hand. Quinn waited until he could see Ally in her entirety, but her hands were up. When Quinn scanned Ally from top to bottom, he also checked the clearing that engulfed his trailer. Around the RAM, past some of the trees, Quinn saw nothing he deemed a cause for concern.

"Sorry to drop in on you like this," said Ally. She spoke like a friend. She grinned at Quinn as he guarded the door. No one knew where he was, no one except for her.

The heat dried Quinn's nostrils. There was no need to sniffle, except Quinn sniffled all the time. He liked that he didn't have to do this now, especially considering how he was nervous. He was feeling flushed and almost jittery.

Quinn's lips fastened and he squinted.

He displayed a firmness that assured Ally that, while she was safe, it didn't change how he was still prepared. Quinn holstered his pistol and stepped aside to let her in.

"Can never be too careful, right?" asked Ally.

"Part of the job," Quinn said. He placed his Glock down on the table.

Now back in the living room, Quinn stood by the couch and the flatscreen. He looked back at Ally coolly.

"How you stay alive, I know."

Gulping down more of his coffee, Quinn grunted.

"Yes, it is."

Quinn stood with his arms folded and was shirtless as he sat stared. "Why are you here?" he asked Ally.

"Actually," Ally said, looking around the room, like she was inspecting the furniture.

Quinn thought maybe she wanted to see if he changed anything. The trailer was the same as it was when the Custodian first moved in. The only difference was it now contained Quinn's clothes and his possessions.

"I came to check in on you," said Ally. "You know, see how things are."

"Why?" Quinn asked.

Checking on Quinn was not part of Ally's job, not even slightly.

"Well, it's just the news," said Ally. "There's so many dead now, and I know you said you were going to take out your targets quickly and without remorse, so...it has been effing quick, even for you."

"No such thing as too quick," added Quinn. As far as Quinn was concerned, he was right on schedule.

"Of course."

"Intel is solid," Quinn said, "and recon is done. Shouldn't be much longer now."

He chose not to provide any other details besides this. It was not because Quinn didn't trust Ally. No, it was because, at this point in the game, Quinn really didn't trust anyone. He wasn't going to break this rule now, even if he liked and respected the person.

"Good," said Ally, still having a look around. "And is there anything else you think you might need?"

"None. Think I'm good for right now." Quinn dismissed the request as soon as it was given. However, he was still curious about why Ally was here now. Recalling how her eyes were all a twitter, she was always smiling whenever she was with Quinn. And so, it was obvious why.

Quinn knew never to mix business with pleasure.

This was another piece of advice given by Priest.

"Good," said Ally. She eyed Quinn with a sparkling infatuation. It was undeniable how she felt about the Custodian. "Just want to be sure, that's all. I gotta make sure state PD doesn't get wind of anything. I know a few people inside, friends from a while back. So far, so good."

"Then keep it that way," replied Quinn. Ally pivoted and made her way back to the door.

"That I can and that I will." About to step through, Ally turned before he left. "Although word to the wise there, Quinn," she said. "Sirius Tenet does have a chief of security."

Head tilted, Quinn gawked. While he was aware of who this person was, he didn't expect Ally to be too.

"He's been known to get...*dirty*."

Ally was throwing Quinn a bit of a bone here. In some ways, it was a favor granted in order to ensure the Custodian's safety and success. It added extra awareness to an already escalating situation. Although Quinn was familiar. Still, he was appreciative and thankful for all of the above.

Quinn bowed his head. He smirked at Ally to show gratitude.

"Keep that in mind," Quinn said.

"All right then," she said. Her hand was on the door. She hadn't left yet. "You have a good night then."

"Yeah," Quinn said. His head was down. He was too busy thinking about Ally in more ways than he cared to admit.

This was only a business relationship. It was a reminder only starting to become more consistent. Assuring himself repeatedly of this new standard of professionalism, it was nothing more, he thought.

Absolutely nothing more.

"Good night."

Ally left Quinn's trailer but after, he lay in bed, wide awake. The only thought that gave Quinn comfort was finding his dad and finishing the job. Although money was still a motivator, Quinn thought about the life whereby he had someone to go home to.

He wanted a life without pain.

Quinn knew he would see Ally again once the mission was over. When he did, Quinn would have more to say. He would do more too. Quinn's head was only in one place now.

———

With all his gear and weapons loaded into his RAM, Quinn emerged from his trailer late the next day. Outfitted in black tactical camouflage, and his EOTech, every compartment Quinn had on his person was filled with a weapon or device.

Quinn held his AR-15 in one hand, and in the other was his bagged recon sniper rifle.

Quinn's Glocks were secured in the holsters around his waist. His heart beat hard and fast and Quinn's OTF was sharpened and ready to go too. The laces on his Viper shoes were tied so tight he could feel them grinding against his bones.

The sun was just starting to set. The sky had turned into a teal shade of gray. Quinn's tonfa was crisscrossed behind his back, as accessible as everything else.

With all the tools Quinn needed present and accounted for, he looked at his Luminox diver watch. Almost six, Quinn's next stop was the Tenet's famous fundraiser. It was set to start in just under an hour.

Although Quinn was never one for spectacle, he was ready to rock and roll.

Locked and loaded, now was the time to bring the noise.

The party was about to begin.

CHAPTER 29
NOT SAFE

THE FUNDRAISER WAS TO BE HELD AT THE BEST Western Plus in Baton Rouge. And, from what Quinn had heard, it was a mediocre accommodation spot at best. It didn't have a four-star rating on Yelp or Expedia or anything like that. Instead, it was a standard, paint-by-numbers hospitality lame-ass shithole of a hotel that was both average and unassuming.

A congregation of uniformed cops stood in the lobby.

Next to this lobby was the hotel's breakfast room, which was roped off because it was where the majority of guests were now grouped. The room was monochromatic, painted with a healthy mix of white and brown shades. Each officer stood among their cohorts, but most were either cops, state representatives, council people, or small business owners. Yet, all of them were called here by the Tenet family to contribute to the benefit's auction. With all the guests assembled, Sirius Tenet was prepared for what he hoped to be a grand opening. He was dressed in his finest tuxedo while Kardinal stood by in his classic red checkered suit.

Both watched the party from the elevators.

"Is the building secure?" Sirius's first question was the most important.

He was speaking about all the brotherhood's knights and pawns now there as security. Standing with his hands folded in front of him, Kardinal gawked at his master and then out into the crowd.

"As of now...we are good, sir, yes." Kardinal guarded the entrance.

A conference room, which was created specifically for this event, was constructed with a smooth dome where gaga photographers took snapshots of the many guests. One photographer was female. She asked everyone if she could take their pictures before heading in through the grand archway. Beyond the doors were round tables, a stage, and a lectern. Above this hung a banner with a greeting written in cursive letters.

Tenet Annual Statewide Fundraiser And Auction.

The female guests drank their mint juleps and the tangy smells of the room aligned well with the decor. There was a hint of dandelion and traces of pinewood and red wine wafting through the heavy air.

"How are we doing on the outside?" Kardinal asked, his finger pressed to his earpiece. He was communicating with the security guarding the hotel's many entries.

"B Team, come in, please," Kardinal continued to speak.

Four guards were by the door near the kitchen. Eyes up, all of them kept their hands folded near their waists and responded to Kardinal's call.

"All clear." Kardinal waited in the kitchen with the bustling waiter staff. The first words spoken by Sirius were centered on one fact only. "Any sign of *him*?"

Him being the Tenet family's *ace in the hole*. They

had called their *consultant*, the one the family called only for emergencies. Kardinal knew him only as *The Dark Man*. Yet, when asked about this Dark Man, Kardinal looked immediately at his boss's hands.

"He'll be arriving soon, sir," Kardinal said. "I'm sure of it."

Kardinal's brows inverted as he gazed. Being the stern and cold bodyguard, his purpose was clear. Kardinal straightened himself out by yanking on his sleeves. Sirius then flattened his jacket against his chest. He moved through the hotel and went about his business. Always with him, Kardinal was his boss's shadow. Tonight, he was his chief guardian in the presence of a possible assassination. He would not leave Sirius's side, not for a second.

He was to be with him, *always*.

"When he arrives," Sirius said, "he'll join the rest of our forces, but should anything happen, you will be the one who answers him, do you understand?"

"Yes," Kardinal said. "I do."

The cacophony of the party drowned out most of Kardinal's words. It made the exchange between Kardinal and Sirius almost inaudible to both parties.

"He has a plan," continued Sirius. "And we are going to follow it to the letter."

"So...you have spoken to him?" Kardinal asked.

Sirius waved at one of the tables. Head back, the boss looked at Kardinal while also being alert.

"Briefly," Kardinal said. "Just keep your eyes open."

Kardinal followed Sirius to a table. Given the urgency of the situation, Kardinal didn't wish to leave his master alone, especially not here, in such a crowded setting.

"Whoever this fool is," Sirius said, "he would have to be more than a fool to try and come after us here. Now go. I must tend to our guests."

Sirius waved his hand again, stepped away from Kardinal, and returned to his session of schmoozing and deceit. Alistair did the same, and both men became preoccupied with their own branches of socializing and flattery.

'Whoever this fool is, he would have to be more than a fool to try and do it here.'

The man in question was no fool. This was something that had once crossed Kardinal's mind. Killing Sirius so publicly, while it was not an indication of someone who was apt and aware, whoever this guy was, he was no idiot. He was not even afraid. He refused to dismiss any outcome.

Kardinal knew the killer would be here soon and they were not safe. Tonight, no one was.

CHAPTER 30
INFILTRATE

Quinn parked his truck a block away from the hotel entrance and sat in the RAM for five minutes without blinking.

This car was given to Quinn upon arrival.

Actually, Quinn was pleased with how similar it was to his own truck back in Wyoming. Concealed in a narrow parking spot between two buildings, Quinn blended in nicely with his surroundings. Although not far from the hotel, Quinn was difficult to see in this crowded strip mall. It was difficult for someone like Quinn to be inconspicuous when he was everything but. He kept his eyes out for security cameras. He parked the truck near a hardware store. Quinn examined two guards poised outside the hotel. Unbeknownst to these nameless men in suits, all of them would soon be killed in the next few minutes.

Quinn popped the trunk and retrieved the Desert Stealth.

This weapon was equipped with a bipod stand and a solid scope. The rifle shot .338 Lupuad Magnum rounds, each one long and thick. The rifle's scope could magnify a target from hundreds of yards away and the quad-rail handguard massaged Quinn's hands. It felt extra snug against his leather gloves. Quinn quaked with delight. This gun was perfect.

All the men stood exactly where he wanted them. And, once Quinn had them, he didn't hesitate to make his next move. Quinn tickled the trigger and eased his finger close. Then, in a bold act of precision, he popped the first guard between the eyes.

The shot was terribly precise.

A bang and then a splatter and then an exploded skull all followed. The first man fell while the second one was silenced from the shock. As soon as Quinn fired one round, he fired another. Spotting the second, with an even quicker reaction, Quinn fired another two into his chest.

Bang. Boom. Bang.

With two dead, Quinn counted down the seconds. The clock was officially ticking.

Switching to his AR-15, Quinn whipped the strap over his shoulder and marched with big footsteps. Quinn left the Desert Stealth in his vehicle. His next move was to enter the building, cap the security, hide, and wait.

Nothing is ever as easy as it seems, especially a kill mission such as this.

Quinn had completed over twenty missions in the past. Even with all their planning and testing, nothing ever goes completely to plan. It's the job of any operative to adapt and alter when necessary.

Soldiers—good ones—are prepared for this. Spies are trained for it.

Assassins are familiar, but Custodians...Custodians are *bred* for it.

Quinn assessed all the contingencies. He weighed all the outcomes and constantly reviewed his plan. Still,

Quinn felt new thoughts entering his mind that didn't belong there. He couldn't explain it, but a new feeling had emerged after his first kill. It plucked at the back of Quinn's eyes and he found himself feeling dizzy, almost nauseous. Whenever a job was easy or going too well, Quinn reminded himself how it could all change in a second.

Despite his successful kills, something was amiss. Quinn sniffled and smelled something bad. It stunk, and then he caught a second whiff. To Quinn, these were just the smells of battle and slaughter. He shook them all aside and rid himself of every last one of them.

As he was prepared to move, the Custodian felt the serrated grip of his rifle. He was sure to watch his six. In fact, Quinn always watched his six. He did this because it was sure to prevent any and all surprises.

Although he was alone, approaching this location was quite the risk.

Still, Quinn worked out all the angles. He was always anticipating as he lent his ear.

He leaned into the door. His hearing was astounding. Many people are gifted with eyesight, an acute sense of smell, or an incredible gift of hearing. In Quinn's case, he was fortunate enough to be gifted with all three.

Quinn neared the door and there he detected several other sounds.

Why Quinn insisted on doing this was a risk in itself.

The first rule was always to keep one's face away from any door. An operative did this in case of explosions or the fact that someone might shoot from the other side. However, Quinn did have his rifle set. The barrel dipped forward. It was still straight, and all Quinn had right now was his gun and his ears.

Strolling in, Quinn continued before firing again. He

suspected a threat behind each corner. In the end, Quinn moved with the shadows. He was there one second and then gone the next.

Quinn was everywhere and he was nowhere.

He was alive and he was dead.

CHAPTER 31
BAITED

THE EVENING UNFOLDED AND SIRIUS AND ALISTAIR were about to take the stage when Kardinal gave them both the thumbs up and signaled to his lord that everything was set and safe. So far, it was. Their expected guest was about to arrive any minute.

Time to execute.

Sirius stood five feet from the crowd and kept his hands crossed below his waist. He monitored his guests and the governor smiled and gave a humble wave to everyone who passed by. While moving to one of the tables, Sirius leaned into his son. Alistair was currently in a conversation with Vermilion's chief of police.

"Let's move our guests, shall we? Come. Let's go."

Next to his father, Alistair had expected the request to come. The reasoning behind it, however, was not theirs. In essence, it wasn't *their* idea. All of it had come at the behest of the man whom they brought in to protect them. Sirius clinked his fork against the glass. It created a chime that grabbed everyone's attention. Sirius stood by the doorway. He looked around and spoke loudly so everyone would hear.

"Hello, everyone. For now, before we start our dinner, I would also like to invite all of you to join us on the patio for a special announcement."

Alistair was there next to his father. He grinned as he looked at the guests. They were the same people whom his father knew from years in this position. The commotion settled and a few moans lingered from the crowd. There were some who were unwilling to vacate the space and go to an outdoor setting.

But this didn't matter. As soon as Sirius was done requesting everyone to move, Alistair located Kardinal.

"Do it."

Hearing his boss loud and clear, Kardinal stepped out of the main room and everyone else proceeded to outside.

"Tell him we're moving the guests like he said we should," Alistair said to Kardinal.

Kardinal was so close to Alistair that their shoulders almost touched.

"Will do," Kardinal said. "Will do."

CHAPTER 32
SILLY RABBIT

QUINN KEPT HIS BACK FLAT AGAINST THE WALL WHEN in the kitchen, which was connected to the hall in the hotel lobby. There, Quinn spotted a pawn armed with an assault rifle. He stood out like a rabbit in a cage. Quinn's played the game as he planned it.

Take out Alistair and force Sirius to run. Then, handle the rest of the security.

Done.

From where Quinn was now, he stood in a narrow hallway outside the hotel's conference center. Quinn counted eight guards. Four were by the door, and another four were spread throughout the kitchen. Quinn looked at the sidearms holstered under their jackets. He assessed their body language. They were so prim and stoic that they might pass for police. Also inferring from their smells, this was Quinn's method for judging the threat level.

Right now, it was minimal. This was the last step before he started.

With men left on his list, some were here—right here!

All Quinn had to do was walk right through this

fucking door. He raised his gun and looked through the scope. The magnification expanded every one of his targets. The first was near the doorway. Head down, Quinn didn't know what was about to happen. As he stepped out of his hiding place, he saw the guard rolling in.

The guard was oblivious to what awaited him.

While the gunshot was quiet, it was not completely silent. It produced a quick, flat-sounding pew and let out a snapping flash as Quinn squeezed the grip. Hitting one guard through the left temple, the shot was so clean it left barely any blood.

Quinn aimed for the second.

Bang!

"Gah!" Down. Owned. Killed.

The second guard gagged after Quinn pierced his forehead. From there, the Custodian only had so much time before the situation escalated into a full-on firefight, end-all-things-good orgy or pure mayhem. Being the only one armed with a multi-round rifle, Quinn's weapon of choice was modified and efficient. And so, Quinn had a clear advantage. With all the other guards obtaining their weapons, Quinn's AR-15 was set and locked.

Quinn pinpointed the others and had each one.

Shooting the third and then the fourth, Quinn capped another one in the gut.

Like hitting a bag of sand, the impact was a flat-sounding slap. The exit wound resembled a grape being squished into the back of a mouth. Only relatively messy, two splatters appeared on the rear wall. It was burst reminiscent to a diarrhetic explosion.

The fourth guard fell and Quinn quickened.

The next assembly of men was five feet away. They watched the exit on the other side of the hotel. On the way down, the slaughtered pawn mumbled something Quinn couldn't hear.

To further silence his attacker—or maybe it was just Quinn indulging in the moment of extreme behavior—he kneed the man in the face and knocked him into the wall.

Down.

With bodies everywhere, Quinn looked to his left and spotted more security on approach. Wielding Berettas, most were nine-millimeter. This was child's play when compared to what Quinn was carrying. Once Quinn was close enough, he smoked all four in a row. Starting from the left, Quinn worked his way across and completed his signature.

Two in the chest, one in the head.

Always.

Bringing this massacre to a close, and with a still functioning scope, Quinn had fired twelve rounds so far. He aimed between his target's foreheads, smoked the men in their skulls, and turned them all into grapefruit.

His AR was so fucking accurate!

Even looking in the other direction, Quinn was confident he could get close. Not quite the same as shooting fish in a barrel, in the end, it was just as simple. When Quinn hit the first, more heads from more knights had exploded. Looking at the juicy gathering of broken skulls and brains, it looked so gooey. The smell was a blend of blood and smoke. So far not a single shot hit Quinn. He wanted to keep it that way. With two security units down, Quinn had come to a door at the end of the hall. Given the rapidity of his AR and the low sound it produced, it was possible no one inside heard a goddamn thing.

Easing his head past the door, Quinn heard more sounds on the other side.

The men were slain in the kitchen, so the waiters and the line cooks were likely frightened and on the run.

Still, the clock was ticking. It was ticking fast.

The police were likely on their way but Quinn had to go forward and finish the job. With time moving against him, Quinn only needed a small window. Through the crack in the door, he gawked and found exactly who he was looking for. At twelve o'clock stood the two leaders of the cult. Waiting there idly, Sirius and Alistair had no idea they were seconds away from being shot dead.

They were also unaware that the cult members acting as security were all toast now.

Looking dead ahead, Sirius and Alistair were among a sea of bodies. Quinn was all bloody from the shootout. He stopped to hold on and think, but was still prepared to move. He wrapped his hand tightly around the stock of his AR. Quinn never tired of holding such a magnificent piece of hardware.

Before going in, Quinn waited. He pushed the barrel in through the door and took a quick peek. What he saw were five men in suits. Amid all the mumbling, Quinn detected the voice of someone who was giving a speech.

He hadn't completely entered this hall as of yet.

No, Quinn was only stepping into another room within the hotel. When he was done doing this, then he would gradually proceed to his next location. Using his shoulder, Quinn bumped the door. With a slight nudge, the door opened, and with another thrust, Quinn moved into this other room.

Scoping the scene, Quinn counted five more.

He was *sure* there were five.

While inside the *new* room, Quinn stood not with five men or with ten. He was not even in the company of fifteen. No, from what he could see outside, there were twenty.

At least.

"Fuck."

Cornered, trapped...*tricked*. Quinn gawked. The men were armed with automatic weapons. Quinn observed the impressive arsenal and accepted he was mistaken in terms of numbers. Among them, there was only one who garnered Quinn's attention.

Kardinal was the only one Quinn could see now.

"Eyes up!"

He shouted at the security team and Quinn listened as the head of security warned as many as he could about the incoming attack. Despite having the element of surprise and superior firepower, Quinn's heart raced as the mission provided him with another surprise.

Quinn hated fucking surprises. Worse than this, he hated fucking tricks.

"Silly rabbit," Quinn said to himself. That's what he was now.

He was a silly fucking rabbit.

CHAPTER 33
TRAPPED

EXECUTING A GUARD, THE AR'S HYPERACTIVE trigger, a solid feature, enabled Quinn to shoot multiple rounds without being burdened by the recoil. The hard-hammering of every round was distributed in careful bursts that produced only fire and smoke. Always aiming for the head, Quinn hit the first target dead center before moving on to the next. Hyper-focused, Quinn had fallen into a state of pure dread. He heard nothing throughout the duration of the slaughter. Taking down another fool, Quinn looked through the Trijicon scope and grabbed more men to kill. Every second was pivotal.

Quinn targeted the others and counted each round.

"Shoot!" This order was Kardinal's.

Quinn knew that asshole's name and his face. Kardinal's choice of weapon? A SIG Sauer, something he had yet to fire. Quinn moved into the room and kept a close watch on Kardinal.

Always, he had him. Always, Quinn was set and ready. Quinn smoked the attackers who were the closest and then shot again. Two in the chest and one in the head,

Quinn tallied up all his kills. Right now, he counted only five. Quinn also knew he had twenty-five bullets still left before needing to reload. The trick during gun training is to aim small and miss small.

But, due to the power of this rifle, Quinn didn't miss a goddamn thing.

What he could see, he saw quite clearly. Still, Quinn divided his targets. His finger grazed the cool steel of the trigger and he enjoyed the feeling of the stock as well as the textured grip.

Quinn could hold this tool for hours and not get tired of it. The pinnacle of firearm ingenuity, it was primed and accurate. Quinn kept his eye on Kardinal and shredded a cluster of new pawns and more knights.

"Go!" Quinn could hear Kardinal's roars. The Custodian's goal was to get this all wrapped up in the next minute.

Find, hold, *kill*. This was all Quinn wanted to do.

He needed Alistair dead. Sirius was on the verge of an escape. Quinn continued to keep count of those he shot.

So far, he was at ten in total.

Now closer, Quinn was within arm's reach as one attempted to get his hand on the gun. Quinn spotted this move from a mile away. The fool wrapped his hands around the AR's stock. Quinn pulled. He felt the force of the brace. This act was expected. And Quinn, while ready for it, quickly turned and used his hips to flip the guard to the ground.

In judo, the flip is known as an osotogari.

It's also quite common in other martial arts too. Quinn depended on the technique as he battled this bold guard. Fortunately, the flip managed to break the fool's grip. Once the man was down, Quinn put a bullet through his left eye.

Quinn kept all the corners cleared. He kneeled and worked his way through two more. The clip was getting lighter and Quinn turned to his next target. He rolled along his arm and somersaulted while keeping the AR secured against his chest. Quinn used his legs and initiated a BJJ open guard so he could bring down the shooter and get at the fool's legs so he could break his stance. Using the soles of his feet, Quinn pushed his opponent's knees and thighs simultaneously. Doing this, he disrupted the pawn's balance and added additional pressure to the tendons. While capable of weakening anyone's ability to stand, in order for Quinn to actually get this guard down, what he needed was leverage.

Yet, the only leverage Quinn could obtain was the pawn's wrist.

Quinn latched onto the guard's wrist and smacked his attacker's legs with the hunk of boot heel. While pushing with his foot, Quinn pulled his opponent's hand. From here, Quinn flipped the man down but kept him pinned with his knee. Chopping the pistol, Quinn knocked the gun away. He looked up and spotted two more pawns.

Tilting the AR, Quinn stared through the scope.

I see you, you motherfucker.

Quinn stayed low to the ground, so naturally, the men's aim was high. But, with Quinn down and out of sight, the Custodian reacted. He put the man he brought to the floor using an jiu-jitsu *open guard* and sent one round straight through another one's eye. The guard's oculars were black and red, and a thin strip of bone flailed through the air like a frisbee.

Another one bites the dust.

More charged and Quinn covered behind a pillar. He had ten rounds left and was so close to the room where

Sirius and Alistair were located. Gun by his chest, Quinn stopped and slid along the panel built into the pole.

Quinn let go of his rifle and placed it behind him. It stayed strapped around his shoulder while he moved to a different weapon. Aware he was being approached, why the men had declined to shoot had left Quinn bewildered and uncertain. If they weren't shit before, they damn well were now. Quinn suspected they were choosing not to waste any ammunition. But, as he opened his hands, Quinn ejected his OTF. His wrist snapped and he held the weapon upside down. He could see a shadow growing from behind the pillar. Observing this, Quinn's hesitation and his mind both fell into the red zone. Holding this OTF, Quinn waved his hand in a circular motion. He brought the knife up and across and then plunged the blade into the man's jugular, slicing his throat. Blood spritzed the Custodian's cheekbones and burst like ketchup spraying out of a bottle.

With one quick squeeze, drops of red peppered Quinn's chin.

Blade down, Quinn understood there was no time to look back. There was no time to even lower his hand half an inch. There was no time to question the whereabouts of Kardinal, and there was absolutely no time to determine how many more were still left standing.

What Quinn did have, however, was a number.

He counted two, not including Kardinal. This was all that remained.

With the last pawn behind Quinn, the Custodian cocked back his right foot and slammed his heel into his attacker's chest. Quinn shattered his opponent like a board.

The pawn gasped and Quinn pivoted. He spun and swung his AR back into his hands like a rockstar playing with his guitar. Quinn fired. He watched as a juicy pocket of bone and brains splashed his chest.

Other pawns opened fire and joined the fun and more shots cratered the plaster and shards flicked Quinn's face. He hunkered. He glimpsed at the door. Right now, Quinn was *not* where he needed to be. He listened to more gunshots crackling over his head, but Quinn had to assume the people beyond the door heard this racket as well.

And they were now ready to run. The clock ticked faster.

Quinn squatted; his foot pushed the carpet. He selected a new spot not far from the pillar. Should Quinn want to avoid what was coming, then he knew he had to make a move fast. And the one Quinn *chose* to make could bring him closer to the door.

Quinn checked his gun. The grip on the stock handle felt tight.

Quinn rolled along the carpet and the bullets zipped past his head. A few did graze his armor but none penetrated. Quinn finished the roll and his legs were now outstretched. He rested on his bent leg and spotted another shooter. The AR-15's modifications made every shot easier. And, with Kardinal by the door, he fired and clipped Quinn's shoulder. A speckle of blood blotched Quinn just seconds before he slipped inside.

"Fuck." Quinn said this as he stumbled into the next room.

He finished his escape while he pulled out the empty clip and reloaded. Everywhere Quinn looked was a body. He marched toward the door and peered inside. He saw a fraction of this new room's interior, and Quinn also saw Sirius Tenet. Clear as day, he was at the table and present despite being attacked.

This was it. This was what he was waiting for!

Although this room did not align with Quinn's schematics, the Custodian wouldn't trust the result.

If there was even the slightest flaw in the plan, Quinn would have to think twice before going forward. What makes a Custodian a Custodian and not a run-of-the-mill assassin is their adherence to the code. It is the constant upholding of unbreakable standards regardless of the situation or the alterations that may or may not follow.

Custodians are required to perform at maximum efficiency at all times. This is something only matched by their deliberate attempts to avoid anything that could further compromise the mission or the code itself.

Here to clean and to mop up, Quinn was also required to make sure whatever forces surrounding the mission were swept up too.

Quinn looked at Sirius. The Custodian was shocked to see they were all sitting around the table. Next to Mr. Tenet were a few guests. Yet, there was no sign of Kardinal as of yet.

Quinn was irked. He saw him walk right through the damn door!

Quinn peeked through this one door. The entire time, he questioned how no one was running.

No one had heard a damn thing.

Impossible!

This new room wasn't soundproof, but then why was everyone inside of it?

Quinn's AR was loud, but because of its free-floating modification, it removed any contact with the handguard. This eliminated any interference within the barrel's harmonics. It increased consistency and accuracy and reduced the impact shift and made for a much more silent shot. Regardless, someone could still hear it. Someone might still react to it.

Instead, Sirius sat by. Right now, he was speaking to four nameless people Quinn couldn't see. The fundraiser was still happening.

All of this was awry, all of it was strange.

Quinn stepped from the door. Should he kick it down and get Sirius? Then he would shoot him and then shoot Alistair too. However, this was not Quinn's original plan. With time still moving against him, Quinn wanted to finish the mission. He wanted to go through this damn door and end Sirius exactly right as he was.

And so, Quinn's plan had effectively changed.

It had been this way as soon as he let Kardinal get away. It didn't add up the way he wanted, but it didn't have to. Quinn had his targets. Although it didn't go precisely as outlined, if Quinn wanted to stop taking unnecessary risks, he would need to pop this mother-fucker right here, right now.

Quinn stayed back. It was such an easy fucking shot.

Quinn could take it and not skip a beat.

If he killed Sirius and Alistair, then Quinn would also have a direct line back to the kitchen. All he needed to do was push through. Checking his watch, Quinn's loyalty to his plan caused further obstacles. It forced him to continuously doubt whether this was in fact the right move to make. Quinn was thinking with his heart and not with his mind. This saying was critical.

In this instance, it was being used as a warning. It was like Priest was with Quinn now and advising his Custodians never to let their emotions obscure their duty.

Quinn would give anything to find his father.

Whatever the rules were, he abided by every last one of them.

The Eradicate order gave Quinn full autonomy. He was free to go outside the lines, if he wanted to.

As he looked beyond the door, he could see Sirius Tenet.

He was still present but still...not moving.

Quinn was more than ready to take the shot. He was ready to end this mission once and for all. Quinn exhaled, pushed the door, and stared at the head table. Yet, Quinn was focused on Sirius and nothing else. And that was the problem.

The head of the cult looked the same. In fact, he looked *exactly* the same.

Standing in the same suit, the man was even holding the same glass as when Quinn saw him last. The main difference here was he was *not* positioned as he was before. He was still on a stage, but the stage had moved unexpectedly. Sirius was still with Alistair, but that was not *all* he was with.

A brigade of men in suits guarded Sirius and his son.

In the company of this army of gentlemen, this new room was not the hall Quinn thought it was. No, it was a *smaller version* of what he saw back in the kitchen.

But how? *How* was any of this possible?

According to the schematics, there was only *one* room. Now there was this one, *a new one*. It didn't make sense, or maybe Quinn's schematics were wrong, which also didn't make sense. Quinn did his best to remain calm. At this moment, Quinn could not deny he had been baited using the oldest trick in the book. It was the old bait and switch, all of which was done by incorporating the use of a mirror.

A big fucking mirror.

Quinn was tricked, duped! And now...*he was trapped*!

Quinn only thought he was seeing Sirius on the other side of the door.

What he really saw was a reflection. It mimicked the interior but directed in a way whereby Quinn could only see half the picture. It was a bloody scheme, and despite this, Quinn lined up his shot. He was ready to slay anyone who might fire back. This was just another part of where he was and what he was seeing.

In the end, not a single man reached for a single gun.

Quinn gazed. The last thing he wanted to do was be overzealous. It was still kill or be killed, and this never changed. With his targets in sight, all Quinn had to do was carry out the final act. The curtain was coming down now and Quinn was smack in the middle of the damn show.

Eyes up and chest out, Quinn was ready. He was ready for the final bow. With everything lined up, Quinn's finger touched the trigger. As he was about to move in, he heard a voice calling from behind his shoulder.

"Right on schedule." A shudder lambasted Quinn. He was assaulted by a myriad of chills.

The Custodian's hands suddenly went numb. All his muscles weakened and a spell was cast on the one known as Kyle Quinn. It stripped him of all his will and strength. Unable to gain any semblance of control, Quinn was aware of why this was happening.

This voice was the precise trigger needed to set Quinn off.

Feeling this immense change, Quinn tracked it back to its original source.

It had come from the only person in the world who possessed any power over him. So, as Quinn stared into his grizzled face, his grip on his gun disappeared. He was now face-to-face with the man he was so desperate to never see again.

"Hello there, son. We've been expecting you."

Quinn gawked at his old man; his mouth gaping due

to the shock and anger he was experiencing at this moment. He looked at his abuser's mottled complexion. His dad's skin had become thicker with age. It looked like leather was being pulled over his dad's skull.

It was then Quinn started to shift and the rest of the Tenet pawns sprang into action.

Fully armed, they fired at Quinn and sent violent volts of electricity through his body.

Surges scattered and singed Quinn's neck and chest and he was put down like a rabid dog. Now a wounded animal, Quinn fought the currents as best he could. Waves rattled every fiber of his being and all his guns were gone. The electricity he was facing now was strong enough to bring down a bull and so, strong enough to bring down fucking Quinn!

Not even he could overcome it.

He convulsed as more shockwaves exploded inside.

Although Quinn would give anything to be holding his knife, he was too weak to hold even air, let alone a goddamn weapon.

Seeing his father, Quinn was furious. His dad was so close and he missed him!

Broder Quinn watched his son take this beating. The plan to lure Quinn was executed to perfection. The Tenets watched Quinn as he fell. Quinn's vision faded and his fingers spread.

"Gah!" With no weapon and no plan, Quinn was finished. Someone could have picked up Quinn's gun and shot him there, but none did.

Custodians are never supposed to lose or back down or *fail*.

However, if Priest discovered that Quinn did not finish the Eradicate, he would not be buried or bereaved. All the deaths of all Custodians was to be reported and recorded. Once they were, another operative would be sent to finish the job.

Yet, most Custodians *did* make it back. The ones who didn't were avenged.

With Quinn torn and defeated, his frail eyes had only one purpose.

They looked at the face of his father. After falling for this trap, Quinn did what he said he never would.

He failed.

This truth rang in Quinn's mind like an incessant taunt. Soon, Quinn eventually stopped hearing the same word. It transformed into another Quinn didn't wish to reiterate. It was one he could not avoid hearing, even if he harnessed all his willpower.

The words just kept repeating over and over again.

Father, father, *father*.

Failure, failure...failure.

CHAPTER 34
DYING, NOT DEAD

THERE'S A SPECIFIC SIGN THAT LETS YOU KNOW THAT you're alive and not dead.

For Quinn, it was the smell. Having ingested an aroma of smoke and bullets, when Quinn's eyes peeled back, one scent emerged among the others. Afterward, Quinn needed time to regain his focus. He was seated with his head bent and felt bruises along his neck, all of them throbbed equally. Quinn turned. He was only taken prisoner once in his life. This never occurred during his Custodial duties. No, this one time occurred back when Quinn was in Delta. He was sent to rescue some hostages from a paramilitary group operating out of China.

Few took him down, and Quinn and his partner found themselves cut up and tied.

Afterward, they were burned and their fingernails were plucked out with tweezers. It was a bad day, like the other things Quinn had faced in his life. Some just came with the territory. Torture was an unavoidable consequence of the game Quinn was playing. He was still playing it now.

"Do you know where you are, assassin?" An eerie voice spoke to Quinn from the dark.

Quinn tried to guess his location.

Deep in the heart of the Louisiana bayous, Quinn found himself surrounded by nature. All the trees were invariably grown. They appeared crooked and bent. Despite seeming like he was outside, the room looked like one found inside a castle.

Quinn assumed it sat isolated in the middle of a dense forest.

It was a castle but a hut too. In there, Quinn spotted some clinker brick along the wall as well as two towers and torches. These lit up the main passage, which was not the traditional arched gate like Quinn had expected.

Instead, the doorway was triangular, and the space was not guarded by any wall. It wasn't protected because Quinn assumed it was owned and sanctioned by the very men who had taken him.

"*Vikaya.*"

The name heard sounded ancient yet also familiar. Quinn blinked.

In the center of the grand construct that was this vast lair, Quinn's first sight was an altar decorated with cadavers and corrugated wood. This was where the victims of the Tenet cult lay during the family's twisted rituals. So much blood had been spilled in this place, even Quinn was sickened by it. When the Tenets said the name of the location, Quinn felt a pinch under his left ear. Something about the name was scary. And, if the name was scary, then the place was worse.

"Vikaya, oh great Vikaya." The cult chanted with their hands raised high in anointment.

Quinn had only heard this from the readings provided

by Priest, though he never thought he would become a prisoner. And yet, here he was, exactly that.

Quinn thought he'd seen Vikaya before. He had, maybe, in his nightmares.

Now, Quinn's dream didn't present him with an exact version.

The place the Tenets called Vikaya appeared to be *made* from Quinn's nightmares. Its walls were rotted. The ground was covered in pebbles and shards of glass. It appeared to be three floors high. Like a castle merged with a cave merged with an old colonial house, it was a cavern someone tried to make into a habitable living space. There was nothing about this place that suggested home. It was a temple, a temple of doom.

Nothing about this temple made any sense to Quinn. He looked everywhere he could and absorbed every detail. He did this to determine exits and places for him to evade should the time come.

It was coming.

The location seemed like it was habitable, at least it used to be.

"In old Vikaya, we lay."

"So...this is the one who killed my own?" Another voice entered the dark space.

The first belonged to Sirius, while the second was Alistair. This was something Quinn only assumed. He was in a dungeon made up of stone walls and collapsed tunnels.

Quinn looked around as his vision began to clear.

Now, he could see Sirius Tenet. He was standing in a suit with the shirt unbuttoned around the collar and wrists.

"Yes, and thanks to the man who helped bring him here," Alistair said, "we now know his name."

"That we do," Sirius said. "That we do."

One by one, here they come, was a thought on Quinn's mind. He looked at the many servants of the cult, the last of the pawns and the knights. There were no more core members left, none except for two. They would all die just the same. Together, these tiny men approached Quinn like zombies. They weren't men, not so far as the Custodian could see. As he held his gaze, he watched each one of them with an unbreakable gaze.

Plotting out the many ways that Quinn was going to take them out, the Custodian did nothing but glare.

I'm going to be standing over all your corpses, Quinn said to himself. *You just don't know it yet.* Sirius inched forward yet Quinn stayed still. He was confined, but Quinn was not without a plan. So long as he had his watch, which he always did, then Quinn would never be helpless or absent of a strategy.

If Quinn was taken, the trick was to appear down and broken.

So, in the chair Quinn was chained to, he sat there slouched. Quinn clicked the button on the side of the watch's face and removed a small pin housed inside. Quinn pinched the pin between his fingers and then inserted it into the keyhole of the handcuff. Quinn shimmied. The entire time he hoped not a single man would get close enough to see what he was doing.

He was not dead. So long as he was breathing, Quinn was still in the game.

And the game was far from over.

"Thank you, Kardinal," Sirius said. He addressed his fixer personally. Quinn's head eased back and he glowered at the Tenet's chief of security.

As the one in charge, Quinn craved to see him die.

Quinn should have killed him when he had the chance. He should have put a fucking bullet in his fucking face.

"Don't thank me," answered Kardinal. "You know who told us how to lure this so-called beast into a trap. If not for *him*, we would not have been able to bring this guy here. He would not be so chained up or with us. He taught us how to play this game, which means he's the one we'll have to reward once this whole thing is done."

"And we will," Sirius said. "In time, but for now, we savor the meal that is to come."

Him. Again, Quinn noted the pronoun while tied to his seat.

Quinn's father was not a man of many faces.

The people who were as capable as him could change their persona quite easily. It was a lot like trying on masks. All could blend in well, but Quinn's father was good at keeping his cards close to his chest. Yet, there was something rattling in Quinn's head now. His dad wasn't changing his appearance so other people wouldn't know him.

The people in the room knew Quinn's father, and because they did, they knew Quinn too.

But there was a smell Quinn's dad presented. To Quinn, it was more than a smell, it was a trigger. It was something that jolted Quinn the moment he sensed it. There was nothing he could do to avoid it. As it trailed through Quinn's nostrils, the man flinched.

Now it was all perfectly clear.

The name of Quinn's father was not mentioned, but Quinn knew he was the one.

He knew exactly who the Tenets were discussing. As the only man capable of fooling someone like Kyle Quinn, his dad was also the same person who taught his son everything he knew. Quinn's mission from the very beginning was to infiltrate and to eliminate.

But there was a problem. There was a flaw.

There was something in the schematic that did not align with what Quinn studied.

When Quinn entered the hotel, he was following a map he received when he first arrived in Baton Rouge. This map outlined how the Tenet's event was to be organized, including seating arrangements and overall layout. Quinn had it all.

This event was old. It had been conducted for years and it did not change, except for today. The event was the annual Tenet Police Charity Fundraiser, and its venue was never different. Priest said this to Quinn. He said it was to be held at the same time of the year and at the exact same location.

So, when mapping out the setting, Quinn knew all the exits and entries. He knew them as they were but not what they had been transformed into. He could pinpoint the security and the passages designed for re-entry. He knew everything that could happen. He knew the whole place inside and out. And, although the event was still ongoing, Quinn hadn't taken one detail into account. He neglected to remember the main ballroom, how it was separate from the hotel.

The guests were there, yes, but then seconds after... they were not.

They moved. Somehow, they moved! Quinn didn't notice. He didn't because he was too busy killing people. They were evacuated for some reason. What Quinn realized now was that reason was him. With no police alerted, Sirius and Alistair Tenet chose the old bait and switch strategy. They would not have done this unless they were told how to do it. And Quinn would not have followed *this* unless he was distracted.

And he was. Quinn was completely distracted.

Always, he saw his father. He was chasing him now even though he wasn't here. No one knew his weaknesses more than Quinn's dad. It was one of the reasons why Quinn hated him so much. Nevertheless, Broder Quinn did manage to get the best of his own son. He knew Quinn wouldn't stop until he came face-to-face with the demons of his past. The mirror trick was so simple. All you had to do was change the angle of the room and make sure the person couldn't see the whole display. It was child's play in the eyes of a master manipulator, and Quinn wasn't prepared for such a trick. He was blinded by something else, something new.

Never put vengeance or vendetta before viability or victory.

This was only more advice granted to Quinn over the years. He could remember exactly who gave it to him. Right now, all Quinn's memories were merging. Right now, Quinn was stuck in a series of endless nightmares he couldn't shake or suppress.

His mind was absolute mayhem. He had to get it straight before it was too late. He was certain he could kill the rest of these men. And, if not for the fact that his father arrived, Quinn would have done it. It would have been done a long time ago.

All he faced now was just a bunch of magic tricks.

They were the playful things conjured by an ultimate magician. It was the same magician who was relegated to the confines of Quinn's fragile mind. He was that man who gnawed at Quinn's subconscious day in and day out. It was a biting that had come from the same person who drove the Custodian to where he was now.

But Quinn could not see him. No, he could only *smell* him.

"He's all yours...sir," Sirius called out to the nameless man.

If Sirius was willing to refer to him as *sir*, then he was someone respected. After Sirius spoke, Quinn's jaw locked and he bit down hard on his tongue.

Venom and rage were all flourishing as Quinn stayed tied up. He was flooded with a hate so corrosive he couldn't see and feel nothing else. Quinn stared and saw a man strolling across the rocky ground. Surrounding him was a haze of eerie smoke. The thick scent stung Quinn's nostrils. His father motioned past Sirius Tenet, and Quinn observed his shadow. It looked the way it had throughout all those terrible and traumatic years.

"Thank you for this," Sirius said. He was now commending Broder Quinn for orchestrating the ruse that brought his only son into their hands. "As always, we appreciate your...*expertise.*"

"You are welcome," said Quinn's father, in the dark, still covered by smoke.

Quinn quaked.

Each time Quinn caught a whiff of his old man, he was thrust back to the time when he was all he could smell. Quinn was back to living the days when he was built into the man he is today: a killer, a maniac, an artist.

Quinn gazed at his father's legs because he refused to look him in the eye.

He heard the ruffling of Sirius's jacket in the background. It sounded crisp and rough, like papers grinding against cheap fabric. Quinn saw Sirius slip an envelope from the same jacket. Obviously now was the time when Broder received the money for why he was brought here, to Louisiana. Quinn had yet to understand what those reasons might be. Quinn's father was a freelance merce-nary. He was someone who worked for the highest bidder.

Maybe he was brought to work for the Tenets and train their security. Maybe, but again, Quinn didn't know for sure. Evidently, he was brought to help the family. He had come to bring his only son down to his knees, like he was now. A grunt and then a sigh belted from Quinn's father's mouth. What followed later was the sound of a hand snatching paper, of Broder Quinn accepting his offer.

"A deal's a deal."

Quinn heard Sirius add this part in later. Further tension rose and yet, Quinn refused to look up. Seeing their legs, Sirius and Broder were now in a standoff. There was some-thing else happening within their exchange. They whispered, and yet Quinn didn't know what they were whispering about. Still, Quinn hated his father, and yet still...he knew him. He knew that money was never a true motivator for Quinn's dad's choices or actions. It wasn't for Quinn either.

When Quinn looked up again, he remembered how his father was too brooding and too fast. Rarely was he ever under anyone's employ, and rarely did he seek to rush such an exchange. And, since he was allowing himself to be now, this change had coerced Quinn into doing more.

He was looking at the situation in a much deeper and more profound way.

"I think that makes our transaction complete, does it not?" Sirius snickered. "You have worked to make us stronger as an organization, and to that end, you have succeeded. After all, that is why you were sent to us, is it not?"

Quinn struggled to hear the last part, but he did hear the first.

As Quinn had noted about the family, when a deal is done, a deal is done. This was something Quinn had also come to know throughout his life as a mercenary. He had also come to understand as a thief, an extractor, a spy, and now...as an *eradicator*.

"The deal always was to bring him to you, yes," Quinn heard his father say. "And I have, but seeing how he is my son and this will be the last time I ever get to see him. I think I'm owed...*just a little time.*"

"Ah," Sirius said. He sneered.

What was once only suspected had now become abundantly clear to Quinn. His father brought his own son to the brink of death, and nothing else was to be done until Broder himself gave the last word. This was something which hadn't been done, not as of yet.

"Very well," Sirius said. "Not long. We have big plans for this one here."

Quinn glared at Sirius. The head of the cult used his head to gesture to the tied-up mercenary. With his handcuffs picked, Quinn already felt the metal starting to loosen. He was close, he just needed more time. Oddly, it was his father—the man Quinn wanted to kill more than all the others—who was going to give it to him.

"I understand," said Broder. "Not long."

The Brotherhood of Cyn left Quinn. Even Kardinal stepped back to let his masters leave.

They retreated into Vikaya and Quinn's arms and shoulders flexed. There was a strain building in his muscles. He stared at the old man dressed in his classic coat and loose pants. Quinn's father was a man who wasn't big on style or appearance.

What he was doing, Quinn believed was unintentional.

He was giving the Custodian the time he needed to escape!

In essence, the more his father insisted on delaying his son's execution, the closer Quinn came to getting back his freedom.

"So...you are here. So...you found me."

Quinn's father's face looked long and moonfaced. It was exactly as Quinn remembered, almost. His dad had a few more scars. Clearly, he encountered more enemies since the last time they were together, which was a long time ago.

"I *didn't* find you," Quinn said, cold and shrill. This was something he hoped his dad would take as a sign. He was not interested in talking to him. But, now that Quinn was trapped, he might as well try. In the midst of doing this, Quinn had yet to lose sight of his objective. What he needed now was time. In fact, he needed all the time he could get.

"Oh, someone else?" said his father. He leered at his son.

"Someone else," Quinn said.

"May I ask *who*?"

"Why do you care?" Quinn snapped. Again, he made no apologies for the malice now being inflicted on him now. He thought he made himself clear.

He. Did. Not. Want. To. Talk.

"I want to know if I still have eyes on me, if I'm still as popular as I once was."

"Popular," Quinn said. He scoffed at the word.

He was disgusted that this was what his dad chose to discuss. Broder was once a strong-armed merc with the reputation of a lion. He prowled and he hunted. Quinn's father ate and he stalked. In the world today, however,

Quinn's old man drifted out of sight. His name meant less than it ever did before.

In a lot of ways, it meant absolutely nothing.

"You're just another abuser," spewed Quinn. "Someone who managed to slip free of his retribution, and now...you're linked to another band of assholes who are the same as you are. Actually," Quinn said, and he spit on the floor. "They're the same ones who are going to get exactly what's coming to them, same as you."

"Hmm. Is that right?"

Broder Quinn was unaffected by the statement. Nothing Quinn said or did could present a real threat. But there was still time for Quinn to prove otherwise.

"And you think I'm part of what these men are a part of?"

"Last I checked," Quinn said, "you work for them, don't you?"

"And last I checked," said Broder. His reply was just as quick. "I have never worked for anyone a day in my life. I go to where the work is, where the opportunities are, and I would think that you, of all people, would know that."

Quinn was quiet. He did know that. Since his father left the Berets, his departure happened right around the time he started training his own son. Broder Quinn didn't enlist or go on a single government-sanctioned op. He was actually quite similar to how Quinn was now.

Quinn hated when people thought he was a mercenary. It made Quinn think he was on the same path as his father. And so, Quinn corrected people when they referred to him as such.

He was more. He was so much more.

"I had you and you know it."

"Maybe," Broder said to his son. He folded his hands and interlocked his fingers. "But then you fell for the easiest trick in the goddamn book there, kiddo. You thought you knew your surroundings so well you didn't expect anything to change. Big mistake."

Quinn held back his words.

He knew everything about the hotel. He was familiar with the location of Sirius and Alistair Tenet. When Quinn arrived, however, there was a shift. When he saw both his targets through the door, it didn't comply with the schematic he had memorized.

They weren't where they were supposed to be.

Quinn didn't know he was standing in an entirely separate room. Now, Quinn insisted this wasn't an oversight. He wanted his dad to know he was tricked by the only man capable of tricking him. This was the reason why Quinn failed and that was all.

"You got sloppy," said Broder, "and sloppiness blurs the lines, and blurred lines get you burned, hence, why you're here now."

"Yeah?" Quinn said. He scoffed at his dad's claim.

"Yeah," said Broder.

Quinn spit and continued to chat with his old man. "And this child abduction ring that's just what, a means to an end?"

Broder Quinn looked at his boy with his eyes deep and dull, like wet stones resting inside his skull. He had an answer in regard to his son's quandary.

"Well, that's...that's a little more complicated."

"Nothing complicated about what you are," refuted Kyle Quinn. "You always saw yourself as an innovator, and now you're working with men who don't innovate as much as they fucking crawl and hide. Couldn't imagine this, but then I'm not that surprised by anything I've seen so far. It's all been so...predictable."

"And yet, here you are," Quinn's father replied. "Besides, I thought you learned how to leave emotion out of the game. I think that maybe that's starting to slip. You're starting to become more, what's the word? *Introspective?*"

Quinn hissed. Too big a word for his old man's vocabulary.

"Of course," said Broder Quinn. "Time will do that to a man, though. Hell, I know it did for me." Broder squatted in front of Kyle Quinn. He pressed his arms against the inside of his thighs and sneered.

"Time doesn't change people," Quinn snapped back. "It only makes them feel regret for the things they did and wish they could take back."

With an unforgiving glower, Quinn looked unfazed by his father's explanation. Deep down, Quinn knew his father had not changed. And just because he was giving him time, it wasn't necessarily for the right reasons.

"And in the end, you're still going where you know you shouldn't." Broder took a long and deep breath. "I have taught you well. I have made you into one of the most fearless and feared men who walk this earth. There is nothing that can stop you, no one who can terrorize you, and none who will keep you down. There's no force you will be unprepared to face, and I'm just sorry you had to be tested again, in this way."

Pervading waves of rage burned inside of Quinn as he fantasized about what it is he truly desired. He kept working his way through the handcuffs while also envisioning his father being somewhere else. He imagined him held up, chained, and taken as a prisoner. Then, he thought about what he would do to him *if* the opportunity returned. And yet, Quinn imagined throttling his father by the neck. He couldn't help but cling to the words spoken. These words, which sounded genuine and like praise, contained hidden meaning.

It was something Quinn couldn't help but grasp.

"I have taught you well. I have made you into one of the most fearless and feared men who walk this earth. There is nothing that can stop you, no one who can terrorize you, and none who will keep you down. There's no force you are unprepared to face, and I'm just sorry you had to be tested again, in this way."

Quinn continued to hear these words over and over again. They were like a virus growing inside of him. They plagued the Custodian's increasingly frail consciousness and it was then that Quinn's arms began to shake. His fingers flicked, and the cuffs loosened, and yet the entire time, Quinn couldn't help but ask why?

Why was his father saying this now?

More than this, why was Quinn given what he needed most and that was the gift of time?

The task of removing handcuffs is nothing more than a simple military training exercise. In Quinn's case, it was a skill instilled since the age of seven. Quinn's dad knew his son could remove these handcuffs. He also knew that Quinn's watch was a weapon. And, if anyone was aware of the application of these items, it was Broder fucking Quinn.

Although Quinn was compromised, this was not a situation he couldn't handle.

In fact, all of it was so familiar. *Intensely* familiar.

It was Quinn's father who helped the Tenet family bring him here. It was also Quinn's dad's idea to have his son handcuffed to a chair. Quinn's father placed Quinn in a situation he knew he could overcome; one he was trained for and knew easily how to defeat.

"I taught you well." What Quinn's dad said was true. Broder did teach his son well.

With five men positioned outside this cavern or cave or whatever it was, Quinn refused to accept this as his final fate. No, nothing could stop the Custodian and nothing could terrorize him. Quinn looked at his dad, who now stood away from his son. He yanked the lapels on his trench coat and tightened the collar against his neck.

On his way out, a bag slipped from Quinn's father's jacket and drifted past his leg.

Broder held this sack. It was the same one Quinn himself had used to store his own weapons. Maybe it was guns or maybe it was knives. Although it was subtle, it was very visible.

It was here.

"I'm just sorry you had to be tested again."

Broder Quinn had apologized once before, but then he was never one for apologies. But, should Quinn's father suddenly adopt this policy now, then it was for a reason. There was one last trick up his sleeves. Broder motioned around the chair and moved behind his son. Then, he held the bag he slipped from his jacket and placed it into Quinn's hands. With one handcuff loosened, Quinn snatched the bag and tucked it behind.

He kept the bag out of sight and so, no one did see.

Quinn squeezed the fabric and held on to two completely *unmistakable* items.

It was not Quinn's AR or his Benelli. It was not his Glock or his OTF. No, what was hidden in this bag was not a conventional weapon anyone could wield except for Quinn. In his hands, Quinn now had everything.

He had his tonfa.

Quinn could feel his dad standing next to him. Quinn also felt the touch of his old man's hand. It was heavy yet at the same time steady. It provided the only form of affection a man like Quinn's father was capable of giving. Even when he was a child, Quinn interpreted it as a guiding gesture. This was his dad's way of ensuring Quinn he was either proud or that everything was going to be okay.

And here, with Quinn armed and almost free, he believed the touch indicated both.

"He's done now," Broder said to Sirius. "You all can have him."

Sirius Tenet drifted into the shadows, the same as the rest of his clan. Sirius, however, was not alone. By his right, was another name on Quinn's list. It was one he had almost forgotten until now.

Tulsa Monarch was still alive and he was here now, watching.

He followed his master through the cave and gave Quinn a sultry wink. Quinn gave Tulsa and Sirius a *see you soon* kind of look because his mission was not yet done. And, Quinn had plans to get out. Still, he had plans to finish what he started.

When Quinn looked at the man he hated, his dad, he was also a man who would ensure his freedom. Each time Quinn fantasized about pulling the trigger and exacting his revenge, he was burdened by some kind of change. Quinn was hit with a new memory. He was forced into a situation whereby all his rage had vanished and he was feeling something new.

Whether it was hope, faith, or both, Quinn didn't know. And right now, he didn't want to.

While Quinn could see his father walking away from Sirius and Alistair, he left the caverns and left Vikaya. Quinn watched as the shadows enveloped his dad and made him disappear.

"Thank you," Quinn said. He squeezed his tonfa.

"It's not often a father gives up his own son," Sirius said to Quinn. "I would know. I also gave up mine."

Sirius was now standing next to Alistair and next to him stood Kardinal. Behind them stood the rest of their brotherhood, which was all that was left. Everyone stared at Quinn, enraged and ready. For Quinn, the looks on their faces were only a pitiful attempt to exact their dominance over Kyle Quinn, who was still a prisoner.

Holding firm, Quinn kept his hands behind his back and played along with this fake act. No one knew he was actually free or what was in his possession. Yet, they also didn't know what was going to happen now that Quinn was free.

The mission was still on.

Quinn had to finish what he started. He had to finish and he had...to win.

CHAPTER 35
MORALITY AND MADNESS

"THE POWER GIVEN TO THOSE WHO SERVE A GREAT promise is a timeless desire, wouldn't you agree?"

Quinn gawked at Sirius after asking this silly question. Quinn assessed the cult leader's posture. Sirius appeared prim, and in Quinn's mind, his pose was strange. He looked like he was trying to channel power while also speaking aloud to everyone in Vikaya.

"But you still think of us as monsters, yes?"

Quinn wanted to respond. He wanted to say *yes*. More than this, he wanted to tell Sirius Tenet precisely what he thought of him and his company. Instead, Quinn opted not to. He wasn't here to talk. And even *if* he was, Quinn was far from the talkative type. He rarely contributed to any conversation unless he absolutely had to.

"You think what we do is evil, do you?" Sirius inched himself closer to Quinn.

He raised his hand and pushed his index finger and thumb together. Quinn slipped the tonfa farther down his hand.

"Well, now you will truly come to understand why we do what we do because you will be a product of it, just like you deserve to be."

Grins formed on Alistair's and Kardinal's faces. Quinn observed these men as they stepped toward him. Quinn's body was now turned.

"You may have this one as tribute," Sirius said to Alistair. "Lords knows his blood will not be as pure as all the others, but something is better than nothing."

Kardinal held Sirius's coat and the man in charge slipped his arms through the sleeves.

Quinn kept a watchful eye on Sirius.

In fact, he was watching everyone and everything.

"Today marks the first of our *three* festivals," Sirius said. He was so joyful his arms were raised even higher. "Appeasement is on the horizon and a new tribute is now ours to take. Certain occasions call for...*optimization*," Sirius lowered his arms slowly. "And perhaps spilling the blood of a true warrior like this will provoke a new change here, in Vikaya, and it might also be one that will bring about greater glory. Soon, a new truth will be granted to us all. Rejoice!" Sirius's voice beckoned. It created a loud echo that coursed throughout the entire lair. Quinn glared at Sirius. He was now jubilant and giddy. "There are greater realms ahead of us! This is how we will live above the rest!"

Sirius Tenet walked toward another tunnel. It was the same passage Quinn's father had passed into earlier. Therefore, as Sirius vacated the space, the master had separated himself from what came next.

And Quinn saw him for what he always knew him to be.

He was a fucking coward. When Quinn's target passed by, the Custodian knew he had not yet completed the Eradicate. But he was alive and he was still breathing, and yet the mission was not yet done.

It was not over.

"And this, I will do anything to preserve," Sirius said. He took a moment to look back. "And I will stop anyone who tries to stop me, especially a foolish merc who thinks he can put an end to something he knows nothing about."

Sirius stayed in the tunnel while Quinn stayed strapped to the chair. Quinn stared at all the men now standing around him. He had more to say despite the fact that his last target was about to slip away.

"I'm *not* a mercenary." Quinn was emphatic and spoke using a sharper tone of voice.

His hands throttled his tonfa and Quinn kept the broad side against his forearms.

"I'm...a Custodian!" Quinn's voice echoed throughout the lair.

Alistair, who was looking directly at Quinn, squinted after hearing the terrible roar.

Now confused, Alistair leered, for it was strange to hear someone refer to themselves in such a way. This was the exact distraction Quinn was hoping for. Jumping from his seat, Quinn erupted like lava exploding from the mouth of a volcano. He was so close to Alistair. Quinn's skull rammed the Tenet son in the chin. His teeth clacked.

"Gah!" Alistair's exclaim sounded muffled.

The second Alistair was hit, Quinn's arms popped out from behind his back and ejected like the wings of an eagle. Now free, Quinn latched his hand around Alistair's neck and performed a good old-fashioned headlock. While his arms and torso were free, Quinn's ankles remained tied.

"Shoot him!" Alistair commanded one of his men.

All the rooks, knights, and pawns from the brotherhood were present and accounted for. They were robed and they were armed. Beyond this cluster of nameless fuck-heads, Quinn spotted Kardinal. Quinn used the other tonfa to whip another cultist. Alistair, in his own spot, used one hand to snag the Bowie Alistair kept in his belt.

This was the weapon he was going to use to kill Quinn, if he damn well could.

No, he could not.

Quinn's arm stayed looped around Alistair. He pulled until this fat fool was all the way back. Using Alistair as cover, Quinn took him straight to the ground. He grinded the soles of his boots into the rocky floor and Quinn spotted another armed pawn.

The pawn carried a Smith and Wesson revolver, and, in an instant, Quinn torqued his hips. Pulling himself around, Quinn whipped his torso. Relaxing his right leg, Quinn let the power of the roundhouse guide him the rest of the way. Quinn brought his right foot down and connected with the hand of the shooter.

Ka-bang!

The shot barely missed the Custodian's shoulder. The round cratered the ground and left a small imprint. From here, Quinn switched the positioning of his tonfa. He reversed the batons and planned to use the long section to strike at Alistair's face. Directly across from him, Quinn could see Kardinal stomping after him. He was coming to save his master. Now with his own gun drawn, it was a SIG. Quinn needed to bring him down same as all the others. Quinn glared at the weapon. He snatched Kardinal's wrist.

If he didn't get the gun from Kardinal's hands, then Quinn was as good as dead.

Quinn's method for disarming an opponent involved a

lot of wrist manipulation. It was this first, and then Quinn would flip the handle up until his opponent's fingers cracked.

But in this case, Quinn had his tonfa to assist him.

Quinn pulled Kardinal's wrist and pressed the tonfa into the fixer's elbow.

"Ah!" Kardinal screamed.

Quinn felt the brace of his weapon against his arm. Kardinal yelled. Quinn pulled Kardinal forward and performed a rough, sloppy throw. The move was not executed as smoothly as Quinn would have liked, so when he did it, Kardinal was nimble enough to land on his arms and avoid a lock and a pin. With Kardinal down, Quinn kicked his gun away. Quinn could see his opponent on his stomach and Quinn hit back with a hard *donkey-kick*. He believed this was enough to still keep Kardinal down.

Hard and fierce, Quinn felt vigilant and alert but was also concerned. He was concerned because Alistair was getting away. More than this, Alistair Tenet was still alive.

Quinn recovered his tonfa, the one he had recently thrown, and lifted it from the ground and placed it in the natural position. With all the weapons secured, the exhilaration from the scrap pumped Quinn up with a powerful second wind. He was now faced with a challenging scenario. Quinn was among armed men and big brawlers. Again, he made sure to remember that his man was now limping toward the door.

Yes, Quinn knew what he had to do. He fastened the tonfa against his arms again. Then, Quinn pulled and felt the cool wood rubbing against his bones. As the second shooter in robes marched in. Quinn answered straightaway. He hammered the man's gun and deflected. After, Quinn swung with his opposite hand, he used his elbow and tonfa and struck the nameless cultist in the neck.

"Ah!" Kardinal continued to scream and scream, as if doing so would help him.

Now that Quinn was using the shorter end, he went straight for the knee. With this, Quinn's goal was to shatter femurs and crack fucking knees. For a second, it was as if all his attackers were made from wood. Quinn used the end of the baton and pounded at the fool's kneecaps. Quinn finished his attack with a clean cut across the pawn's jaw. With the broad side, Quinn cut and slammed the fool upside the head.

The jaw was fractured and knee was broken. Quinn's goal did not change.

He flicked the tonfa and gripped the handle. Now, Quinn was holding the weapon in reverse. Seeing the shooter fall, the man's nose was gushing and crooked. Quinn hammer-thrusted the pawn in a clean, parallel strike to the head.

Quinn pounded the bone and the power of the impact sent a rattling sensation through his arm. Followed by a vibrant pop, it sounded like Quinn had struck a marble countertop with a wooden mallet. This was enough to make Quinn feel only a hint of pain. Splitting his attacker's head, a death-induced gargle seeped past the lips. Quinn saw the man's head turn into a misshapen sphere akin to a bruised tangerine.

To his right was Kardinal, still down.

With no time to second guess himself, if Kardinal got away, then Quinn knew he would get to Alistair. And, should Kardinal get to him, then Quinn might never finish the mission. Amid all the doubt, however, there was also Quinn's father. He ensured the Custodian's freedom. And if he was willing to free Quinn, then he held no true loyalty to the Tenets at all.

He was a consultant, if that.

Broder had taken the Tenet's money only to purposefully lead the entire cult to their death. Doing this, now his own son was convinced it was so he could succeed. His father actually wanted to see Quinn finish the job. He wanted Quinn *to win*.

CHAPTER 36
LAST MAN STANDING

WHEN QUINN SAW KARDINAL, HE TWIRLED HIS tonfa and marched through the secret lair known by the cult as Vikaya. Ready to take on anyone else who lay beyond this secret passage, when Quinn looked at Kardinal, he delivered a straight kick hard into the fixer's midsection.

"Gah!" A choking sound emerged from Kardinal followed by short, straining bursts of fleeting air.

Should Quinn have been in the octagon, this would have been like that Anderson Silva kick and set the tempo for the rest of the fight. On his knees, Kardinal's fighting style was always poor. When Kardinal fell, he spit to rid his mouth of any lingering saliva. He glared at Quinn.

"Kill him, Kardinal!" Alistair's raised voice was done out of frustration and impatience.

He was loud and his voice was fractured. He was out of breath so early in the game, but Alistair chose to flee. However, his arrogance compromised this pathway. The fact that Alistair had declined to save himself allowed for Quinn to create a new order of execution.

He was next!

Quinn stormed after Kardinal. Quinn squeezed his tonfa and went straight for his opponent's body.

Kardinal hooked left and struck Quinn's earlobe. But, by the time the blow landed, it was already too late. Quinn rammed his shoulder into Kardinal's gut. Then, using the tonfa as a sickle, hooked Kardinal and forced him to fall to the floor. There, Quinn would do the nasty. He would not let Kardinal stand again. In fact, Quinn wouldn't even let Kardinal kneel. He jabbed Kardinal's thighs. This quick stab throttled Kardinal's tendons. From here, Quinn broke his opponent's stance.

"Ah!"

Quinn held the tonfa naturally now and felt the same brace from the weapons like he always did. He scanned his opponent for potential striking sections and went to them. He pounded Kardinal's knees. The fight continued and Quinn predicted it was only a matter of time before something changed. Quinn didn't take Kardinal for being this kind of man. After Quinn pumped Kardinal with the tonfa, the head of security revealed a weapon of his own.

Kardinal's hands slipped out from behind his red jacket and removed two swords.

"You're not the only one who can get up close and personal," Kardinal said.

Now with both of their weapons, a circle began to form between them as they both eagerly anticipated who was going to make the first move.

"Never took you for the type," Quinn said, tonfa up.

"Never was," replied Kardinal. "But then someone taught me that in any fight, you gotta be prepared for anything. He also said that the person I was likely to face did have a weakness for blades and other surprises."

"We'll see," replied Quinn. His plan stayed the same.

"Come on." Kardinal invited Quinn to make a move. The metal in Kardinal's hand flashed before clanking with Quinn's tonfa.

Quinn knocked away Kardinal's blades and pushed the batons even harder into his forearms. Quinn protected himself from Kardinal's vapid, haphazard cuts. Kardinal kept the swords by his chest and did exactly as Quinn had expected. He stomped with his swords cocked back. Like always, Kardinal was off balance. What Quinn needed now was to get Kardinal's blade out of the way. Quinn's highest hope was he would shatter these swords. For Quinn, he could fasten Kardinal's swords between his tonfa. Quinn might be able to trap them, and once he did this, he'd jam them inside and break the steel.

It would be difficult but not impossible.

Hell, this was a phrase Quinn could carve on his fucking tombstone!

Nonetheless, Quinn was far from that day. He collided with Kardinal's blades. Then, using the short end of his tonfa, the tonfa acted like some brass knuckles. Quinn punched, and the tonfa stayed tight near Quinn's fingers. Quinn aimed for Kardinal's left cheek. Kardinal leaned in, and Quinn clipped the fixer just under his nose.

"Ah!" Kardinal yelped.

Quinn swung. He was bloodied up, but far from broken, and so, he was far from through. Quinn spun the tonfa out. He held the batons now like baseball bats. He slammed the weapons in a series of unrelenting and angry thrusts. Quinn continued to deliver this epic assault, but amid the clanging metal, vibrations coursed through Quinn's stiff hands.

Kardinal fell. To Quinn, this was significant. It meant only one thing:

Progress.

Breathless and sweaty, pockets of dark puddles appeared across Kardinal's body.

Quinn prepared for another jab. He studied his weary opponent while, in the background, a watchful spectator stood by and watched. Alistair Tenet was eager to see who the victor would be. He wanted to see who was going to win in this never-ending fight to the death.

"Finish him!" Quinn saw fear in Alistair's gaze as he shouted the command.

If Alistair Tenet was smart, he would have run. Instead, he chose to stay. He didn't run, because Alistair Tenet wasn't smart. He was, as Quinn knew him to be, a coward. And yet, choosing to stay was another indication of who the son of Sirius really was.

It was foolish to think they ever had Quinn against any ropes.

If the fight was still going, then Quinn was still in control.

"Do it, Kardinal!" Alistair shouted again.

Quinn peered back for only a second. He watched Kardinal acknowledge his master's call and afterward, saw him lunge at Quinn like a poorly trained fencer and deliver a semi-on-target riposte. Quinn's tonfa was in two different grips when he dodged Kardinal's jab. Quinn lifted the weapons over his head and held them high, like a pair of twin axes. Generating momentum and power, Quinn's strike was the best one yet!

In one fell swoop, Quinn clattered the broadside of Kardinal's sword. And, in another bold attempt to break the fixer down, Quinn snapped Kardinal's swords in two pieces.

Quinn broke them! He broke the blades!

Quinn whacked Kardinal in the throat and shattered his windpipe. Kardinal hit the floor and convulsed while

Alistair stayed by the door. Now shaking, Alistair could have run then, but like before, he chose to stay.

He didn't run, but he should have.

Quinn glared at the Tenet son. He flipped his tonfa, spit, and grunted.

"*Run.*"

CHAPTER 37
LAST ROLL

QUINN EXECUTED KARDINAL AND THEN THE Custodian kipped-up using the classic martial arts move to get back to his feet. Lifting his ankles behind his head, Quinn pushed out with his legs, and then popped himself up to a standing position. Quinn's kill list was not done and still, he was loyal to his plan. And now, Quinn observed a change he was pleased to see.

Alistair wasn't running. Alistair was *returning*.

Despite the forewarning and despite not having a clear shot, Alistair cocked his shotgun.

He lowered the weapon, and the Tenet son bounced in a poor attempt to look intimidating. Quinn gazed at this pathetic amateur of a man. It was so sad, Quinn could laugh. The fool lifted the Ithaca. It was so high it was perpendicular to Alistair's shoulder. Alistair let go of the trigger and the first round cratered the gravel floor.

Creating an upturn of smoke and pebbles, remnants sprayed Quinn's face as he leaned back.

"Ha!" Alistair yelped before lifting the weapon up again.

Quinn marched. First order of business was to get his hands on the gun. Admittedly, the Ithaca was not Quinn's taste. Nevertheless, Quinn snatched the barrel. Then, with a quick trick of the hand, Quinn flicked his opposite arm upward. He stripped the gun away like it was nothing.

"Gah!" The move was done in a matter of seconds. Alistair's lips moved and he was mumbling incoherently. Still holding the gun, Quinn swiped the weapon up and across. He used the handle as a cudgel and whacked Alistair's jaw.

Alistair dropped while Quinn performed another trick of the hand.

He relied on another disarming technique that only the elite operatives knew how to use. They can take away their opponent's weapon before they even know it's gone. This piece of advice was given by Quinn's many sergeants. It was also one he'd learned to perfect over the years. Now knocked to shit, Alistair knelt before Quinn. The Custodian wielded Alistair's shotgun as if it were his own.

Quinn escaped his torturous demise, and this was not Quinn's first time whereby he found himself pinned down. As Quinn wielded the Ithaca, new thoughts began to assimilate. Quinn could see Alistair's arm was broken. He could also see it bleeding. Alistair's hand was wrapped around this damaged limb. His complexion was pallid and his footsteps weak. Quinn had him marked clearly and yet, he chose not to take the shot.

With the barrel aimed down, Quinn interfered with the weapon's trajectory.

A Custodian's job is to clean. If Alistair is alive, then technically, the scene is still dirty. What it needed was a good sweep. Quinn cocked the Ithaca and emptied the weapon. The empty shells trickled onto Alistair's chest, and the son of the cult leader landed face-first into the dirt.

He squealed and he whimpered.

After Quinn obtained Alistair's shotgun, he didn't forget to get his hands on his two beauties. Until now, they had not led him astray. Quinn clutched his tonfa both like two sticks.

Alistair Tenet was the second to last name on Quinn's kill list. He was also the right-hand man—or the right-hand son—of the man responsible for the mass murdering of women and children. He was kind of a hopeless soldier, and when Quinn looked at Alistair, he was complacent. He could not fight back. And so, Quinn knew exactly how to finish him.

"I have to commend you," spit Alistair. "You really are one crafty motherfucker."

Alistair's last words actually sounded complimentary. They were given to the person about to kill him. Quinn was halfway through the tunnel when he glared at the helpless man.

"Nah," Quinn said, securing his grip on his tonfa. "I'm just professional."

Quinn watched Alistair's face gradually rotate. Still holding the tonfa, Quinn aimed for the back of Alistair's skull. He grabbed a handful of Alistair's hair and pulled. Alistair's body arched. The back of his skull was pressed into Quinn's chest. Quinn pushed the tonfa into his forearm.

Alistair was right where Quinn wanted him to be. He was secured and going nowhere.

Quinn jabbed.

Relying heavily on the tonfa handle, Quinn pummeled with a punch capable of denting steel. After he struck, a muffled thump echoed from Alistair's quaking mouth. His brain was now mush. Every part of him felt ruptured and shaken. Blood began to spill through Alistair's ocular cavities and then trickled along his jaw.

Alistair lay with his arms spread cruciform. He wasn't breathing. Quinn observed his body. Soon, he would be only a rigor mortis cadaver.

Beyond the tunnel, anyone could be on the other side waiting for him.

Sirius was likely on his way home. Quinn checked his watch. Now, it was well after midnight. And, if the head of the family was planning to go, he was probably on his way to doing this now. While Quinn couldn't step out unless he was armed, the tonfa would do little if he was so out in the open. To Quinn, he would most surely be. Quinn turned back and swept what he could find. He picked up the Ithaca as well as a few shells and stole a Beretta from one of the pawns. Even with these weapons, there was no place for Quinn to take cover. So, if Quinn was going forward, then he was going to be facing down more cultists.

Each one waited to see Alistair. Quinn kept the tonfa behind his back as he marched through the tunnel. Before he could go on, Quinn had to make sure he wasn't noticed. Beyond the entrance to Vikaya, Quinn spotted one of SUVs used as a transport to Vikaya. The vehicle was parked in front of the rocky pathway and in front of it were two men in black suits. Casually, they faced one another and shared a smoke.

At this hour, coins of moonlight touched the ground.

When they saw Quinn, the men flinched and reached for their sidearms.

He was right. There were more.

Way more.

CHAPTER 38
QUICK SWEEP

QUINN TREKKED TOWARD THE PACK OF WANNABE tough guys and very bad killers.

The men stared at Quinn as he crept out of the dark.

"Mr. Tenet, sir? Is that...is that...*you?*" The speaking man was glib.

He didn't know who was *really* coming out of this tunnel. It could be Alistair or it could be someone else. The man also wasn't wrong when he referred to Quinn as Mr. Tenet. Quinn kept the pistol tucked behind his left thigh, then, hoisting the man whose skull he'd cracked open, he stepped into the light.

"Sir?"

What the men saw—in fact all they could see—was Alistair Tenet. Yet, Alistair's head was tilted too far back and his body appeared ravaged. Quinn was holding Alistair up, like a doll. He was presented as nothing more than a broken version of the man he *used* to be.

"What the..." All the men stared at Alistair's corpse.

Each one was distracted by the brutalized appearance of their employer. Quinn snapped to attention and quickly got to work. Quinn popped out from under Alistair's dangling arm and dropped both guards with headshots.

Quinn then tossed Alistair's body aside and spit. The doofus left a bad taste in his mouth.

Alone in the Louisiana swamps, Quinn had no clue how he was going to find his way back. He needed a minute to collect himself. In Quinn's possession were his tonfa and the Ithaca shotgun stashed inside his shirt. The tonfa stuck to his sweaty back, but the pistol Quinn had was a Beretta. It had only a few rounds left. None of this would be enough to finish the job.

What Quinn wanted now more than anything was his gear. He wiped the blood off his face and walked up to the pawns recently executed. Quinn kicked their bodies over and patted them down. Looking for the keys to the car, Quinn recovered a set from one of the pockets.

Quinn unlocked the SUV and looked into the trunk. He was prepared to toss everything he had inside. To his surprise, the family was dumber than Quinn had anticipated. Quinn examined the contents stored in the trunk and then he came to realize that what he was seeing was no accident. This was yet another bone tossed Quinn's way. It was given by the same man who gave him his freedom.

"Son of a bitch." Quinn ogled a new cache of precious items.

Inside was Quinn's body armor, his AR-15, his Benelli, his Glock 34 and his 26, and also his OTF knife. It was everything Quinn had while at the hotel. It was everything he thought was taken from him. It was all here, exactly as Quinn left it. They were all there, along with a fat stack of ammunition. It was another gift from his father. Even Quinn couldn't figure out how his dad pulled this off. It was a huge misstep that the Tenets had over-looked. It was so big it was fucking embarrassing.

Quinn didn't care about the reasons. Maybe his dad was never working for the Tenets, and maybe Priest had made sure Quinn's father was in the picture, someway and somehow. Yet, despite his dad's good deeds, it would not erase the other bad ones he committed. And yet, Quinn couldn't help his feelings of gratefulness and appreciation. Without them, and without his dad, Quinn would not have been able to set this trap, but he did. And, because he did, Quinn was here.

He was free. Quinn tightened his vest and holstered his 34.

At well after midnight, Sirius Tenet was likely at home eagerly awaiting the call to confirm whether Quinn was alive or dead. Mr. Tenet would receive no such call.

The only news he would be given was one of failure and doom. The time to Eradicate had finally come. Quinn was ready to finish what he started.

It ends tonight!

CHAPTER 39
THROUGH THE WALL

In his office, Sirius Tenet sat primly behind a robust desk and looked out his window, solemn as he gazed. This might be the last room he ever saw. Outside, Quinn peered in and examined the paneled walls and mahogany bookshelves of the Tenet manor. Every picture showed something that was truly important to Sirius Tenet. On his desk was a letter opener and a quill. There was an emblem etched into both of these tools. This emblem was a circle with a straight line dividing its center. There was a face concealed within this one loop. It was the mark of the king's hand. It was this very symbol that Sirius and his whole family had ingrained into all of their possessions. It had been theirs since the day they called this state home. Along with all of these miscellaneous items, there was also a framed photograph at the corner of Sirius's desk.

Inside the hand carved border stood a picture of Sirius when he was in his early thirties.

He was with twelve other men. Sirius looked so young in the picture. It was one taken from the earliest days of the brotherhood. Along with this, there was an image of Jacque Synthianas sketched by some local Cajun artist. And next to this picture was a photo of robed men and children. The pictures of kids who stood with Sirius were many. None of these children were his. There were many framed images of little girls, some as young as four. As an elderly man, Sirius was endowed with a certain toxicity. He carried a potent mix of all things inappropriate, misplaced, and just plain weird. Yet, in the end, Sirius made no attempts to hide what it is he truly wanted nor did he apologize for what he was willing to do.

Sirius twirled a cigar between his fat fingers and stared out his office window. This window was small. It was crisscrossed with beams. Outside was an aggressive rustling that echoed from a cluster of bushes. Quinn watched as Sirius lit a fresh cigar. Fully outfitted, Quinn stepped out from the plants and approached the regal manor. Holding his AR-15, the gun was fully loaded as Quinn stared through the scope.

The Tenet house was secured.

There were two surveillance cameras posted outside its main entrance. Quinn was also aware that Sirius Tenet was not alone. When Quinn marched to the front door, the rage he channeled so far was still very much inside. More than this, it was growing.

Quinn let go of his rifle and ejected his OTF. His footsteps were tepid and careful. Quinn glided in toward a pawn outside. Another fool was there smoking a cigarette. Quinn eyed the asshole's neck.

"Errr..." The man grunted.

Quinn grabbed the man's chin. As soon as he jerked and tried to break free, Quinn jammed the weapon straight into the man's jugular. As the blade entered, a clean cut one inch wide appeared along his flesh.

Quinn let go and the fool fell.

Quinn didn't care about the cameras. He had entered the Tenet's property like he owned the place. Eradicate was freedom. He had plenty of it still left. Quinn clutched the rifle and pulled the gun to his chest. Quinn pushed the barrel behind the door and peeped into the foyer. The interior of the Tenet manor was as impressive as its exterior. The marble tiles gleamed beneath orange light that resembled a lantern's light. Quinn moved past a swirling stairwell and looked at the shadows cast by two guards. Quinn's AR was fitted with sound suppressors, but the rounds could still be heard as Quinn was set to fire. How a Tenet managed to summon this much security was another peculiar detail regarding the family.

Where did they come from, and how did they get here so quickly?

In Quinn's opinion, most of these *pawns/knights* looked like they *could* be ex-military. Based on how they walked and shot, they were rigid and absent of expression. Quinn suspected maybe they were Army, but definitely not Marines.

No, Quinn knew a Marine when he saw one.

"What the..." Another fool balked as he inconspicuously stepped out from his hiding place.

This one looked too familiar. A name immediately popped into Quinn's head. Until now, Quinn had almost forgotten about this one last person. He was a name on the list, but not one written at the top. Quinn hoped to get to him, yet he was blinded by his revenge. He considered himself lucky to see him here now.

"Tulsa fucking Monarch," Quinn said.

"Uh, who are you?" Quinn ignored Tulsa's question and scanned him from top to bottom.

He was a low-level guy affiliated with the Brotherhood. Supposedly good at disguises and very slippery, Quinn saw him back in Vikaya but here he was now. Now in mid-stance, Tulsa was about to reach for his gun. Before he could, Quinn capped two clean shots and watched as the dumb fuck hit the ground. Scratched off as easily as a lottery number, Quinn was back at it.

Bang. Bang. Bang.

Easy execution. Truthfully, Quinn didn't check to see if Tulsa was dead. He simply stepped over his limp body and moved on. Above Quinn's head was a crystal chandelier. In the foyer, across from this space, sat the kitchen and the dining hall. Quinn spotted something else there.

He could hear footsteps and tried to determine the patterns behind all of these movements. For now, it seemed like it was only *two* footsteps. But, as soon as Quinn had a visual, he killed another pawn trailing around the corner.

Pop. Pop. Pop.

This new pawn fell to his knees. Quinn finished him off with a shot to the face. Quinn minded his environment. With his ear to the ground, he detected new sounds. The next one he heard was a vicious exclamation. It boomed from outside his purview. Sharp, Quinn was ready to shoot again. Unlike the last three, the next target engaged while Quinn ventured to a different approach.

The target withdrew his blade. It was almost the same length as Kardinal's.

Quinn slipped the rifle off his shoulder and held it across his chest. Quinn sighed and looked at yet another sword. Perhaps this was a common tool of the cult, Quinn thought. However, this new guard was a wild man. He hacked up Quinn in big, directionless swings.

Quinn was now dependent on his AR-15. He kept one hand on the handle and the other on the handguard.

Quinn parried. He deflected everything while wielding his rifle like a short staff. Quinn did keep his attacker at bay. Still, the man fought to try and cut Quinn wide open. As this man insisted, Quinn kicked him in the shins and forced his opponent down to one knee.

Then, lifting his gun, Quinn pointed the barrel at the man's temple.

Quinn let go and split the man's head.

Removing the empty clip, Quinn smacked in a fresh one. Heavy yet also comfortable, thanks to the gun's flared magwell, the clip went in easily. Quinn trekked through the mansion. He went left and then right. Quinn expected another fool to attack with another sword, which is exactly what happened.

Quinn released his AR.

This next attacker was a brand-new breed of belligerent asshole. This new man raised his foot to kick and Quinn brought his arm down to complete a low block. Keeping his foot secured against the floor, Quinn forgot about how good a gun's recontoured grips could feel and how straight they fired. Quinn blasted the guard three times before moving on. Quinn blew another one away and knocked a new man in his face.

The other fool pancaked while Quinn did away with his AR-15 and pulled out his Glock. He marched down a long hallway and did his best to navigate the long passage.

How far was he from Sirius's office?

Quinn counted the inches to measure the spatial connectivity. He continued to do this while holding his Glock with two hands. Steady, Quinn sidestepped to the door. Quinn nudged it open with the edge of his boot. He was greeted not with more cult members but by a decrepit old man.

Sirius sat slovenly in his wrinkled suit. He held a drink

in his slanted hand. He waited in front of his burning fire-place while Quinn was gifted with one last opportunity. And yet, rather than executing Sirius Tenet, another surprise emerged.

Sirius was cordial. He smiled at the man who was here to kill him.

He raised his cigar and hissed.

"Welcome," Sirius said to Quinn. "I'm so glad you're here."

CHAPTER 40
DEAD AT DAWN

ALTHOUGH QUINN DIDN'T PULL THE TRIGGER, THE need to pull it plucked at his very nerves and taunted him as he stood compliant for whatever reason.

All of this further reminded the Custodian about how he had not yet finished the job. He was able to kill Sirius, and certainly, he could and he would soon enough. He just hadn't decided when or how. Quinn wanted to savor Sirius's final hour. For the Custodian, this was something earned and cherished. It was also something to be enjoyed. Quinn moved in and kept his 34 aimed at Sirius's forehead.

"Where is he?" Quinn's tone was forceful and impatient. Either Quinn was going to be told of his father's location or he was going to kill Sirius with a single bullet.

The last Tenet would decide.

"Aw, yes," Sirius said. He sounded slithery and weak. "He said you would ask about him when the time came, but don't worry, he's not far. And where he is, well, let's just say he's waiting for you to come and find him."

Quinn held his aim. All it would take was one for this

fucker's lights to go out. Quinn, however, was more surprised to hear how his father was involved with Sirius and the true nature of their relationship. Broder Quinn was the source of Quinn's suffering. It was the same suffering that gave Quinn control over his enemies. It was also the same force that brought him here, to this one moment where he could end it all.

"I will not ask again." The threat Quinn made was clear and yet, it did not dawn on Sirius, not completely. It also did not dissuade his confidence. Quinn eased the trigger of his 34 while the elderly head of the cult chose to speak again.

"I know you're here to kill me," Sirius said, "and I know you have killed many to get to where you are now. Even so, I do have something you might want. I promise I will give it to you, if only you will give me something in return."

Quinn was irked by the last-minute proposal. If this was Sirius Tenet's way of negotiating, then he was very bad at it. There was nothing Sirius could say to change Quinn's mind. Quinn never listened to the begs or pleas from any of his targets. He was already waiting longer than intended. So, the act of executing Sirius Tenet could not be any easier. Quinn was deadlocked and he was ready. And yet, Quinn could not finish.

His curiosity was palpable. It was also unavoidable.

Quinn needed to know. He needed the truth.

"Please," Sirius said. He pointed to a chair in front of his desk. "Sit."

An intolerant sigh expelled past Quinn's fastened lips. Then, he slid into the chair, but the grip on Quinn's gun did not change. With the barrel aimed low, Quinn kept his eyes on the door as well as on Sirius. He relied on his peripherals to do most of the watching. Quinn stayed away from the windows. There could be a sniper nestled somewhere around the house. Quinn planned for everything. He lifted his gun and waited for the old man to speak first.

"Can I get you something to drink?" In Sirius's hand was a glass of scotch.

The slick brown liquid was presented to Quinn, who did not answer. Yet if Quinn had, his answer would be no.

Hell no.

"You must have worked up quite a thirst erasing my family and destroying the brotherhood that has carried my bloodline for generations. Impressive work."

So far, Sirius had said nothing interesting to Quinn. Nevertheless, when seated across from this disturbed man, there was one statement said before any others.

"If you move," Quinn said. "I will kill you."

A smile pushed aside Sirius's blubbery cheeks and he playfully raised his hands. He was showing Quinn he meant no harm, but the Custodian didn't care what Sirius said or did not say. Quinn's 34 stayed right where it was. He would be watching Sirius closely.

"Please, you're already going to kill me," Sirius said. "You and I both know I was dead the moment you slaughtered my men, killed my son, and walked through my front door."

Quinn squinted. Clearly, Sirius Tenet was aware of his fate. He did not deny what was to come, though he could not prevent such a certainty. Even so, Quinn asked himself, what did Sirius have to say that was so important?

"And now," Sirius continued, "so long as I still have a few breaths left in me, I would like to at least try and understand this man who has come so far to end my life. I want to know why he has, but I also want to know what makes him think he is any better than me."

Silently, Quinn reflected.

Better?

Better than Sirius Tenet and his minions of pedophiles and child killers?

Better than the vast network of predators, kidnappers, and creeps?

Throughout Quinn's career, both as a soldier and as a Custodian, he had never once killed a child. He was also never given an order that required it. Quinn never raised his hand to a female unless she raised hers first or was trying to kill Quinn because all Quinn's missions were outlined by a code—*a creed*. It did not apply to all Custodial missions, but so far, Quinn remained true to the no women-no children rule.

Quinn was a professional and a dutiful servant. He was this and nothing else.

"You did well."

Sirius's comment pertained to all the men Quinn had killed. Most recently, it pertained to the trap Quinn had escaped. This happened when Quinn vacated the Tenet's cavernous lair known as Vikaya, and now, he was here, where it all began. All of this was admirable, according to Sirius. Again, Quinn squeezed his Glock tightly. He wanted it, needed it, but had not yet taken it.

"I want you to know I respect your skills," commended Sirius. "I admire how you managed to take out Kardinal and all of my other men. That was all so very impressive."

"Not quite as impressive as the ones who made them," Quinn said.

He was speaking about the Brotherhood as a whole. He was referencing all the members involved in the abductions over the years. Quinn was speaking specifically about the murder of dozens of women and children spread across Louisiana.

This required equal attention.

"Oh, I didn't *make* anyone," Sirius said. "But I know someone who could. That is why you're here, is it not? You wanted to find him?"

Sirius did nothing to indicate he was alluding to Quinn's father. After hearing this, the Custodian replied to Sirius in a cold tone of voice. "Just here to do a job. Just here to clean up a mess."

Cleaning was Quinn's duty, and finishing was his oath. He still planned to.

"Yes," Sirius said, "a job which you do very well, but then I know what it is you do, because I clean too, you see."

The trigger to Quinn's gun, for some reason, felt warmer. Should Quinn's grip change only a millimeter, he'd blast Sirius Tenet straight through the forehead. Quinn would do that and finally put an end to this menial conversation. Still, Quinn hadn't moved an inch.

"You kill for two reasons," Sirius said. "Either you're being paid to do it, or you do it because you're good at it, because you *like* it."

Quinn kept his Glock aimed dead ahead. He had Sirius exactly where he wanted him, just as he had all along. If this was where Sirius was going, Quinn was already done listening. Yes, Quinn enjoyed the thrill of the hunt. Yes, the idea of killing a person who was trying to kill him provided a certain degree of exhilaration. At times, Quinn loathed admitting this.

Sometimes, he denied the pleasure and the wonder.

"Most refuse to face such truth," Sirius went on, "but most shamelessly admit to the first. Why? It's as though money makes sense while a lot of other reasons never seem to."

Quinn watched Sirius. He shook his head and sighed.

The Brotherhood of Cyn killed on the basis of belief. Their loyalty was to an entity conjured from peril and despair. They didn't kill in the name of money or materialism. Money was what they acquired after their dirty deeds were done. It was not what caused the deaths of so many.

"Do you like to kill?" Sirius asked Quinn. The Custodian held his position and said not a word. "Judging by how good you are at it," added Sirius, "I'd say you do. I also imagine you've been doing it for a very long time. Is that also true?"

Quinn counted the days. He knew precisely how long it was.

Too long.

For every day Quinn was alive, there was someone out there he was ordered to seek out and destroy. For every man he killed, there was a memory and a new face to recall and then to forget at the same time.

"And it's difficult for me to imagine that you'd become this good," Sirius said, "if there wasn't at least a part of you who enjoyed committing such heinous and ghastly acts."

While Quinn chose not to speak, he was already uncomfortable. It was not because Sirius was speaking the truth. It was because, with each attempt to actually talk truth, Quinn was inserting logic where empathy didn't exist.

"Yes, I know what you're thinking," Sirius said. "Wise child killer pontificating about the reasons why he chooses to do what he does. But, last days, last words...you can be certain I'm going to say what I want to. I know, deep down, that you, me...we're not so different."

Quinn glowered. The comparison forced him to feel a throbbing in his fingertips.

The only way to stop it? Pull the damn trigger. Do it, Quinn. *Just fucking do it.*

"A long time ago, when it all began, I thought I would never understand too," Sirius said. "I thought I would never want to partake in such horror or suffering. But then I began to see how, in the end, for the sake of me and for the sake of my family, certain sacrifices needed to be made."

"By appeasing a nameless god?" Quinn snapped back at Sirius. His patience was fleeting. His will to tolerate Sirius Tenet was going soon.

Pull the trigger. Just pull the fucking trigger.

"Nameless?" asked Sirius. "So, is it better to kill in the name of something unknown than to kill for yourself?"

Quinn considered the question. No, he never killed in the name of anyone else except himself. Well, perhaps he did. He didn't actually know. Quinn didn't speak to this. He chose to ignore it like all the others.

"Or is it exactly the same?" asked Sirius. "You think I'm worse because I don't follow a no women and no children rule? Why, because someone at some point decided that their lives were more precious than others? A life is a life, my dear boy, and ending one is ending one. I might be a monster, but I'm a monster who exists in the same world that so many others do. It's the same world you're a part of, whether you choose to believe it or not."

Quinn turned his gun. He thought about this world Sirius had mentioned. It was the world of predators and prey. Among the killer elite, Quinn was part of all the danger and destruction. He'd ventured into the world of animals, hunters, thieves, and butchers. Even now, he could see the faces of those he'd slain. He could see all the blood spilled, and weirdly, everything Quinn saw now looked exactly the same.

When Quinn killed, it was because it was his job to kill. Sirius, however, killed for duty.

He killed because of his faith. Worse, better, or maybe it was all the same?

With each question asked, a new thought entered Quinn's mind.

He was not a child murderer, yes, but a murderer...he still was.

"You might think you're above those you kill," Sirius lectured Quinn, "but we all do the same thing, see? We just do it for different reasons."

Quinn angled his gun so it was completely horizontal now. Still, he had yet to fire. The Custodian tsked. This was the longest Quinn had ever waited before finishing a mission. He could not bring himself to do it. He was trapped in a shell of conflict and doubt. This was something Priest had warned Quinn about. He spoke about the burden that came with having a lack of conviction. It's what happens when you run the risk of becoming a prisoner to your own creed.

"The world is filled with killers and villains," Sirius lectured, "and depending on who you're hunting, you're either deemed as one or the other, when in reality...it's all the same. Lives are taken and people are destroyed. See, a long time ago, I accepted that it doesn't matter who you kill so long as you're willing to admit who and what you are. This is something I have never denied, because I have always known who I am. The question is...do you know?"

Quinn reflected on who he was. This, he knew. Kyle Quinn was a problem solver. And the problems he solved were only fixable by means of a bullet and a blade. Yet Quinn's standards did not change, and they never would.

Do you think about the lives you have taken?

How do you determine what a life is worth or not worth?

All these questions assembled in Quinn's mind and he couldn't stop a single one.

Do you even care?

This one proved to be the most troublesome of all.

A tremor slithered through Quinn's once-solid hand. The time to execute and finish this fucking job was now. Yet, he had not done it.

"But it is...as I said," Sirius continued, "a world of killers. And you are in no position to lecture me about the differences between good and evil. You're a lion, roaming his kingdom. It just so happens that you're the hunter who goes after more experienced prey."

Predator versus prey. Quinn always was the predator. This was true.

His prey was never those unable or incapable of defending themselves. Every person who fell by Quinn's hand did because they were not highly skilled or highly trained. He never killed someone out of enjoyment or pleasure. It was not a ritual; it was a mission. It was a duty and it was a calling.

Sirius raised his cigar to his mouth and stuck it between his wormy lips.

"We're always hunting, Quinn."

For the first time throughout their entire conversation, Sirius had chosen to address Quinn by name. Quinn hated how it sounded coming out of Sirius's mouth. He glared at Sirius and his Glock felt heavier.

In this way, Sirius was urging Quinn to let it go.

He was urging the Custodian to finally fire his weapon and end the life of the man he had come so far to kill.

"Still looking for our next meal," Sirius continued. The cigar remained between Sirius's nicotine-stained teeth. Sirius huffed a cloud of smoke, and it was during this moment of sheer smugness that Quinn came to see the great monstrosity at the center of his homily.

Quinn was now contemplating his own morality. He looked deeper at the contradictions; the comparisons Sirius had made. And there was one truth that emerged among the many justifications. It was the same truth Quinn was observing now.

No, they were *not* the same.

"I just like to enjoy mine," Sirius said. He pulled his cigar and let out a fat, sulky breath. "Because I know it's mine to enjoy. It's real."

Real.

Yes, thought Quinn. The reality of his actions would always be a part of who Quinn was.

There was no regret, but then there was no absolution either. Quinn was without shame and doubt. He was without anything that would allow him to see Sirius as anything more.

Sirius was nothing more.

"So," Sirius said, "are you going to do it or are you going to just—"

Bam!

In the middle of Sirius's seemingly thought-provoking question, the Custodian sprang from his chair and blasted Sirius Tenet the fuck away like he should have from the very beginning. Arm stretched, Quinn shot his man right between the eyes and Sirius's brains ejaculated onto the bookshelf. All that followed was the smell of smoke and the crisp sounds of compelling silence.

Once he finished the Eradicate, Quinn did nothing but wait.

With his arm still extended, Quinn looked at the fallen man who was the last to be executed. Sirius, a man in his seventies, was neither immobile nor brittle, but he was completely unprepared for what had come to pass. Throughout this pitiful attempt to teach Quinn a lesson, it was a blatant decision to try and change the Custodian's mind.

And, while some poignant points were made, Quinn agreed with none of it. In the end, killing Sirius and his men was the only *part* of Quinn that could not be altered. Quinn refused to be persuaded, convinced, talked down, or negotiated with.

At last, it was all said and done.

The mission was finished—the Eradicate was completed.

Almost.

CHAPTER 41
NOT FINISHED YET

HANDS DOWN, QUINN CHOSE TO LINGER AMONG THE dead and bask in the quiet just a little longer, like he enjoyed being among the slain, which he did. Turning back toward the door, Quinn removed his phone. Dialing Priest's number, Quinn waited to hear Priest's voice. Halfway out of the Tenet's house, Quinn stepped over more bodies and then spoke into his cell.

"It's done."

Soon after Quinn spoke, Priest answered with a voice full of relish and joy.

"Excellent. Absolutely excellent."

When Quinn left the mansion, he raced back to his safe house. It was time for Quinn to get packing and to start moving. But his father was still missing. Since he saved Quinn, he felt like he should let him go, almost.

And this word *almost* was repeating in Quinn's head like a bad song.

Now that the torches were lit, the cops would soon be on the lookout for the person responsible for the death of Louisiana's most affluent families. Unable to stay, what

Quinn needed to do now was get out. He gathered his weapons and gear. Quinn chose not to think about his father. Quinn's dad made the choice to save his son. Quinn didn't ask Sirius about his father when he killed him. Due to this fact, Quinn found himself doubting why he accepted this job in the first place.

Did he really want to kill his dad, or did he just pursue the kill for his own sake?

Quinn was haunted by this feeling.

Unloading his AR-15, his Benelli, and his Glocks, these weapons had done quite a lot during Quinn's time here in this state. Quinn inserted them all in a utility case and removed his vest. He placed this along with a few other items brought with him and continued to load.

Quinn's tonfa, the weapons that saved his life, were kept the closest.

Should Quinn still need them, and he doubted he would, he wanted them to be set and ready. Soon after he contacted Priest, Quinn called Ally too. Quinn told her the similar news.

"Jesus," Ally said through the phone. "You get 'em all?"

Quinn placed the case into the trunk of the SUV. Adrenaline still pumping, Quinn replied.

"Yeah." Quinn's voice was hoarse. It cooled once he informed Ally that he had eradicated the entire brother-hood. "I'm packing up now. Need to get going."

"Right."

Quinn and Ally's conversation was brief but neces-sary. Once Quinn had gathered everything, he left the SUV he'd taken back at Vikaya. His RAM was back at the hotel. Quinn didn't care. It wasn't even his truck. Although he suffered worse injuries in the past, what Quinn felt now was a burning in his right arm. There was a bend in the bone. It was not a fracture, but it still hurt like a motherfucker.

"Ah." Quinn gagged and retrieved a first aid kit from behind the couch.

He opened the box and snagged a handful of bandages and a bottle of alcohol disinfectant. He tore open the packages with his teeth and spit out the paper. He dabbed the wound when a light in the living room suddenly turned on.

Quinn unholstered his Glock 26 at the sound of the flick. It was a smaller pistol, and one Quinn only used a few times during the Eradicate. His fingers were taut against the Glock's handle. Quinn stared into the light and at a man seated on the couch.

Even with a weapon drawn, this man did not flinch. In fact, he didn't react at all.

Choosing to remain absolutely still, as soon as Quinn saw the shape, he recognized the figure.

"See you...made your way out. Nicely done there, boy. Nicely done, indeed."

Quinn glared. This interaction was inevitable.

He knew he would come and find him.

Hands up, Broder Quinn surrendered. The Custodian gawked at his father and waited for him to come further into the light.

"I know you probably thought I was going to leave you for dead, but in the end, what kind of father would I be if I didn't help my own flesh and blood?"

"What are you doing here?" Quinn's reply was cold as ice.

"Here?" retorted Quinn's dad. "I came to see my son so I could commend him for a job well done. The Tenet family is quite a big fish sort, and the fact that you managed to get to all of 'em is quite impressive, even if you did encounter a few bumps along the way."

Quinn's Glock remained high. He was tense as he focused on his old man. But, even with all the hatred and anger burning inside of Quinn, his gun remained unused. As of now, nothing happened.

"You were working for them, were you?"

"Working?" replied Broder Quinn. "Nah."

Broder Quinn outrightly denied his involvement with the Tenet clan. He did this while making a clicking sound with his mouth. He interlocked his fingers and his hand bounced off his chin.

"It was just, as you know, part of the game," he said. "And it was the only game I knew how to play."

Quinn's head moved side to side. He was disturbed by his father's justification. Never would he admit to the darkness housed inside any person, including himself.

"You think any of what you say matters? Do you think any of it matters...to me?"

"No," said Broder. "No, I don't, but I thought I would still give it a try."

Quinn glowered. He continued to let the reality of what was happening take hold of him. If his dad was here, it was to do more than just commend. It was also to react.

"Try?" barked Quinn, his finger easing into the trigger. "How about you try saying you're sorry? Sorry for everything you did and that you continue to do. How about you admit that you're no different than the monsters you serve? How about the fact that you're still allowed to sit here and breathe my fucking air is a gift, a privilege you don't deserve. You stand in front of me without experiencing the consequences. This is all a good grace someone like you should never receive. Why don't you just say what you know I want to hear?"

Quinn's father grinned and he leaned back and chortled. Quinn heard the conceited laughter, and his dad's lack of regret was evident. Quinn felt angry. He felt sick. This was the best one he would ever get from his old man.

"Apologize, of course," said Broder Quin. "It seems everyone wants an apology these days. Everyone wants their fair share of pity, but the world is not a pitiful place, old champ, and there is nothing for me to apologize for. I wanted to build a warrior, and that's what I did, and that's what kept you alive. So, if you really want me to say I'm sorry, to grovel, and to admit that what I did to you is wrong, then first you have to admit something there too, Kyle."

Kyle.

Everyone Quinn knew referred to him by his last name only. Now, more than ever, his first name was being used quite often. Kyle was a name reiterated only by the one who named him, so he hated hearing it.

"I want you to admit that, if not for me, you would not be standing where you are now," said Quinn's father. "You would not be one of the most feared men on this fucking planet. I want you to tell me that you would not trade it all in for a normal life, and you admit that." Broder's Quinn voice beckoned in his son's ear as he continued to rage. "And I'll admit the rest."

Quinn's gun hand lowered. He sighed and then he snickered. He thought a man like his dad could change. Quinn was even willing to give a man like him the benefit of the doubt, at least in this regard. Yet, as Quinn's eyes rolled back, he looked at his father with a slack-jawed gape. He wanted to throttle his old man because now Quinn knew the truth. He always had.

Some men don't change. Some people *can't* change.

"Then you know what I have to do now, don't you?" Quinn asked.

"Yes," Broder Quinn's response was trite, but it was better than nothing.

He turned and he leered at his son. "I do."

Quinn snapped to. He was furious. He was still hurting from the previous fight. Quinn's bones could still be broken. Still, Quinn had enough energy to fight on, to go forward.

Quinn knew any move he depended on now would be totally predictable. And so, Quinn started with a technique even his dad wouldn't see coming. Quinn's body moved in a straight line. The flying knee was not a technique Quinn was ever taught by his dad.

Instead, it was something Quinn learned from dozens of other fights he'd participated in.

Flying high, Quinn knocked his dad into the wall, and the fight the Custodian had craved for so long...had finally begun.

CHAPTER 42
THE CLASH

Now in an epic clash of titans, the battle between Quinn and his old man had elevated from encounter to a no-holds-barred romp—a non-stop, relentless fight to the death worthy of the great Roman gladiators; the brutal warrior killers from the bloodiest pages of ancient history. Both men knew the other so well that nothing produced could be countered or anticipated.

None of it was surprising.

Engaged in an all-out war, Quinn and his father were unhinged, for this was the moment Quinn had been longing to have. Despite his age, Quinn's father was still very impressive. He was big and burly, and the techniques he taught, after so many years, still remained. He struck with the utmost precision while his son targeted all the primary areas: the ribs, the pelvis, and the groin. And yet, Quinn's dad reacted using Shotokan karate. Delivering low sweeping blocks, most of his counters were powerless to stop his son's fury.

In addition to Quinn's mean straight kick, the Custodian knocked his dad down to the floor. Watching Broder Quinn crawl, Quinn grabbed his father's collar, hoisted him up, and whipped him fiercely into the television with a mean pelvic throw.

Broder smacked the plasma screen, which popped off the wall, then fell and shattered. Quinn spit and his dad coughed. Broder retrieved a jagged piece off the broken television screen and held it like a knife.

This was an all too easy plan of attack.

"You..." His dad was exhausted. He wheezed as blood dripped from his mouth and his teeth were covered beneath a thin layer of red. "You...really...want to...kill me, don't you, boy?"

Quinn refused to answer. Of course, Quinn wanted to!

His chance to return the malice his father had brought upon him had finally come. It was Quinn's opportunity to make his abuser suffer. It was Quinn's chance to show his dad what this pain looks like from the other side. This was his moment—his time for vengeance and retribution.

"You'd kill your own father, would you?" Broder Quinn grinned as he held up his *knife*. Head shaking, Quinn's eyes widened and his jaw was locked. He ground his teeth as he glowered.

Another trick?

If so, it was a pitiful one at best. Quinn spun and, after a rapid twist, executed a solid spinning back-kick that smacked his father dead center. Broder Quinn's legs buckled as he hit the floor and Quinn pushed his knee against his dad's throbbing throat. Compressing the windpipe, gradually Quinn cut off the oxygen to his dad's brain. Quinn could now see his old man getting weaker. Down and dying, should Quinn wish to quicken this process, all he had to do was deliver a chop to his dad's neck and he'd be done for.

The fight was over.

A horrible way to go, the death was neither swift or painless.

But then, it might also be the kind of death his father deserved.

Although Broder Quinn had saved his son today, nothing would erase the terror and the torment from years before. He could not relinquish Quinn from his suffering, nor could Broder erase his path to total destruction. He had molded his son into a dangerous man. Quinn knew this, but it was not enough to exonerate his father. It would not provide his father with solace during his final moments.

No, Quinn wanted his dad dead and gone, but now that he had the chance to fulfill this dream, things did change. Quinn defeated his father and had, at last, watched him fall. And yet, Quinn felt pressure and he was willing. He felt exactly as he did before. Quinn lifted his leg and gasped. He grimaced due to the shame. And then, he released his dad from the hold.

Honor.

Quinn stood and backed away.

Risen.

Looking down at his trembling hands, Quinn surrendered. Showing mercy and compassion, even against the greatest foes, new qualities were being bestowed upon him now. And Quinn could do nothing to resist their power.

They were suddenly a part of him.

Releasing his father, short bursts of air cut against Quinn's throat. Quinn watched as his dad breathed as another quality had miraculously overtaken the Custodian. Quinn had chosen to be defined by his newfound empathy and his need to become something more. Quinn could not let his father go unless he told him the truth.

"You're my nemesis," Quinn said, hunkered near the couch. "My greatest enemy in my life." Quinn's dad gasped and he rubbed the back of his neck. After being spared, Broder smiled. "And I guess the only way that I thought I could fix myself was to be in the worst fight I could have ever been in, and that fight is with you," Quinn continued. "I know you wanted to make me into something better." As Quinn said this, his hands slid down to his stomach. "I know it was all you had to give. But that's just it," Quinn said. "I did become better, better than you. I'm stronger, faster, harder, and more brutal. I'm not just a soldier, never was, and never will be.

"I'm like you in the ways that matter and in all the ways that don't. And I see now that what I've been doing all along is..." Quinn struggled to catch his breath and so, he struggled to say these next words. He also recalled the days he had mentioned. Doing this, a sob crept up his throat and he immediately forced it down. Now was no time for tears. "It's all just been one step toward not knowing who I am, what I need, or what I want, because beneath all the hate, all the anger, and all the pain, still I can't...I can't do it. Still, in the end, I'm you, and you're... me."

Quinn's father let out a big sigh of relief or maybe it was one of disappointment. Quinn couldn't tell. Whatever it was, Quinn didn't care. It was enough for him. He was now, officially, incapable. He couldn't do it.

Quinn could *not* kill his father.

"So, I don't want to know you," Quinn said. "I don't want to ever see you again. I want you gone and disappeared so just be that. Be gone."

Quinn trekked toward the door and left his father

behind. This was what Quinn's dad deserved, and while Quinn could see that now, he could also...understand it.

"Be gone, and never come back." Quinn was turned all the way around.

In doing so, he broke the cardinal rule when finishing an enemy.

Never give your back to your opponent. Yet, after Quinn did this, he grabbed his bag and listened to another cautionary phrase.

"You have sacrificed a winning stroke in favor of your beliefs there, my boy," uttered Quinn's old man. "And, in doing so, you have forgotten your place and your surroundings!"

Broder Quinn knelt with a gun in his hand that he had pulled from an unknown location. Perhaps it was the original weapon brought to kill Quinn or maybe it was something his dad had the whole time but had forgotten about. Whatever it was, it didn't matter. Now aiming for Quinn's head, the Custodian saw the weapon and shuddered. With the pistol turned, Broder fired and blasted Quinn as he jumped through the kitchenette. The bullet pierced a propane tank stashed under the sink. Unleashing a cloud of putrid gas, Quinn glanced back and watched his dad as he removed a lighter from his coat.

Light sparked; Quinn gawped into his father's devilish eyes.

"You should have killed me when you had the chance!" Shouting passionately, Broder tossed the lighter and a tiny flame flickered as a powerful explosion destroyed the inside of the trailer. In the back of Quinn's mind, he asked himself if this was another test?

Was it another way for his dad to see what his son was capable of?

Perhaps.

Or maybe it was exactly as it appeared. Maybe it was Quinn's dad fighting back.

"No!"

The entire home was set ablaze as Quinn sprinted to the nearest doorway. While flames spread in perilous waves and seared everything in sight, the windows were reduced to molten shards. A super-heated cloud singed Quinn as he escaped. Quinn landed smack on the rustic plains seconds before additional flames rose in big flashing triangles. They cracked and burned, and the roof peeled off like the lid of a tin can. In the center, tendrils of smoke danced before ascending up into the sky. Quinn coughed specks of dirt and fragments of mortar. Now sweaty and dirty, Quinn lifted his head from the smoldering ground and felt the smoke creep into his nostrils. He felt the grass clinging to his cheeks. In the distance, the sound of rolling wheels echoed from the winding road, and a voice shouted out.

"Kyle!" Ally was here. Somehow, she was here.

She hurried after Quinn as the burgeoning fire continued to engulf the safehouse.

"I was coming to see you," Ally said, "and then I saw the fire from the road. Good thing I came, huh? We—I—need to get you out of here before someone else sees. Come on."

Quinn, still shaken, wobbled to his feet. Ally pulled Quinn from the dirt, and though he could stand on his own, this assistance helped. Given how sore and how broken Quinn's legs were now, he shuffled along as additional waves of pain assaulted his tender body.

Ally helped Quinn into her Jeep. Then, she hurried around to the front of the car, jumped in, and looked over to see what she was missing.

"Gotta get you outta here," Ally said again. "I'll fix you up. Don't worry."

Quinn held his breath. He wasn't worried.

Actually, he was smiling.

CHAPTER 43
THE UNSAID

QUINN'S HEAD BANGED AGAINST THE WINDOW IN Ally's car, trounced from the toll the fight with his father had taken on him. It was more of a personal toll than a physical one, but now exhausted and bleeding, Quinn barely escaped before the explosion in his safe house occurred. The last face seen was his dad's. And now, the only words the Custodian could speak pertained to one request.

"No hospital." Quinn could barely utter a single syllable.

He forewarned Ally with whatever energy he still had left inside. Quinn looked up and saw a back-split house on a street corner. Ally stopped directly in front of it. Quinn asked no questions. Ally moved to Quinn, and thankfully, he was able to get himself out this time. Quinn latched his hand on the handle above the door. Ally proceeded to place his arm over her head and shoulder.

Together, they motioned across the long pathway that led to Ally's front porch.

Quinn hopped along. His back hurt the most.

Inside, Quinn was placed onto a wicker chair and Ally raced through her kitchen. She pillaged her cabinets for a first aid kit. Moving like she was in the ER, Ally cracked open the white case. She plopped herself down next to Quinn and placed her hand on his knee. Quinn examined the inside of Ally's house. It was quaint and was so tidy Quinn felt like it could be in an issue of *Good House-keeping*.

This was so much better than a hospital.

"All right. Let's get this shirt off, okay?" Ally was gentle as she touched Quinn's aching body.

The Custodian removed his shirt that clung to his chest. Now off, Quinn's torso was covered in scratches and scrapes, all dripping wet.

"Jesus," said Ally.

"I know," Quinn said. His injuries varied in shape and size. Quinn coughed and Ally slid her chair in closer.

"Got to get cleaned first," she said.

Ally busted open a pewter bottle of hydrogen peroxide. She doused a cloth and soaked it before applying the damp rag. Quinn slouched. He inhaled while keeping his eyes closed because what came after sucked but he was prepared.

"Okay. This is going to—"

"Sting," Quinn said. "Fucking aye, it is."

"Yeah," said Ally. "Aye."

Ally dabbed each of Quinn's cuts with a moist cloth. A boiling burning tingled the Custodian's muscular torso and Quinn bit down on his tongue until the throbs ceased. He was used to pain. Quinn's strategy for overcoming all of it was to think about something else, to be somewhere else.

Disinfecting wounds was not Quinn's main trigger.

The most agonizing experience of his life did not

come from burning things but, instead, from *removing* them.

"You're okay," Ally coached.

Quinn's chin moved as he nodded. He unclenched his body and gradually opened his eyes. Quinn could see Ally. She was by the table. Her hand was on the kit.

"I know you've had stitches before, I'm sure," said Ally.

Quinn chuckled. Yes, he had.

Ally sewed the wounds with steady hands. She worked the needle and the thread like a seamstress. Diligently, she sealed up Quinn slowly and efficiently. As Ally finished the operation with the utmost care, she cut the thread with her teeth. Quinn rested his head on one of the chairs. He sat in Ally's surprisingly cozy kitchen and began to heal. Now resting, Quinn did manage to sit up and look at the rest of Ally's home.

"Here." Ally handed Quinn a bottle of rum. "This might help."

Quinn yanked the drink from Ally's grip and tossed back what was inside. He gulped down the delicious brown juice, so spicy and smooth it flowed easily down Quinn's gullet. Filling his stomach, Quinn basked in the sensations. With the entire bottle done in a matter of seconds, Quinn felt energized. He could stand but chose not to after he saw Ally approaching the table.

"Whoa," she said. "Easy there. Don't get up too quickly now."

Quinn knew the rules. This was not his first time as a patient. He smirked and Ally guided Quinn along. He grinned and was so happy to have Ally with him. Actually, Quinn couldn't believe Ally fixed him up as well as she did.

She was a great fixer, in more ways than one, she was.

"You still need time to rest." Quinn felt a blush starting to form.

Almost smiling, Quinn reached for Ally's hand and caressed her fingers. He delivered a sweet gesture of kindness that could only be interpreted one way.

"Thank you," Quinn said.

Ally gazed into Quinn's hazel eyes and stared at the man who endured more than she cared to know. Quinn's leer intensified.

"You're welcome," replied Ally.

Quinn looked at his Luminox watch. He had been with Ally for almost an entire hour, and that was too long. He needed to get back to the airport and get the hell out of Louisiana. However, although leaving was a top priority for Quinn, Ally was more than eager to take him to his jet.

Yet Quinn couldn't go without first thanking her for what no one did.

She saved Quinn's life, and that was everything.

"So...I guess this job was what, more dangerous than others, huh?" Ally asked.

Quinn nodded and smirked. He answered Ally despite not having to.

"You have no idea," he said.

"You're right," Ally said, drinking her coffee. "I don't."

Ally turned and broke eye contact with Quinn.

"I wish I could explain more," Quinn added, regret clinging to his every word.

"I wish you could too," replied Ally. She was both skeptical and derisive, and Quinn respected Ally enough to tell her the truth. In the end, Quinn expected she knew why he couldn't.

"I'm sorry." Quinn sat straight and he exhaled. He fell to his knees and further basked in the relentless numbness. Thanks to Ally, he'd stopped bleeding.

"I know," said Ally. "I know."

"For what it's worth," Quinn said. He turned so he could look at Ally. "I'm really happy you came when you did."

"Well, when I heard that Sirius's body was uncovered," replied Ally. She smiled and her hand rested on Quinn's arm. "I figured you were done and wanted to get out as quickly as possible."

Quinn hissed and he laughed. That's exactly how he felt.

Quinn felt the last pulling of the thread and the last gouging of the needle. After, he sat up, he extended his arms over his head and stretched. It was a good healing session, and so, the feelings of pleasure were enamoring for Quinn.

"Wait," she said. Ally scurried from the sink, where she dropped off the bloody needle and thread. "Let me help you with that."

Ally's hands still felt warm and Quinn wanted to feel them for longer. He wanted Ally, and yet, he refused to say a word about it. He refused because Quinn just wasn't strong enough.

He was strong in some ways, but weak in others.

Despite all Quinn could do, he still could not do this. He could not tell Ally the truth.

CHAPTER 44
FAREWELL

When Ally was done bringing Quinn's shirt down to his stomach, the beaten mercenary held out his hand and nodded. "Thank you."

"And again," said Ally, sly and with the same blushes as before. "It's no problem at all."

A sullen look began to show on Quinn's face. He wanted to stay and would have if he could.

"I..." Now Quinn wanted to be mindful. The words were all there, but saying them was a struggle. Whenever it came to showing affection, the staunch and seemingly unaffected mercenary clenched up worse than a schoolboy.

Words weren't enough, but what Quinn was going to do next absolutely was. "We gotta go."

"Right," said Ally. "Of course."

She gave Quinn a forced smirk. The two walked out the front door. Despite sharing not one moment but several, the two immediately went about their business as if their time together was platonic.

Was it something to be read into, or was it nothing at

all? Quinn didn't know. Like he had assured himself, one day he would.

Now in Ally's truck, she sped along the highway and beat all the traffic to the airport. Quinn admired Ally's driving skills. He could only imagine what she would be receiving from Priest in these tight cases. Approaching the perimeter fence, Ally flashed her faux bureau badge to the security guards poised there and busted into the airfield and drove straight to the hangar and toward Quinn's Cirrus Vision SF50 jet. Still, it was being secretly held there. When Ally passed through the wide-ranging doors, Quinn examined the entire hangar. The reason why Quinn was allowed to keep his plane in this location was because Ally's influence and how she reported it as an escort for a POI. It was a nice spin. Thankfully, it allowed for Quinn to hightail it the hell out of this place. He was so desperate to get home. It was the only thought that occupied Quinn's mind.

"Okay," said Ally. "There she is."

Quinn examined his jet. The sun reflected off its sleek exterior and accented its curves and ridges. It was and always would be Quinn's pride and joy.

"Yeah."

"Are you sure you're good to fly?" Ally asked Quinn, glimpsing at his wounds. The state he was in was as good as someone like himself could be. Still, Quinn fought through the pain until he felt okay, ready.

"Yes."

"All right," Ally replied to Quinn. "Then I guess you're good to go."

Quinn was about to be on his way like Ally said he would be. However, Quinn couldn't simply leave without giving Ally a proper farewell. Regarding Ally's most recent actions, Quinn was never one for mixing business with other things. In this case, he just couldn't resist.

"You take good care of yourself," Ally said, "and I will —" Before Ally could say more, Quinn sprang and, in a bold and risky move, pulled this gorgeous woman in. Planting a fat kiss on Ally's warm, tender lips, in a solid display of gratitude and lust, passion, and joy, Quinn followed his heart and mind.

It was also a sudden turn of action that took Ally completely by surprise.

Quinn pushed until Ally's eyes opened wide. While he didn't know how she would take this committed and surprising act, in the end, Quinn was confident in the end result. He believed Ally would be receptive enough to not push him aside. Quinn felt Ally's soft hand touching his face. It was gentle and cool. When Quinn was done, he stepped back and let his hand slip to Ally's shoulders. Still holding on, Quinn leered and replied.

"I will."

"Be in touch?" asked Ally.

Still smiling, Quinn backstepped toward his plane. He responded with a casual squint. The sun was shining bright. Quinn's apathetic gaze was followed by a nonchalant shrug. While Ally ogled Quinn, he could see that his kiss had sent beams of infatuation straight through her heart.

Ally was as touched and enamored as the Custodian. *Damn*.

"Definitely."

"Okay, well..." Like a smitten middle schooler, Ally waved and Quinn scampered toward his jet.

"Goodbye." Quinn waved. He would be thinking about this his entire way home.

If not for Ally, Quinn would not have been saved. In

more ways than one, she saved him. In more ways than one, Quinn was exactly that: he was saved. Thinking of Ally, Quinn came to admire all the qualities he'd taken for granted. He could feel Ally's lips and his heartstrings played. He was whisked away, slipped into the cockpit, and counting down the minutes until he was where he wanted to be. For Quinn, that place was his home.

His mission was done, but more than this, he felt fulfilled.

Despite not killing his father, Quinn breathed easier, knowing he had done something that could be called a good decision.

Quinn felt rich; satisfied and awake. He supposed this was how most people felt whenever they did a good thing. Quinn meant what he said. He was going to be better.

And for once, that was enough.

For once, *he* was enough.

CHAPTER 45
BACK

QUINN LANDED BACK HOME AT A QUARTER PAST NINE, and, just like that, he was in his farmhouse, his favorite place. Marching straight into his bathroom, he ran himself a hot shower, and was in the stall for over an hour, the water splashed Quinn's chest and face. It was so warm and satisfying Quinn didn't want to leave. When he was finally done, he stepped out while dripping wet. Lugging into his bedroom, Quinn plopped himself face-first onto the mattress. He was asleep seconds after hitting the blankets.

Before every mission, Quinn was aware he might never see this place again. And so, should Quinn get the opportunity to do so again, he made sure he enjoyed it. Quinn woke after a long and fulfilled rest. He grabbed his phone and browsed through some recent stories. The Tenet family murders, according to Louisiana's press, were still under investigation. As one article described, Sirius and Alistair were not quite as innocent as they appeared nor were they as giving as presented.

When Quinn read this, he just could not stop laughing. Skimming along, Quinn continued to browse more stories. In another article, Quinn read how there were no leads on whoever was responsible for the Tenet's *eradication*. This was actually a word featured in one article. Not a single journalist, however, had discovered who was to blame for the family's demise. And with the investigation ongoing, the police promised they would have a suspect in custody soon.

Quinn was informed of this as well. Afterward, his smile grew as he raised his mug up to his face and drank. No, they would never find him.

Now that Quinn was done with the mission, a meeting with Priest was next on the list.

Due to his recent mission's parameters, Quinn didn't have to explain or report. Still, Quinn imagined he would hear from Priest soon. As of now, this had not happened. So far, Quinn had not received a single call from anyone. This was something that usually happened within the first twenty-four hours of a mission's success or failure.

Drinking more coffee, Quinn was deep in thought. The words of Sirius Tenet continued to plague his mind. Quinn analyzed his moral code. He recalled exactly what was said. It was then Quinn began to see the faces of all those he had killed. Now reflecting, Quinn refused to believe Sirius's comparison. How Quinn felt and what his new future would be were ideas he refused to dive into, at least not now.

Quinn stood on his porch and watched as the sun penetrated a cluster of cirrus clouds that occupied the blemished sky. Screams of terror sounded in Quinn's head like car alarms. Everywhere Quinn looked, he could see someone else in pain and someone who would do anything to have it taken away. Quinn walked back into his house wearing a pair of spandex boxers. After returning, he came across a blinking icon flashing on his laptop. Quinn slid into his chair and moved his mouse to open the desktop.

Checking his email, Quinn saw one message.

It was from Priest. Quinn clicked, the screen maximized, and he read the message.

We should talk. I'd like to. Soon.

Quinn wasn't surprised to see this. As Quinn knew, it was inevitable that Priest would reach out. Quinn also thought it might be a sit-down. Priest, who operated out of Washington, somewhat, traditionally, he and Quinn would decide on a halfway point. When Quinn replied now, he asked where Priest would like to convene. A few minutes later, Quinn received his response.

45 Elmsbury Road and Fifth Street South. Noon. It's in an office. A receptionist will point you. Don't be late. Be seeing you, Quinn.

But that's close.

Quinn emailed back and Priest sent a response seconds after.

Very. Just be there.

Priest signed all his messages with the letter P. Quinn knew where he was supposed to go. Quinn had visited this Elmsbury spot before. Quinn had met Priest there after another mission was concluded only six months earlier. With the Eradicate order and an entire criminal enterprise wiped off the face of the fucking earth, Quinn presumed this did require his attention.

Apparently, they did. The Custodian, however, did not.

Quinn returned to his bedroom to put on something more appropriate. Along the way, he passed his weapon's vault. After the fight with Quinn's father, and the destruction of his safehouse, Quinn made note of some precious tools that needed replacing. He had received half his payment. A Custodian's salary was fixed regardless of the job, and it was always the same:

One hundred and fifty thousand.

Half was sent up front and the other half was given once the job was done.

This was a policy Priest made absolutely clear.

Seventy-five thousand was deposited into a secure account. Quinn received a notification once the money was transferred. Quinn's jet was housed inside his barn, which he converted into a hangar. It was renovated along with the rest of Quinn's house. The field around it was tilled and paved into a runway. Quinn walked toward his RAM truck. Quinn's 1500 was a big, black beauty strong enough to roll over any tumult and conquer all forms of inclement weather.

He could even break through a brick wall with this beast. When Quinn drove to the location specified by Priest, he listened to the radio as it played his favorite tunes.

God damn, it felt so good to be home.

It took no more than twenty minutes to reach the place. Quinn exited his RAM in jeans and a muscle shirt. All stitched up, his right arm needed the most time to heal, but it was getting better. Quinn's shoulder stuck out compared to the rest of his arm. Walking ahead, Quinn strolled into this robust office building.

He cut across the stark lobby and didn't pay any attention to anyone. Quinn's Oakleys covered his sunken eyes. A few people looked his way, but not many. Quinn was a square peg in a round hole. He stepped along the gleaming tiles with inverted triangles and approached a pleasant secretary now sitting behind a desk. She was a woman with red hair and glossy lipstick who extended a kind look toward the Custodian.

"Here to see Raymond." This was Priest's real name. Raymond Priestly.

"Yes," said the receptionist, eyes on her computer.

Quinn was unsure if she was actually looking up Priest's name. She could be arbitrarily tapping her fingers against the counter in order to seem busy. Quinn checked everyone's hands and faces. Even here, anything could happen.

"Yes," said the receptionist seconds later. "Floor number five."

Quinn nodded and stepped back.

"Appreciated." Quinn's hands were folded as he walked to the elevator.

Quinn pressed the button to the fifth floor. When he reached that level, the doors opened, and Quinn was in a room with paneled walls decorated with photos of old America. Carpet bristles scraped Quinn's sneakers as he scoped the scene.

Quinn tried to see if there was anyone standing too close.

So far, Quinn was alone. The door to the office was half-opened. Quinn took a peek inside.

"Quinn?" The voice was undeniably Priest's.

Why he insisted on being in this room was beyond Quinn's understanding.

"Yeah," Quinn said, lowly.

"Come on in. Glad you're here."

Into this private space, it was not quite secured. And yet, when Quinn came to the door, he felt it was mannerly to knock. It was unnecessary, but still, Quinn minded his manners.

He continued to look inside and he had no doubt it was Priest.

Quinn could never be too careful. At any moment anything could change, and always, Quinn was ready. He was ready even when he didn't need to be.

"We have a lot to talk about."

CHAPTER 46
A NEW QUINN

PRIEST'S OFFICE MIGHT BE PLAIN AND SIMPLE, BUT HE was certainly not a plain and simple man.

For now, Priest's space consisted only of a desk and two shelves, and there was a mess of papers strewn along the floor. Priest looked like he was playing the role of a businessman and the other people who worked in the same building had no idea it contained a top SAC operative. Priest employed elite mercenaries and assassins. He ordered such people to destroy anything that threatened this nation's security and its prosperity. He was also a man responsible for the deaths of hundreds of people, all ordered to die at his command. Wearing a black suit, Priest's hair was combed flat against his scalp. Once he saw Quinn, he jumped up from his chair and scurried toward the fatigued Custodian.

"Welcome back, my brother. Nice to see you here, healthy and of course...alive! Good God, are you ever alive!"

Immediately after mentioning this, Priest followed up with an entirely different question.

"Jesus," he said. "Look at those cuts. This one got a little hairy, did it?"

Quinn made his way to Priest's desk. He didn't have much to say regarding his cuts and wounds. Quinn responded absentmindedly. "Just a little."

"Right. Please, have a seat," Priest invited. "We got a lot to talk about. I know this wasn't required, but hey! A lot to say. A lot to know."

Priest was cheerful and confident. Quinn's personality was completely opposite. So often, Quinn enjoyed that it was.

"Hmm." Terse yet also casual, Quinn was well aware of the reasons he was here now.

"So...I take it everyone is...gone? Eradicated, so to speak?"

Quinn tried to think about what else to say. Eradicated was exactly how Priest would describe Quinn's most recent mission.

"I mean, Ally has been filling me in," commented Priest. "Turns out some questions are adding up, but she's keeping an eye on all that. She's working with the local enforcement to sweep it all under the rug. Doesn't matter what they find because they'll never find you," Priest said. "I mean, at least you're here and not over there, am I right?"

Quinn nodded. "Right."

"Yeah." Quinn took a second to admire the setting.

It was so different from where he and Priest shared their previous encounter. They were on a greasy mat on Quinn's farm. Here, everything was lighter and brighter, cooler and more contemporary. Quinn actually felt like there was room to breathe.

"But, it's done, yes? Tenets are all dead?"

Quinn nodded at Priest. The Tenets were dead, but not Quinn's father.

"Down to the last man, but..."

"But?" Priest asked.

"My dad, he's...he's not..."

"What?" Priest said, waiting for Quinn to say more.

Quinn didn't like to admit he didn't end his dad like he planned to do. Quinn didn't feel he needed to. His dad was only Quinn's incentive to accept the mission before. He was not the primary reason behind it. And, so far as Quinn was aware, he didn't *have* to kill his dad.

It was his choice, and he chose not to. Quinn shook his head to show he didn't kill his father. Afterward, Priest leaned back and said nothing.

"Are you all good, though? Still?" Doubt clung to every one of Priest's words.

"I'm still breathing," Quinn said. "And that's enough for me."

He pushed aside all the commendations. Right now, Quinn wanted Priest to get on with the rest of their boring exchange. Priest thought his Custodians were invincible. He relished in the idea that, no matter where he sent them or where they were ordered to go, they would always succeed. They would find a home.

"Proof of death?" Quinn was usually tasked with bringing this evidence to Priest.

It was something he chose not to submit. His Eradicate allowed him to do this.

"Watch the news," Quinn said. "You'll see it's all there."

Priest continued to show a slick grin and then he pulled open a drawer next to him to remove a fresh cigar. Holding a shiny cutter between his fingers, Priest gestured to Quinn with the fancy tool and clipped the end of his butt.

"Imagine I will." Priest inserted the cigar into his slick mouth and lit it up.

The flame brightened Priest's enthusiastic demeanor. To Quinn, he looked a lot like Sirius Tenet right now. For a second, they almost looked like they were exactly the same.

"Very good. Half of your money was deposited before you left," Priest said, "and now that you're back, I'll make sure you get the rest. You know I'm good for it, but there's still a lot to process, a lot to explain. This job, as you know, was different."

"I do," Quinn said.

Priest cackled and then he fidgeted with his flare. Quinn listened to the tool hiss as a blue stream of fire flickered from the end. Quinn watched the fire sear Priest's cigar.

"And since we did something new," Quinn said, "I was hoping you might be open to...letting me do a few more with a similar purpose."

"Well, our whole game is pretty set here, Quinn," Priest said. "You know that better than anyone. But, if you're hoping for another Eradicate, I'm sure that will pop up again sometime in the near future."

Near was the operative word in Priest's statement.

"I'm sure it will," Quinn said, "but that's not all I had in mind."

Quinn kept a close eye on Priest. What he said was more than he ever had about any mission before. In the past, Quinn only reported. He dropped off photos and was advised about his next mission and that was all. And usually, his duties were to say nothing and to hear nothing. Once it was all said and done, Quinn would return home and wait for the next call. Now, however, Quinn was the one pitching missions. Despite not being allowed to do this, it didn't stop the Custodian from saying what he wanted to say.

"Oh?" inquired Priest. "And pray tell, what *exactly* did you have in mind?"

"I want things to be different from now on," Quinn said. "I want to *do* things different."

Smoke wafted in front of Priest's smiling face and highlighted his shrewd, unaffected demeanor. Quinn was aware of how Priest would react after saying what he did. Priest was the contractor and Quinn was the operator. Both were respectful enough not to tell the other how to do their job.

Nevertheless, Quinn had something to say. He was going to say it.

He bled and he fought. He almost died too many times to count. And, what kept Quinn fighting was different than before. Now, Quinn could see. He could feel that something new had hatched inside of him. He was looking at his abilities from a different perspective. He was given a glimpse few had ever received. He was given the chance to be better and to be freed of his demons. Perhaps Quinn could bring retribution to those who deserved it. Perhaps, he could make the world better by washing away all the scum that infected it. And for Quinn, he was going to start with *kids*. He was going to kill anyone who hurt, tormented, and killed kids.

"Oh," Priest said. He pulled out his cigar. "I see. So you want to change our directives a little bit, do you?"

"Yes," uttered Quinn. He was being terse on purpose. "I guess you could say that."

The less Quinn explained, the better...for now.

"Well, you know," Priest said, "when you signed on for

this gig, you knew the risks, the parameters, the outcomes, and you couldn't alter any of them. It wouldn't change, because it couldn't change."

"Yeah," Quinn said, "and they don't have to."

Quinn observed his boss.

Priest's head moved and tendrils of smoke swirled above his cigar. Quinn liked to think he was intriguing his employer in ways he hadn't before. Quinn rolled his fingers up into his palm. He wanted his fists to be nice and tight, and they were. They were so tight they were shaking.

"I want to make sure that what I have can be used for something more," Quinn said. "Maybe something better."

"Better?" Priest snarked.

Quinn recalled the faces of Sirius Tenet, Alistair Tenet, and Kardinal. Quinn saw them and all the other disgusting vermin he recently exterminated. He remembered how long their reign was before someone came and ended it. It was Quinn's job not to question the morality or to judge the character of those he eliminated. A Custodian was not a lawyer and Quinn was no judge or jury. He was an executioner tasked with cleaning and removing, and that's all he was supposed to do.

So, that was all Quinn did and all he had done.

But what Quinn was proposing now was an entirely new trajectory. Yet, this was something he was in no position to request. Nonetheless, Quinn was willing to try. He was willing because now, he actually had a choice.

Quinn nodded.

"Evil, the kind so bad it causes other people to wake in the middle of the night shaking."

Quinn could see the faces of all the dead children once again. He was haunted by the victims the cult had taken. This idea plagued Quinn. Having outlined to Priest what his new plan would be, he could think of nothing else and it only made his heart burn harder with hatred.

"I want to find these people," Quinn said, "the cretins, the vermin, the scum. I want to find them all, as many as I can, and I want to take care of them, and just them. I want them all dead and gone."

Quinn was quiet. He hoped Priest would say something soon.

"Eradicate *forever*?" Priest asked.

Quinn nodded humbly. Bad men were always integral to their missions.

Not mandatory, for Quinn, amid all his victims and all the prey, there were always a few who didn't necessarily harm children. Quinn was also not a force of justice or reckoning. Quinn killed without remorse. However, now in the place he least expected, a new idea was born.

It was an idea Quinn never thought would come to fruition. It did.

Quinn stood with his fists behind his back and described his future role as a new Custodian. Still desired, it was never accepted. Maybe it would be now.

"And that's all I want to do," Quinn said, "and all I will do if you still choose to keep me around." This was a clear declaration. Quinn's mind was already made up.

Priest heard the rest of the pitch.

After, he rolled his cigar between his fingers, and Quinn watched as his lord gawked from his desk. One of the rules for being a Custodian is you never abandon your mission and you never surrender. This is true not only regarding your enemies and the threats you face. No, for Quinn, it was true for him and the others who were part of this very same guild.

You cannot leave.

This is the way it had to be: the law and the way it had to remain.

Priest made a clicking sound with his mouth. Quinn could see he was amused. He was still digesting Quinn's proposal, but still, Priest's response was rhetorical and one the Custodian did not expect.

"Who are you, Quinn?" Quinn found himself feeling puzzled and irked by the question. It was a strange one. With his eyes locked on Priest, he looked ahead. He was now pensive. His lips were clamped so harshly his eyebrows wrinkled.

He knew exactly who he was.

"Because I know who you are," Priest said, "maybe... even better than you do."

Priest lowered his cigar down to the table. Quinn spoke in a hard, cutting tone of voice.

He wanted to be absolutely clear.

"You don't know me, Priest, not really."

The two masters of their craft were now trapped in a tense stare down. It was created because both men were loyal to their perspectives. Yet, in what seemed like an exchange of platitudes, Quinn's reason for saying this was only starting to make sense.

"Well, I don't know what's here," Priest said, his hand moving in a circle. The here Priest mentioned was Quinn's exterior, what was on the outside and not inside. "But I do know what's there, *underneath*."

Priest pointed at Quinn's chest. Quinn blinked fast. The claim was a direct contradiction to Quinn's previous thought. No doubt, Priest had a way of getting under people's skin. He knew how to burrow and how to tunnel into the back of other people's minds. He enjoyed plucking chords and pushing buttons. He liked to provoke fury, provoke pain. Wise and manipulative, deep down,

Quinn believed Priest did not know who Quinn was, not really. Still, Priest claimed he did.

"I know what's there," Priest continued, "what festers..." Priest's teeth cut against his lips. He looked like a hungry rabbit. His eyes were wide as he mentioned Quinn's so-called desires. "And what you've kept buried inside is the very thing," Priest said, "that you see whenever you go off. It's what shows whenever you're ready to show people exactly what it is you're capable of."

Quinn was familiar with this process. When he did go off, so to speak, Quinn saw red and only red. And all of this was accessible due to his willingness to embrace his inner animal. It's what kept him hungry and it's also what kept him alive, though not well.

Actually, Quinn would never call himself well.

"This isn't about me anymore," Quinn declared. He was attentive, same as always.

"No, but it is about what's to *become* of you," added Priest. He emphasized the one word, *become*. "I know you want to believe that there's some grand design to all of this," Priest continued, "some greater idea that surrounds who you really are and what you really want. You want to believe there's something profound and noble in what we do. But you know that's still not who you are and it's not the person you will be in the end."

Quinn predicted what Priest might say next. As of now, he had commented on Quinn's choices and aspirations. Like the many heroes of old, Quinn's pursuits were about nobility, grace, and honor. These, however, were not Quinn's observable characteristics. In the end, Quinn was not born for anything other than destruction and murder. This he knew, and yet this, Priest refuted. Still smoking his fat cigar, what Priest had said almost broke Quinn's spirit. The Custodian felt that with each new sentence delivered, his calmness was further disrupted.

Quinn was hurting more than he cared to admit.

"This world you're a part of, it's not built on these ideas," Priest said, taking another puff. "This is a game of conquerors and worms, of people who know how to endure, how to climb, and how to clean." Priest exhaled. His heavy breaths were done out of intolerance and fatigue. Quinn was aware of everything Priest said. Quinn didn't need to hear Priest describe it again. "And I know you want it to be something else," Priest said, "but it's not going to be that way."

Quinn was again fully aware. To wit, he only had one response.

"Why?" Simple and direct, Quinn was also being confrontational. His response challenged Priest's point of view and Quinn was not going to abandon this idea so easily.

If Priest demanded it had to be one way, then Quinn would demand the opposite.

"We're not heroes, Quinn," Priest continued. "We might get a few bad guys here and there, sure, and we do have a code, yeah, but what we do, it's not a philosophy or something that absolves us. We seek and we destroy. We remove and we make sure the country we love is kept safe and protected. We play by the rules and we drive in a very narrow lane. We preserve a cause, but that cause is not our own. That's what we do. That's who we are."

"Who we *used* to be," Quinn slickly replied. "Not who we *are* now."

This was Quinn's only defense for standing his ground. He was not going to surrender his agenda or adhere to the same protocols as he did before. Now, Quinn wanted to consider his next missions and follow a new and possibly better path. He was no longer asking anything from Priest. No, now he was the one giving orders. He was the one being heard, possibly for the first time ever.

"You know of all the things I thought would happen, you building a conscience was the very last."

Quinn gazed at his employer and bit his tongue.

"And of all the things I thought you wanted no part of," Quinn replied, "I thought killing children was where you drew the line."

"And it is." Priest's reply was so quick it was practically a worded belch.

"Then prove it," Quinn said. "Help me find more of those bad people," The bad people Quinn mentioned were like his father. If Quinn found him once, he could find his dad again too. Still, what Quinn discovered about himself now, he believed, was more valuable. Now he knew exactly who he was and what he wanted. "Help me do things right," Quinn continued, "so we can be better than we were before. All of us can be better."

Priest rubbed his cigar with his fingertips and smoke blew out into Quinn's face. When it seeped into his nostrils, Quinn found himself feeling tickled. Hearing everything said, Quinn pitched a new direction whereby he and Priest could conduct their business. With the revelation Quinn was now experiencing, he knew it wasn't something Priest would be so easy to accept.

He was a contractor and he was an operator. Quinn couldn't question the morality of each and every foe. He couldn't conduct a character assessment of those who appeared on his lists. Should Quinn do this, then the entire Custodial role might implode. Priest, Quinn, and all the others would be out of a job. It was a nice idea and an honorable one too. Still, it was not possible. And yet,

Quinn was not backing down. He was not taking no for an answer.

"No guarantees in this business," Priest said. "You know that, and what may or may not happen isn't the same as what is necessary and vital to our own survival."

Quinn nodded and pretended like he understood. There was more he wanted to say and even more he wanted to know, but he had said enough, with only a little more left to say.

"Then, let me prove it to you," Quinn said. "Let me *show* you."

Priest sighed and grinned, both amused and impressed with Quinn's persistence. He admired it, and so, he fed into it.

"You still couldn't bring yourself to kill him, could you?" Priest asked Quinn.

Quinn looked at Priest feeling only shame. Quinn hoped Priest would not speak about this. Nevertheless, when it came to probing people, there was no one more skilled or talented than Priest. There was only one person Priest was referring to. On this point, Quinn had nothing to say.

Quinn's answer was no.

"No," Quinn said, "but..." Quinn took his time before asking Priest the all-consuming question he had yet to ask him. "How did you know, Priest?" Quinn asked. "How did you know where my father was?"

After this, Quinn had more questions.

Why was his old man with the Tenets? How did Priest know where to find Quinn's father, and what was he doing in Louisiana?

All were valid questions and all of them hurt Quinn equally. He fought through the pain by thinking about what lay ahead. He remembered what he could do now that he had a new conscience, a new direction, and a possible new mission.

"I thought you wanted your old man dead," Priest said, referring to Quinn's father. Quinn still believed his old man to be his greatest enemy. "And I needed him dead," Priest said, "and I threw you a bone, because I thought it's what you wanted. I see now...it wasn't, not really."

Priest, now downcast, was upset because he wanted Quinn to kill his own father. The fact that Quinn didn't bothered Priest, almost to the point of irritation. While Quinn still cared about his dad, he saw him as an arrow that pointed to other bad men. And there were plenty of them out there, too many in fact.

"The world is the way that it is, and no amount of anger, death, or good intentions will ever change that."

Quinn gawked. He had no doubt Priest believed everything he said. He was someone who saw the world in only one way. His credibility in this regard couldn't have been better.

"People always think they can make the world a better place," Priest said, "and those that try are usually the ones who fail. We don't fight for change as much as we fight for the people who fought for us. In doing so, we ensure that the best parts of this country remain intact. And for now, that's the best we can hope for."

"Maybe," Quinn said. His arms slid behind his back and Quinn replied with another unwilling-to-back-down response. "But then again...maybe not."

"*Ah,*" Priest whispered. "And you think that this new moral high ground can actually work? You think you can *make* it work?"

Quinn's jaw slacked and then locked. Standing tall, like some kind of prideful hero, he felt like a misshapen, poorly rendered version of Captain America. There were only a few words left for Quinn to say. "It will." Quinn turned. The cigar in Priest's mouth continued to burn, but the smoke was now fading away.

"Well," Priest said, "then, I guess we'll just see... won't we?"

Although Priest's response was riddled with skepticism, Quinn understood there was still some convincing left to do. Killing people was Quinn's game. Now, it just had to be the right people.

Quinn took a step back. He thought the meeting between him and Priest was adjourned.

Before heading back toward the door, Priest changed his tone, and he was more emphatic as he addressed Quinn for the last time.

"I know this is about *him*," Priest said to Quinn, singling out his chief weakness. "It's always been about *him*."

Quinn turned and glowered. "You think it is," he said, "but it's not."

"Yeah," Priest said, dubious and still smiling. "Where is he then?"

Quinn stood in the doorway; his body partly turned as he replied.

"Does it matter?" Quinn begged this one question and felt the need to state something else to go along with it. "You just *used* him," Quinn said. "I know your game, Priest. It's all just one big dirty trick, isn't it?"

Priest nodded and his smile widened to the point where it dominated the entire lower part of his face. *Maybe*, Quinn thought to himself. *Maybe everything Priest said and did was part of a game, a game Quinn didn't want to play.*

"It is, but then again," Priest said, "this is a business of dirty tricks, so how surprised can you really be when one grabs hold of you tightly and refuses to let go?"

Quinn said nothing. He wasn't surprised. This was another undeniable truth Priest had chosen to reveal. Indeed, this was a nasty business. Wrought with lies, ulterior motives, and conniving, vindictive decisions. Priest tested the conscience of every single participant in this game and Quinn did whatever he could to avoid doing this, but Priest was right.

How could Quinn possibly think he was above it all?

He wasn't because no one was.

"Why didn't you kill him, Quinn?" Priest asked. "Why didn't you kill your father?"

Quinn blinked and he recalled this moment as it happened back in the safehouse. He remembered when he was in a deathmatch that nearly cost him his life. He remembered all of it and then listened as Priest asked, "Why do you hate him so much, and yet, you didn't want to see him die?"

"Because," Quinn said, "he was not ready to die."

Quinn eyed Priest as he sat behind his desk. Priest rolled the dead cigar between his fingers and ended the back and forth with an askance. Still, Quinn didn't clarify his statement. Priest didn't ask Quinn to and perhaps...all of this was a story best left for another time.

"If you say so, Quinn. If you say so."

Quinn was supposed to complete his exit. His hand was still on the door leading out of Priest's office, and as Quinn clasped the cool handle and was inches from stepping through it, he was about to go until Priest said something that made Quinn stay.

"Since we're talking jobs," Priest said, "I do have one for you that doesn't involve you settling a family matter. It's a little different but also a little the same too. It's taking out some pretty evil dudes who have been known to hurt kids, sort of. However, it *might* offer your chance at the retribution you just said you wanted."

Quinn pivoted so he could face Priest. This new offer sounded like a compromise.

"Retribution?" When Quinn said this word, goose bumps trickled along the Custodian's forearms. They tingled Quinn's back, and suddenly, his injuries felt a little less painful, almost like they were cooling.

"And maybe," Priest said, "you might even be able to feel like the good guy you're trying to be now. It's yours, if you want it."

Quinn contemplated the possibility. His mind was spinning as he had yet to leave Priest's office.

Did Priest say what he just did? Did he mean it?

Would he grant Quinn a mission that fit his new parameters and something that was suited to Quinn's new brand of justice?

Full of focus and with so much on his mind, Quinn's heart accelerated. He answered Priest, and the word said just scraped against his throat and was barely heard.

"Yeah," Quinn said, in a brooding voice. "Hell yeah."

CHAPTER 47
HOME, FAMILY, FUTURE

QUINN RETURNED HOME AND STOOD ON THE PORCH of his modern farmhouse and basked in the morning sun. Leering at the unblemished horizon, a red glimmer shined quaintly in a straight line. Quinn felt like a Neanderthal coming out of his cave. He didn't know what to do now. The day seemed so open, so uncontained.

Some time had passed since Louisiana.

Quinn slept more and trained less. Now was his time to rest and recover. Quinn skipped his breakfast and drank two fat cups of coffee. He leaned against the veranda post, closed his eyes, and enjoyed the cool morning breeze blowing in from the tilled fields that engulfed his super property. Alive as Quinn was now, he was also happy, at least in a way not felt in a while. What he felt could only be described as an elusive satisfaction and an extreme sense of self-awareness. All of this deepened the more Quinn considered his new and possibly better future.

Most people experience a change of heart at some point in their lives. Parents express regret and criminals show remorse, pioneers lend perspective, and relationships can be mended with time. Quinn was the same man he always was, yes, but now he was gifted with the opportunity to alter his life and shape it in a way he never thought possible.

For this, Quinn felt peace. Though not the life he was made for, it was the same part he traded away. Quinn learned how to accept and how to cope. It was the early morning days like this where Quinn asked himself:

What if he could?

It was the dream of damn near every assassin to come a point in their careers whereby they can finally stop killing. Although everyone who called themselves a warrior loves to fight, a part of them wishes for the fighting to come to an end.

Although Quinn embraced his life, he asked himself *what's fighting if not for something real? What's war if not a battle toward some kind of good?*

Almost done with his coffee, once Quinn was finished, he tossed what was left over the porch and onto the grass. Standing in a clean pair of boxer shorts, Quinn stomped over the flakes of grass and proceeded away from his house. It's been two weeks since he stepped foot onto the mats; a staple of Quinn's daily routine, and an intricate part of his healing and his constant growth. It was, and always would be, one of the main tools keeping Quinn sane as well as alive. The cool surface brushed the Custodian's feet and Quinn looked at the punching bag dangling from a thick chain. He saw his bokken, his knives, and his tonfa. It was warmer when Quinn fell into his kamae. Now in his aikido basic stance, Quinn kept his right foot in front of his left and his back leg straight and locked. He kept one arm extended while the other was curved. He was stable—balanced—and was set to perform the basic movements.

Splaying his fingers by his forehead, the sun shined against Quinn's solemn, focused face. Feet firmly planted; they swooshed as he swept them across in a circular motion. He thought about Priest and could even still hear his voice.

Not what we do.

When combined this way, these four words coerced Quinn into recalling something new. He remembered how he heard a similar phrase spoken by certain people. He remembered those who didn't like to change or compromise. On other occasions, Quinn heard the words spoken as, *"Not who we are and not what we believe."*

And yet, they all had the same meaning to Quinn now. The purpose was to exonerate and to absolve him of his many sins, in a way. It was to do all of this because people refused to take responsibility for their choices and actions. But Quinn's mind was made up. This new change was something he desperately longed to build.

Sun rising with each passing second, Quinn continued to slide his feet back and around. Five minutes into his training, Quinn's phone vibrated and flashed. Quinn cleared his throat as he looked at the blinking device.

It was the one he used for work. He had no idea who was calling him now.

Quinn figured it might be Langford, the gruff bar owner who hired Quinn to work security whenever they needed an extra guy. It could be him, or it could be one of Quinn's old Delta pals, maybe someone who wanted to chat or offer work as a bodyguard. This was another job Quinn used to earn a little extra when not performing his Custodial duties, not that he ever needed any extra money. Quinn held his phone and saw a message written there. It was from neither of the people he had anticipated. Since it wasn't any of them, the revealing of this person did brighten Quinn's morning. He was enchanted when he saw who messaged him.

Kyle, it's Ally. Hey, how's it going?

Ally messaging Quinn was completely unexpected. And yet, Quinn read the greeting and watched as another notification popped up shortly after.

How are you feeling?

Quinn didn't know how to respond. He thought he wouldn't hear from Ally for some time. He answered as best he could.

Fine. You?

Quinn returned the message and waited. Ally had patched Quinn's wounds and after the safehouse exploded, she helped him in a way that was non-repayable. If not for Ally, Quinn would not have made it back. Having done an impeccable job with Quinn's stitching, even now, Quinn's wounds were in a good place. In effect, Ally had saved Quinn's life. More than this, she was a better person than him, and so, this made Quinn wonder:

Why was she interested in speaking to him when she didn't have to because the mission was over?

Quinn sat on a tall box outside he used for jumping and stretching. There, Quinn held his phone with two hands and watched as the messages continued to pop up.

Good. I know you're back home, but just wanted to check in. See how you were doing.

Ally's following messages were clear and endearing. How was Quinn doing?

Few cared to inquire about this. It was as Priest said: so long as his Custodians are alive, then the rest can be mended with time.

For a moment, Quinn thought about him and Ally,

maybe as more than just friends, maybe even together. Such an idea soon became as invasive as Quinn's other thoughts. All of this was unlikely, but Quinn dwelled on it as if it actually was possible. This thought gave Quinn what he desired most: happiness and a second chance.

He was alone now, but maybe someday he wouldn't be.

As Ally sent Quinn another message, he was charmed by the wit and cordialness of their conversation. It was sparkling and better than the others Quinn and Ally had shared. Now, Quinn knew what it felt like to be missed. He was the one who was breaking the rules, choosing to bend a few now because he could, all of this was a part of Quinn's next endeavor.

He returned every message sent from Ally and thought more about his life and the day when everything could, possibly, change.

But for now, for today, Quinn wanted to know more about what tomorrow would bring. Maybe it would reveal how things *could* be, and maybe Quinn would someday have a future that was entirely his own. *Maybe.* For now, Quinn had work, *lots of work,* to do. He was Kyle Quinn—*Kyle Quinn the Custodian*: baptized in fire, sworn to uphold his creed, to defend the weak, to rise to honor, primed for retribution, and ready for the next fight certain to come.

ACKNOWLEDGMENTS

I extend my warmest gratitude to James Reasoner, Jake Bray, Mike Bray, Patience Bramlett, Sean Forbes, Rachel Del Grosso, Amy Briggs, and Ellie Folden, and everyone else at Rough Edges Press and Wolfpack Publishing for allowing me to share stories about my beloved antihero, Kyle Quinn.

I will always be forever grateful.

Thank you, Jon McManus, Douglas Martin, Jan Clausen, Melodie Campbell, David Bergen, Brian Drake, Mark Allen, and Michael Black. Thank you, Brent Van Staalduinen and Mark Manner, both of whom gave time and encouragement when needed and patience when it was never asked. I would also like to thank a man who is more than a friend, but a mentor, Mr. John Corr. I thank Naben Ruthnum, Lucy S. Snyder, and Andrew F. Sullivan, who have taken time out of their very busy schedules to look at my work, and I offer my gratitude to all my family and friends, including my fellow teachers, good and decent colleagues. Thank you, my buds, Greg Zavitz, Brent Duguid, Andrew Francella, Dave Franciosa, Steve Legge, Christopher Barrett, and other like-minded geeks, and thank you to my guardian angel, Sharmaine.

I thank my best friend and brother, Cody, and my sister, Jenna, who is a relentless voice of concern. I thank my father, a good and decent man, and I thank Bentley, the current love of my life. Above all else, I thank my mother, Sheila. She was the first fan of this series and the first fan of everything I do. Mom, you are an amalgamation of encouragement, power, strength, and truth, which is often inconvenient, but most importantly...of love.

Thank you for being my greatest fan and thank you for following me on my many journeys. I always know where I'm going, and because of you, I am never lost.

A LOOK AT BOOK TWO:
EVISCERATE

*The adrenaline-fueled sequel to Eradicate, a thrilling
new chapter in Kyle Quinn's fight for justice.*

After dismantling a child-abduction cult and confronting the
horrors of his past, black-ops mercenary Kyle Quinn, known as
"The Custodian," emerges with a renewed purpose: to protect
the vulnerable and eradicate the worst of the worst. But leaving
his past behind is easier said than done, especially when his next
mission forces him to face an enemy as cunning and lethal as
himself.

Tasked with taking down a revived Sinaloa Cartel in Austin,
Texas, Quinn steps into a shadowy world of human trafficking
and terror. With a new leader, a dangerous product flooding the
streets, and untold power at their fingertips, the cartel threatens
the very fabric of Quinn's country. But they aren't his only
challenge.

A mysterious assassin emerges—one whose skills and strategies
mirror Quinn's in chilling ways. As the deadly game unfolds,
Quinn is forced into a battle not just for survival, but for the
truth about his own identity and the purpose of his fight.

With everything he thought he knew crumbling around him,
Quinn must decide how far he's willing to go—and what he's
willing to sacrifice—to bring justice to the darkness.

AVAILABLE FEBRUARY 2025

ABOUT THE AUTHOR

Jarrett Mazza is a graduate of Goddard College's MFA in Creative Writing Program in Plainfield, Vermont as well as The Humber School For Writers.

Before completing his terminal degree, he studied writing at the University of Toronto School of Continuing Studies and comic book writing under Ty Templeton and Andy Schmidt. He has had stories published online in the GNU Journal, Bewildering Stories, Trembling With Fear, Aphelion, The Scarlet Leaf Review, and Toronto Prose Mill, The Fictional Cafe. His work is featured in anthologies by Silver Empire Publishing, a best seller, Zimbell House Publishing,NBH Publishing, MuseWrite Press, twice by Dragon Soul Press, Gypsum Sound Tales, Hellbound Books and The Ginosko Literary Journal. All are available on Amazon for purchase. He was also an Honorable Mention for the Freda Waldon Award for Fiction, nominated for an Indie Book award, and was featured as a visiting author for the nationwide We Read Canadian event in 2020. His mystery short story was published in an anthology under the editorial supervision of Michael Bracken and was published by Down and Out Books. He is currently a pulp fiction writer for the companies Airship 27 and Stormgate Press and Rough Edges Press.

He lives in Hamilton, Ontario.

You can follow him on Twitter @JarrettMazza